CODE OF SILENCE

CODE OF SILENCE

A Ben Reese Mystery

Sally Wright

This first world edition published 2008
in Great Britain and 2009 in the USA by
SEVERN HOUSE PUBLISHERS LTD of
9–15 High Street, Sutton, Surrey, England, SM1 1DF.

Copyright © 2008 by Sally Wright.

British Library Cataloguing in Publication Data

Wright, Sally S.
  Code of silence
  1. Reese, Ben (Fictitious character) - Fiction
  2. Archivists - Fiction 3. Ciphers - Fiction 4. Murder -
  Investigation - Fiction 5. Detective and mystery stories
  I. Title
  813.5'4[F]

  ISBN-13: 978-0-7278-6679-0   (cased)

All Severn House titles are printed on acid-free paper.

Typeset by Palimpsest Book Production Ltd.,
Grangemouth, Stirlingshire, Scotland.
Printed and bound in Great Britain by
MPG Books Ltd., Bodmin, Cornwall.

One

S he saw it herself by early evening – the fact that one small decision can change life for ever. It can call down death, prevent murder, alter private and public history, channel the course of nations in a hair's breadth of a second.

In her case, it was what to do on her lunch hour.

Explain to Carl Walker? Talk to Carter Clarke first, before she saw what she had? Develop the photos while Tom went to lunch?

Miriam Gold chose the darkroom.

And lived long enough to regret it.

'Hey, Tommy. Is now a good time?' Miriam's earnest, young, inquisitive face was searching the short smiling lieutenant's, as she pushed open the half-closed door to Arlington Hall's Photographic Department.

'Hey, Miri. Sure, come on in. I'm on my way to the cafeteria. What'd they have for lunch? No, don't tell me. I don't want to hear it.'

'I pack my lunch, so I never know. Thanks for teaching me, Tommy. I couldn't have learned nearly as quickly without your help.'

'It's nothin'. It's been fun.' He was scrawny and awkward-looking when he didn't have a camera in his hand, like a big-boned rosy-skinned twelve-year-old, instead of what he'd become – an army photographer who'd filmed the liberation of two German concentration camps before he turned twenty-one. 'So you wanta be Margaret Bourke-White shooting *Titans of Industry*?'

'No, landscapes. Clouds moving across mountains. Ansel Adams better watch out, right?' Miriam Gold was edging toward the darkroom, pulling her bag off a narrow shoulder, adjusting her glasses on her nose.

'Good luck with *that*! Adams is in a class of his own. Listen, I gotta collect some work on the way back, so I'll prob'ly be gone 'bout an hour and a half. Just leave everything neat, OK? And lock the darkroom door.'

'You know me, reliable to the point of stupidity.'

'You? No. You think for yourself.'

'Sometimes I don't, and don't understand why. I'll leave the key in the box in your desk.'

When Miriam Gold left the darkroom an hour and twenty minutes later, she'd already zipped a small Manila envelope inside a compartment in her purse. She'd adjusted her sweater-set, and tugged on her overcoat, and pulled out her orange ID badge (arranging it so the photo faced forward on top of her old brown coat), thinking about what was left to tack down before she talked to Carter Clarke.

She left Building A in a hurry, the ugly, institutional barrack-like warren they'd thrown up overnight, heading back to Main Building, running across the soggy brown lawn toward the original Arlington Hall – the big white-pillared, red-brick building that had been a girls' school before the army took over during the Second World War.

She waved to women in and out of uniform, said hello to two male book-breakers, hurrying on without stopping for anyone, glancing at her wristwatch, then back at the upper windows where Carter Clarke could've watched.

She'd been sitting at her desk for less than a minute when General Clarke's door opened, and he stalked through it into her office with a trench coat over his arm.

'Congratulations, Miri.'

'Sir?'

'You ate lunch away from your desk. Was there one other time? With Bill Weisberg?' His eyes were watchful behind his glasses, but the narrow mouth had started to smile and the formal face he put on in public softened as he studied hers. 'You've been looking tired, Miri. The pace here would weaken an ox, but don't push yourself. I mean it, not so your health suffers.'

'No, sir. I won't.'

'How would I get anything done? Where would I find another assistant as fluent in as many languages who has your other talents?' He was shrugging on his raincoat, staring at her intently, considering the hunched shoulders, the pinched mouth, the nervous droop of her head. 'You *are* all right, are you? There's nothing wrong you want to tell me?'

'I'm fine, sir. Thank you. Tired, sir, as you say.' Miriam looked down at her desk, her plain features looking plainer, her skin mottling as she blushed.

'A toll has been taken on all of us, which hardly diminished at the end of the war. That reminds me—'

'Sir?' Miri had pulled a pad of paper toward her and was reaching to pick up a pen.

'I've come to the conclusion, considering the recent break-throughs, that a celebration's in order.' General Clarke (tall, thin, unbending) swiveled toward the hall door. 'Give that some thought, Miri. Something special for Meredith Gardner and Cecil Phillips, now that they've both earned a place in history. For the rest of the team too. A dinner dance, at the Willard Hotel? They seem to enjoy that. I'll have my wife phone you Monday to consult on a suitable date.'

'I'll be happy to help in any way I can.'

'This morning's work is in your safe. If you can manage it, I'd like the week's extracts finished this afternoon. I won't be back tonight, but I'll be in early tomorrow, I expect by 0600.'

'You'll be in town at the usual location, if we need to reach you?'

'Yes.' He smoothed his clipped brown mustache and pushed his glasses further up his nose. 'Go home early today, Miriam. That's an order. Relax this once for me.'

'Thank you, sir. I'll try. There is one thing—'

'Oh, Lou Benson stopped to see you. He said he'd drop by later.'

'Thank you. I'll phone him after you leave. There is one matter I do need to raise with you, sir. It's rather a—'

'Could it wait until tomorrow? I'm running behind now, though if you think we should, I can—'

'No problem, sir. We can talk first thing in the morning. I'll be in early myself.'

'Fine.' General Clarke walked toward the door that Captain Robert Louis Benson had just opened, saying, 'Come on in, Lou. Make her go home early.'

'I'll try, sir.' Lou Benson saluted and stood back, so Carter Clarke could walk past. 'Got a question for you, Miriam.'

'Oh, so I should be surprised? Benson, the born inquisitor?' She smiled when she said it, her dark eyes teasing him behind her usual watchful intelligence.

'That's what I get paid for, right? Persistence and curiosity?' Lou Benson's wide wise mouth was smiling cryptically off to one side, while he lit a Lucky with a Zippo.

'I wouldn't know. None of us here understands what you do.'

He ignored that, the way she'd known he would, and said, 'We need you to talk to a group about Muggeridge. 1933. His year in the USSR. How the Western press reacted. Why you knew to order his books from England before they were published here. Friday lunch. Does that fit your schedule? The large meeting room in Building B? Right at twelve fifteen?'

'Sure. I can do that. You're gonna end up a historian, Lou. Writing about us weirdos. Telling the world what actually happened.'

'Think so?' He was grinning down at her, his brown hair combed perfectly, his officer's uniform well fitted and immaculate, thick black eyebrows as inquisitive as ever above cool analytical eyes. 'There're worse things I'd be good at I guess.'

'Yeah, and I'm too young to hear about them.'

He laughed before he said, 'I'll see you Friday, Miri.' He was already out the door by then, heading toward the center stairs. 'Remember to bring a bag lunch.'

'Have you seen Carl?' Miriam Gold was looking at the girl at the desk next to Carl Walker's, in a room absolutely packed with desks – with people using the same desks, facing each other across them, with bent backs and concentrated eyes staring at strips of print.

'Carl Walker?' It was freezing in the room, and the young woman, like most of the others, was wearing a hat and coat. 'Not the new Carl, who—'

'Right. I've never known Walker not to be here at four.

Have you? Unless there was a meeting of everybody working on the problem, and today we aren't—'

'He had another kind of meeting. I don't know where. Training someone they've just brought in. I think here. Not in DC. It might've been over with the radio guys.'

'When he comes back will you tell him I need to talk to him? It's urgent. Tell him that. Urgent. Tell him that if he doesn't get in touch with me before the end of the day, I'll stop by his apartment between six and six thirty.'

'OK.' The young woman was staring at a page of printed columns, running her finger down the five number strings, with a pencil clamped between her teeth.

'Cathy?' Miriam Gold waited. When the young woman was looking at her again, she said, 'This is a very serious matter. It's extremely important that I talk to him tonight, so don't forget to tell him, OK? Between six and six thirty at his apartment, if he doesn't find me first.'

'Sure. Yeah. I'll remember. He came in to work at four a.m., so I'm sure he'll be home by six fifteen. You know how he is. Following schedules he makes to the minute. Arriving at four a.m. Going home at five thirty, even if he comes back later.'

A plump man in a gray winter coat, on a night-time street in Arlington, Virginia, collided with a tiny woman carrying a cardboard box tight against her coat. He took his hat off and smiled at her before he said, 'Excuse me. I wasn't looking where I was going.'

It was she who hadn't been watching, which wasn't like her at all. And even then, her small brown eyes didn't glance in his direction. Miriam Gold hurried on, walking into a blustering wind, clutching her box against her chest.

A black purse dangled from an elbow. A brown feather hat slid slowly to one side at the same slant as her glasses. The sausage-roll of dark brown hair that had started out on the nape of her neck was hanging half undone. The sturdy heels of her brown Oxford shoes snapped against the pavement as one shin after the other hit the thick folded-up hem of the belted brown coat she'd bought second-hand her freshman year in college.

She didn't see the store lights inside the steamy windows,

or the restaurant signs hung with Christmas bulbs above the
crowded sidewalks, or the flocks of cars running for home,
with their headlights shimmering on the oil-slicked puddles
speckling the shining streets.

She hugged her package and stared straight ahead, a look
of anguish on her thin plain face – a raw face, exposed and
undefended, a wiry child's with a high bony nose on a woman
close to thirty, a grown-up outsider who's faced the worst and
decided not to let it kill her.

Her mind was fixed on understanding, the way it had been
since the day she was born with a gift of mind that had taken
her from a cold-water walk-up on Delancey Street in New
York City to Barnard on a scholarship, during the worst of
the Depression.

She poked and argued and berated herself, as she rushed
along Washington Boulevard. She blamed the man who had
it coming. Then looked at her life, and what she'd come from,
and asked why it was happening again. Why we often do that
– face the same problems time after time when they're not
even of our making? Why couldn't she get away from it, no
matter where she turned?

Anybody could see she'd gotten as far as she could, with
what she'd known to do. Far enough her family wouldn't talk
to her. Nor would the family friends.

It was just like a religion to them. Though they were the
ones who sneered. 'Religion's the opiate of the masses, Miri.'
Her mama had said that day after day, as long as she could
remember.

Their intentions were good, she had to give them that, real
concern and compassion. They wanted Utopia here on this
earth, where we're stuck with flesh and blood men.

Mama and Papa deny what they don't like, that's where
they're culpable. Bearing in mind that denial's human. We're
all guilty in our own ways, but it's an unexamined reaction
with them. A willful, mindless swallowing of blatant prop-
aganda.

Hitler was great when he was Stalin's buddy. She'd listened
to that too many times. 'The reports of persecution, they gotta
be exaggerated, Miri.' Then the second he and Stalin fell out,
it was, 'Hitler, he's a monster!' Which she could've told 'em
to begin with, if they would've listened.

How many times did her Papa say, 'This Muggeridge guy can't be talking the truth. Uncle Joe wouldn't massacre the peasants!' And then when it finally leaked out, even in *Time* in 1940, all over everywhere after the war, he'd say, 'You gotta break eggs to make omelets, Miri. You wait, he knows what he's doing.'

Now it's Bill, doing worse than they could. And the un-examined life is mine, making me want to scream. Letting myself get used like this, like an ordinary simpleton dupe!

I can't stand by and watch. I can't. With Mama and Papa I didn't have a choice, but now with this I do. A clear, sworn duty's what I've got. And why I should hesitate one single second I couldn't begin to say.

Bill Weisberg didn't care about her. Even if he did, what difference would it make, if she looked at the greater scheme – the only context that mattered in circumstances like hers.

Susannah had been right, and that was a bitter pill. One she'd have to swallow. Since she'd told herself it was sour grapes. The pain of the jilted. Everywhere, and always. When one look in a cracked mirror should've shown her the truth.

All the women I've mocked for being used should come back quick and haunt me. All he ever wanted was informa-tion, and that's exactly what he got. A little here, a trickle there, a reference to a colleague. There was no other reason he would've wanted me, not when he'd had Susannah.

Stop now before you start cryin'. You've been rubbing salt in that wound all day. Now you need to concentrate on how to explain to Carl.

Getting him the copies was the main thing. That would make it far more unlikely that Bill would try to silence her. Short-term, or long.

A significant question, whether he was violent. One she couldn't answer. She'd never seen evidence, one way or the other, of what he'd do if he were in danger with his back against a wall.

She'd need a way to defuse him when he found out she knew. And formulating that sort of tactic should've begun weeks ago. She had no appreciable attributes for this kind of situation. She was no good at dissembling. She couldn't

double-deal. Whatever she thought was there on her face for
the whole world to see.

She'd just climbed the steps of a dingy brick apartment
building on the north side of Pershing Drive, and she leaned
the box against the right-hand wall while she pressed Carl
Walker's buzzer.

She wiped her left eye with the back of her hand, and waited
for him to answer. Then said, 'NO!' out loud, as a woman
stepped out and glanced at her as she passed.

*Carl's the original creature of habit, he's gotta be home by
now!*

This time he wasn't. And Miriam told herself to push
someone else's button, and get ready to run through the
door.

She climbed the dark rickety stairs to Carl's apartment on
the fourth floor, the stench of cigars and fatback bacon hanging
in cold damp air. She stopped in the center of a dark narrow
hall and set the box on the creaking floorboards in front of
Walker's door.

She'd prepared for the possibility. She'd brought the books,
and the rest to make it work, in case Carl wasn't home. Or
Bill had started to follow her, without her being aware.

She pulled a small jar of rubber cement out of her leather
bag, and squatted on her heels while she opened the cardboard box.

She took out a pad of paper and wrote a note telling Carl
she was moving to a smaller apartment and needed to give
away books. These were ones she thought he'd like, and she'd
call him that night to explain in detail.

She slid the note under the door. Then wrote another like
it that she taped to the top of the box. She pulled out a very
thick hardback book, and unscrewed the lid on the rubber
cement.

A little more than an hour later, Miriam Gold stood in the
hallway of her own apartment building phoning Carl Walker
from the payphone.

He still wasn't answering, which made her say, 'Son of a
pup!' the way her father did, imitating his rumbling Russian
accent, before she hung up the heavy receiver and waited for
her nickel to shoot out the slot.

She climbed the stairs to the third floor – and found her door unlocked. She knew she'd locked it. And she stood and stared at it, feeling her heart hit the front of her throat, then drop inside her stomach.

She thought about not going in. Weighing options, worrying for half a minute – before she pushed the door open as quietly as she could. The hinges squeaked the way they always did.

And Bill stepped out of the bedroom.

He said, 'Hi. Where you been? I thought we'd go out to dinner.' He was tall and dark-haired and had a large wide face that wasn't what anyone would call wildly handsome, but when he smiled the way he did then he looked charming, and kind, and intriguing – a man who's done things, and lived everywhere, and knows what women want.

'I don't think I will tonight, Bill. I'm not feeling very well.'

'No?' He stepped over to her and shut the door behind her, before he leaned down to kiss her mouth. 'Come in the bedroom. I got something I think you'll like.'

'Let me make a cup of tea first.'

'Come on, honey, I want to show you now.' He'd wrapped his arm around her shoulders and was pulling her toward the bedroom door.

'Can't it wait a minute? I—'

'Look what I found for you.' He led her into the bedroom first, then went back in the living room to turn on the cabinet radio next to her bedroom door. He shut the door, and turned to face her, then walked past her to the window and yanked on the swollen sash. 'Man, it's hot in here. How can you stand it? Staying here's worse than it'd have to be with every room this hot.'

'What?'

'The hot-water heat you can't turn off.'

'I know what you meant, but I—'

'Pick up the magazine on the bed.'

It was hers. *Life*. She'd bought it the day before.

'Look what's under it.'

There were five photographs under the *Life* – two-by-three-inch black-and-whites.

Blood had begun to pound in her ears by the time she finally said, 'Bill—'

'Yeah?' He pulled her up against him from where she'd

sat on the bed, grabbing her elbows, pinning them against her sides. 'Clever girl, hunh? Taped to the top of the medicine cabinet! Why would you do this to me? I thought you loved me!'

'That's not the point, is it?'

'There couldn't be some other explanation, beside the conclusion you jumped to? You actually think I'd compromise the work? Do you?! Miriam? You? Knowing me like you do?'

'It looks clear enough to me.'

He let go of her arms, and shoved her on to the bed, then swiveled to face the window. 'It ever occurred to you I could be meeting these guys for Carter Clarke? Feeding them disinformation he wants them to get? Crap! I thought you loved me. You can't love me and believe this and do what you're doing now!'

'If what you say is true, Clarke will know what to do when I talk to him, and no harm'll be done. Right? Bill? No harm will be done! But I've got to tell him what I know. You know that. You know what's expected of us. You know what we agreed to.'

'Yeah? What evidence you got beside the pictures?'

'I heard what you said, on the payphone outside the Teahouse.'

'When?'

'Six or seven weeks ago. A Sunday afternoon.'

'Go on.'

'I saw what happened in the park twice. And when you got picked up this morning by the guy from the embassy in the Packard. The trash can too. As you can see.'

'And those are the times you got the pictures?'

Miriam nodded, and clenched her hands in her lap.

'What about the list?'

'Kinda speaks for itself, wouldn't ya say?'

'Who else have you told?'

'I don't want to talk about it.'

'What d'ya mean by that?'

'Light me a cigarette, would you, please?'

He pulled a Chesterfield out of her pack, and handed it, lit, to Miriam, before he lit another for himself. 'I can't believe you'd think this. You, of all people.'

Neither of them said anything. He stood. She sat. A small, thin, nervous-looking woman in a shapeless sweater-set and wool skirt that was no color, and no style, but fought with her cheap pink pearls. 'What did you mean before? About the heating when you stay here. What else did you—?'

'You have other copies of the photos?'

Miriam hesitated for less than a second, then shook her head while she French-inhaled like a half-grown child hoping to look sophisticated.

'Tell me exactly what you've done. Come on, Miriam, now. Did you talk to anyone else, or make prints from these originals?'

'I'm taking them to Carter tomorrow. I just got them done today. Why were you searching my room?'

'Why?! Oh, I don't know, why would I?'

'Bill—'

'I saw you watching from the grocer's shop when I got in the car this morning. I'm not stupid, and you're not the operations type. Can't you see I wouldn't do it? I wouldn't betray the Hall!' He was looking out the window, at the alley between him and the side of a warehouse without windows or doors. He shoved his gloved hands in his topcoat pockets, then leaned out to look at the corner. 'Come over here a second. Who's that at the entrance to the alley? You sure you haven't talked to anybody else?'

'No, I told you.' Miriam got up off the bed, and walked across to the window. He put one arm around her shoulders and pointed to the end of the alley.

'Where? I don't see anybody.'

He shoved her then, with both hands, picking her up and throwing her out, watching her slap on to cold wet brick, her arms and legs mangled.

She'd screamed on the way down. But she would've anyway. Whether she'd jumped or been pushed.

He dropped her Chesterfields on to the bed, picked up the photographs and put them in his wallet, looked at the bedroom for what shouldn't be there, at the living room too, as he put on his hat, and locked the door behind him.

He took the back stairs to the alley, passing no one and hearing nothing but a door or two opening, and voices calling somewhere up above.

Miriam lay on the east side, almost a block from his end of the alley, and he pulled his collar up and walked the other way, thinking about Susannah, wondering where she could've gone, and what he'd have to do to find her.

Two

It had been an unsettling day. An intensely disturbing one, if the truth were known. And Carl Walker only began to come to grips with it as he drove north on High Street in Columbus, Ohio, heading home to Worthington.

No one could have known that. His face didn't begin to change. He'd trained it years before, so the green-gray eyes gave nothing away, and the shy smile that made him better looking came and went for colleagues in the parking lot, while the mind behind it went its way.

He'd finished the last of his planning for fall term at Ohio State (curriculum notes, committee reports, graduate-student evaluations), and there'd been some satisfaction in getting it out of the way. But a thick, heavy, settled oppression had been weighing him down ever since.

He knew exactly where it came from. It was where it was leading, and what it implied, that was giving Carl Walker pause.

A woman had walked toward him in the quad who'd looked like Miriam Gold. He'd stopped in his tracks, watching her coming closer, turning to watch her walk away – till he'd realized people were noticing, and he'd forced himself not to stare.

Her glasses hadn't been the same, but the dark glossy hair, and her small delicate frame, and the strong distinct features that reflected at least a shadow of the look – the serious concentrated other-worldly look – he'd admired so much on Miriam.

Miriam had not been a pretty woman. Even he wouldn't have said that. It was the measure of her commitment – the physical imprint of what that was – that was so unusual and so striking. The engrossed attention that would sweep across her face when she was searching for the right word while translating a passage (or considering the truth of a statement, or what could be proved, and what, finally, couldn't) – *that* was what would transform her face into something so rare and beautiful it had made him hide his own eyes so she wouldn't know what it meant to him.

When she'd smiled, it was a free, open, true smile that came from what she cared about. With wonder in it much of the time, and tenderness too, that was childlike. And if he was wholly truthful with himself, there hadn't been a day since she'd died that he hadn't wished he could see it.

It was ten years, nearly. And he still had no doubt how it had happened. He'd never believed she'd jumped. She'd had no reason that made any sense, even if Weisberg had ended the affair. And that was the story he'd bandied about, being the kind of worm he was, before he left town so abruptly. Without telling Carter Clarke, of course – that had been incriminating in itself, leaving minutes after the suicide verdict without informing his boss.

Miriam wouldn't have killed herself. She wasn't emotional in that way. Nor had she been spineless. Miriam had survived extreme deprivation, and been toughened on the way through. Hunger. Persecution. Forced emigration. Poverty. Isolation. Miriam stayed fixed to her principles even when they'd alienated her entire extended family, and hers had been an immigrant family firmly bound together. She would *not* have lost the will to live because a man she'd known for six months or less had decided to throw her over.

Carl had never doubted that. And now, *finally* – now that he'd found what she'd *given* him to find – he knew how Miriam had died as clearly as he knew why. He could kick himself for overlooking it for so long. For not realizing there had to be more to it, and working harder to find it.

It was some consolation that he'd rightly predicted in '47 that Weisberg would disappear. Two years later, as it turned out, out in California, as soon as he'd been released from prison for refusing to talk to a grand jury. That disappearance hadn't surprised Carl at all, and it gave him confidence now.

For he was equally convinced that Weisberg would come back. With a different name. With a different job. Someday

Weisberg would come looking, out of pride if nothing else. Wanting what he'd lost then, claiming it as his own.

Carl knew he'd done what he could do. He'd come where Weisberg would, when Weisberg learned where Susannah was. Not through any great brilliance on his part, but because of Patricia Bennett.

Patricia had helped Susannah disappear, and was still the only person Susannah had told of her whereabouts. Patricia saw better than Susannah that Susannah needed protection, and she kept Carl informed and hid his involvement from Susannah.

Weisberg was at a disadvantage without Patricia's help, but he had intelligence, and an over-abundance of hubris, and it had to be only a matter of time.

And yet how long could Carl waste away there? Writing meaningless articles. Translating works he cared little about. Teaching students what they didn't wish to learn.

Of course, none of that mattered as much as the manner of her death. The cruelty and the arrogance, *that* caught in his craw. The way Weisberg ripped her life from her acted as a goad still.

It may well have been a subjective interpretation, but Carl liked to think that once Weisberg was done with her, she would've come to care for him. She nearly had, before Weisberg arrived. Or so Carl still believed.

Yet, simply to know she was alive and well, striding down a street on this earth, able to study and write what meant most to her. To both of them, if it came to that, in the times in which they'd lived. *That* would've been enough for him, even if he'd wished for more.

But preparations remained to be made. And the next time he saw Ben Reese he absolutely had to raise the issue of Ben's experience in the war. There was much Reese could teach him that could fortify Carl against Weisberg when the need arose. And yet, he'd told Reese nothing. His own caution and reticence continually holding him back.

Carl still assumed that in time of need the documents would engage and intrigue Reese. But the death of Reese's wife could work against him. Grief might prevent Ben from taking up the work. All Carl could hope to do was approach him intelligently, and leave the rest to fate.

Carl told himself he ought to set a date. So that after some specific day, if Weisberg hadn't appeared, he'd move home to Maine to take up work that attracted him. He wasn't yet forty. Much of life lay before him. There he could see his family, and walk the forests and the rocky coast he missed everywhere else.

Why was he so discouraged? He mustn't lose sight of the salient fact that this was where Weisberg would come.

Carl tuned the car radio to the classical station, but kept the volume low. Still unable to shake the sadness that had curdled his insides since morning. For he did know, regardless of what he told himself, that he *could* be entirely wrong.

Weisberg might *not* return. If what he'd heard seven years ago were true, and he *had* been seen on the other side. They'd be bound to treat Weisberg well. He'd find himself made much of. He wouldn't wait in food lines, or share a room in a crumbling barrack with three families or more.

But he did so savor the emoluments of life. Good food. Fine wine. Beautifully turned-out women. Carl couldn't imagine Weisberg choosing to make it a permanent home.

He could've gone on to Egypt, where an Englishman reported having seen him. Weisberg had spent his childhood there, after his parents fled Odessa, and the underbelly of Cairo would present a certain allure for one with his proclivities.

Yet he did so enjoy being an insider that Carl expected Weisberg would want to get back in the business. On the fringes, at least, with an eye on the players. Though there were other likely locations, Berlin foremost among them.

Lennox wouldn't let it rest. The one positive aspect of the whole complicated business was that Lennox would keep Carl informed in whatever manner was allowed.

Making what Carl had chosen the only option he had.

She belonged to him. That's the way Weisberg would look at it. Perhaps more significantly still, a woman who'd loved him had left him, artfully arranging her life so he'd been unable to find her for years. That would eat away at him, and eventually make him reckless.

If there was any truth in Carl's assumptions. He might be simply a self-deluded fool. Living life in the shadows. Feeding on lies and distortions.

Still, putting all personal thoughts aside, the tragic results of Weisberg's treachery were of far greater significance. The damage he'd done couldn't be underestimated, and no one who understood what was at stake could overlook his role.

Yes, but what would he himself do if it turned out he'd been wrong? Pack it in, as the Brits would say? With a muzzle in the mouth, in the gray of winter? Or stand up on his two hind legs and make a better life?

Carl Walker rubbed his narrow forehead, then pushed his sunglasses up his nose, as he stopped at the light in Worthington, a block south of the Captain's Inn where he planned to eat an early dinner.

It was a few minutes before five, but he knew Bobby would let him in. They'd chat in the kitchen for a moment or two, if the front weren't ready to seat him.

He'd turned off the radio, and was gazing at the light, when two men walked out of the real-estate office on his left, three buildings further on toward the Captain's Inn.

The light changed, and Carl drove closer to where the two stood on the corner by an easel displaying rental ads for North Columbus and Worthington. The shorter man pulled a photo off the board, and handed the other a key.

Carl Walker stared, his hands clamped hard on the wheel, and then whispered, 'Weisberg!' before he stuck his arm out the window to signal a left-hand turn.

He drove along the side of the inn, pulled into the third drive beyond it, and turned around toward High. He parked on the right next to the realty, turned off the engine, and opened a newspaper, pretending to read while he watched the men talking on the corner.

Bobby Chambers, wearing his chef's whites and carrying a wide wicker basket, walked toward the vegetable plot he'd planted in a sunny corner behind the Captain's Inn. He'd just dumped the weeds he'd pulled into the fenced-in bin in the back, and had stopped to light a cigarette, while he gazed at his rows of tender new lettuce.

He was humming a mountain song his mother had sung when he and the rest were young. And as he sat down, for the first time since dawn, on the warm brick steps, he was thinking about the gardens they'd grown at home in Black Mountain.

He'd hated the work then. Even though he'd known exactly why it'd had to be done. That could've been part of why he'd hated it – that it was one of too many tedious necessities when there wasn't cash money coming in. You had to be hoeing, weeding, hauling water, liming the outhouse, shoveling horse dung, pulling worms off tobacco – chopping it down, too, and tying it up, killing yourself to get it cured right – picking blackberries up and down the mountains, sweat stinging your scratches, making it feel like you'd scrambled across all of North Carolina.

The garden had kept the ten of them alive, with the squirrel they'd shot, and the rabbit. And he could still see his papa, a thin yellow hand-rolled in his mouth, hoeing between the rows when the sun was hotter than blazes on Black Mountain, and his momma was picking pole beans with Eliza Joy on her back.

A lot had happened in the years in between that'd changed the way he saw things. The war being the main one. You couldn't go through something like that and come home the same.

The GI Bill was the best of it for him, him and plenty of others. He'd gotten himself on-the-job training and real credentials he could take all over from a brand-new cooking school up in New York State. It gave him a future he could look forward to, doing something he liked.

Course, I gotta give Beth Morland credit. Seeing how we lived like she did, when Papa took care of her aunt's cabin. She never has thrown my family in my face in any way at all. But that don't mean nothin' in the long run. Her and me, we ain't going nowhere. The gap's too big today yet, with her daddy what he is, and my family bein' so—

Bobby stared at the brown Ford sedan getting parked across the road. He smiled first, and waved at Carl, then let his hand drop while he watched.

Why is Carl just sittin' there, holding a paper in front of his face, watchin' them two up the road?

Three

'Ben, it's been three months since Jessie died, and it's time you got out of the house . . .' Richard West was smiling when he said it, lying in an antique dentist chair at one end of his living room, holding a pre-war receiver against his ear, using his you-know-I'm-at-least-half-teasing voice, before he laughed out loud. 'Very clever, but you know what I mean, for something other than work . . .'

'Then think of that poor man whose seat is next to yours! You know who I mean, the thin fellow, painfully shy, who . . . Carl, yes. One can see there're very few he feels able to talk to, and it meant a great deal to him that you and Jessie would ask him to join you after the concerts.'

Ben suggested that Richard take his tickets, but Richard told him he couldn't. He had to meet a graduate student, and finish an essay for *National Review*. 'Ben, please! Do it for Carl Walker. Support the Columbus Symphony.'

Ben said he was up to his elbows restoring an old painting. And Richard sighed, and relit his pipe. 'There was more life in Jessie Gerard Reese than any other woman either of us has ever met, and she would *not* want you to do nothing but work yourself to death, and stare at your living-room walls . . . True. Yes, I'll grant you that. You do stare at your landlord's sheep, but I see no reason to laugh!'

Richard listened, and shook his head, then snorted into the phone. 'Of course I'm meddling! *I* know you'd rather I simply folded my tent and silently stole away, but . . . Excellent! You have my unmitigated, undying respect. Let's hope they do justice to Beethoven's Fifth.'

Richard West dropped the receiver on the heavy black cradle that rocked unsteadily on his stomach, hoping he wasn't pushing Ben Reese more than he ought to risk. He wasn't a man who'd take pushing. *And how can I, of all people, presume, when my own experience is so dissimilar?*

I never could've done what he did in the war. I, who sat gratefully in England cosseted at Bletchley Park. I can't understand what he went through, or its lasting effects. What would I know of his grief? Or of what will help him recover?

It is a shame the dog died. He was good for Ben once Jessie was gone, keeping him company as he tramped the fields at every hour of the night.

Richard West ruffled a hand through his thin auburn hair, smoothing it toward the side finally, before drumming his fingers on the phone. He lay for a moment, with his hands on his chest, humming the beginning of *Rhapsody In Blue*, absently typing the word 'morning' on his vest, asking himself what lemons might be left for making veal piccata.

Ben Reese sat still and straight, his hands on the arms of the green padded seat in the balcony of Veterans' Memorial Hall, asking himself why he was there – and why Walker wasn't. Carl Walker had never missed a concert. Not one since his sister had started the Columbus Symphony shortly after the war.

Ben adjusted his tie, before he looked at his watch – at the empty seat on his left again too, and the empty one on his right. Then he stared at the orchestra tuning to the concert-master, trying not to make eye contact with any more of the nodding acquaintances he and Jessie had waved to, the look on his own face, set and distant and carefully self-contained.

Carl would've understood that. He'd sat on Ben's left, year in and year out, arriving early, leaving late, making sporadic conversation about teaching Russian and German, asking more about Alderton University (where Ben was an archivist and Jessie'd taught English), revealing next to nothing about himself, personal or professional.

Ben never would've said he knew Carl, but he did know he felt sorry for him – a quiet, lonely, soft-spoken man with no apparent family or friends since his sister, Evelyn, had died. Carl had told Ben at her funeral that he'd never missed a concert in honor of her dedication, and wouldn't on his deathbed – that he'd even driven from Washington when he'd worked there years before.

But it's five minutes of eight now, and he's nowhere to be seen. Which makes me wonder if—

'Dr Reese?' It was the woman behind Ben, leaning over his shoulder. 'May I lay my evening jacket on the seat beside you? I don't know if you remember me, I'm Celia Jergen. My husband's Chairman of the Physics Department at Ohio State.'

The husband nodded vaguely in Ben's direction, but didn't look embarrassed the way Ben would have, if his wife had dropped his title into a stranger's lap.

Ben told her to put it in the seat on his right, that Carl was still expected.

'I was so sorry to hear about your wife. It's good to see you out again taking an interest in life.' She was a large woman with a sheep-shaped head and nervous blue eyes.

Ben heard himself say, 'Thank you,' while he felt his face clench, muscle and skin tightening against sharp-edged bone. He wanted to say, is that what I'm doing, taking an interest? You know me well enough to know, when we've never had what I would call the beginning of a conversation?

But he didn't. No, he tightened the reins. He sat and kept his mouth shut, telling himself she meant well.

And how would she *know what to say, when you never have with anyone else whose husband or wife died, so stop expecting perfection.*

I hope Carl hasn't had an accident trying to get here on time.

Ben fidgeted during the Ravel and the Mozart. He stared at the conductor, then counted violinists, his mind still on the empty seats waiting on either side.

He went out during the intermission, and ran across to the phone booth at the corner of Broad and Bell – but didn't find a listing for Carl Walker in Worthington.

The operator told him the number was unlisted.

And Ben walked toward his car, wondering why Carl had an unlisted number when almost nobody did. And who he knew at OSU who could dig up Carl's home number.

Ben was in bed by midnight.

And awake again at one.

He'd dreamt about Jessie, lying beside him, laughing against

the side of his neck, her head nestled on his shoulder, sliding
her left hand across his stomach, till he turned and kissed her
large soft mouth, pulling her close the length of his body,
taking her ear lobe gently in his teeth – when he woke up in
an empty bed blinking in a pool of moonlight.

He pulled on his shorts and slipped out through the study
without turning on the lights, carrying the pack of Camels he
kept in the old oak table that had been Jessie's desk. He only
smoked when he'd dreamt about her.

Or when he'd dreamt about his war in Europe. Blood. Death.
Body parts. The dreams that left him sweating. Caught behind
the lines again, having to search the corners.

Those dreams always ended the way his own war actually
had, with him bleeding on to a stretcher strapped underneath
a Piper Cub, flying under the ack-ack fire through the tops
of snow-covered fir, hearing himself scream in the dark before
the landing knocked him out.

So this wasn't that. And that's something.

This is sadness. This is just grief.

*Nothing neurotic here now. Nothing you wouldn't expect.
If you hadn't made assumptions about the path your life would
take.*

Ben smiled, a quick self-mocking grin, as he stepped out
on to the front porch, and sat in one of the bent-twig chairs
Jessie had bought in Kentucky.

It was still and cool, and the sheep in the pasture twenty
yards away looked like small shifting oval clouds in patches
of swirling mist. Some drifted slowly, tearing at dew-covered
grass. Others slept, curled up together. Some lay tucked into
shallows scattered in rolling ground.

Ben watched and listened, and told himself to think about
it then, that trying not to worked when he was working, but
not in the middle of the night. *Get the letter and find a candle.
Then go back to bed when you're done.*

March 1, 1957

Dear Ben,

I've been thinking about you this week while you've
been working in Philadelphia. It's brought the war back,
unexpectedly: all those years of waiting for your letters;
of following the news with heart-pounding fear and

bone-wearying worry; of not knowing where you were and what you were facing, afraid it would have been even worse if I actually had.

I didn't call it fear then, or worry, either one. We kept those moments private here, to keep from unraveling one another. Every father, every brother, every son in the States; every woman with a husband, son, brother, or boyfriend in Europe, and the Pacific, fought the same anxieties. Your work was riskier than some, as you know better than I. And that I kept to myself as well, the way you did then, and have since you've been home.

Wherever you were when you wrote the last letter, I knew meant nothing by the time I got it; that intelligence would send you to any army that needed a scout behind the lines, and all I could do at home was pray.

Pray, and read your letters over and over, and be thankful you were who you were. That's really all we ever can do, isn't it (in a war, or out of one) – pray and take the next step required. None of us can get ourselves home from the grocery store with our brains and bodies intact. Yet we act as though we can. We take our lives for granted, when all of us know better where we keep our silent secrets hidden from our own eyes.

I'm not saying that I've been afraid for you while you were gone this week. First of all, there was no good reason to, and secondly, you know me. I hold myself together. I'm not generally sentimental. I love my work and lose myself in it. I like being here alone, with Sam and the sheep and the cats in the barn, with woods and fields that tell me to watch and listen every second.

You have been on my mind, though, a great deal more than normal. And I feel the need to talk about it.

You're the only man I've ever met that I could have married. Your mind and soul make me whole, and amaze me too, as you very well know, to say nothing of your body (which was the first thing that attracted me to you, though that wouldn't have taken us anywhere if talking to you hadn't been what it was).

The things you wrote from the front – who else could have done that in just the sort of way that suited my own peculiar character? (I can hear you paraphrasing

Samuel Johnson, 'Being likely to die at any given moment concentrates the mind wonderfully.') It's what you believe, and what you think is important in life, and the way you stand on that when pushed; it's the interest you take in all kinds of things that I know nothing about; it's the way you play, and make me laugh, and surprise me daily when I least expect it – it's made me better than I could be without you, and comforts me deep in my bones.

This isn't well written. I could do better if I weren't so tired. I was soaking in the tub, smiling at the way you were playing with Sam the other night when you put your T-shirt on his hairy old head, and I suddenly felt compelled to haul myself out and dash this off before I climb into bed. I'm teaching George Eliot tomorrow, and need to be at school by six.

If anything happens to me, at least you'll have these lame, limited words (with excess alliteration) to help remember me by. I love you, Ben. I thank God every day that He brought you home, when, and how, and in the shape He did. That first year and a half when you were in the hospital was indescribable. The fact that you lived, and ended up whole, despite the pain and countless surgeries – we saw how much we were given, and it changed us both for ever.

Do not let this flattery go to your head, however. Due to your many deficiencies, I will continue to beat you at Scrabble without pity or mercy.

I appreciate the way you keep the furnace stoked too. Absence makes the cold heart grow fonder. Coal shoveling's a pain in the back, especially in my blimp-like condition.

Your reasonably honest, but obstreperous, consort,
Jessie Gerard Reese

Ben folded the letter and laid it on the table. Then lit another Camel.

At least today I could see her when I tried to picture her. Yesterday was disconcerting. Trying and drawing a blank.

So pay attention to what she said. You got home. They put you back together. You had twelve years that were better than anyone has a right to expect. How many scouts like you had that? How many Rangers either?

Ben was thinking about their last afternoon, when they'd walked the west woods after work, throwing a tennis ball for Sam. She'd heated up pot roast, while he fixed the kitchen faucet. She'd read him *Persuasion* as he'd made a fire. They'd sat on the sofa and talked for an hour, starting with the student Ben had bailed out the night before for being drunk and disorderly.

They'd talked again about how to raise their baby, once it actually arrived. Then moved on to that week's news – the horrible treatment of Negro men and women on a bus in Birmingham, Alabama; the plight of Hungarian refugees, who'd run from Russian tanks, and were now in the US. Jessie had graded essays then, while Ben deciphered a pioneer letter he'd found in Alderton's archives.

He could almost see the faded ink and smell the musty paper, so he told himself to stop right there. To leave the rest of Thursday night alone, and think about who she'd been.

He'd been stunted, in a way, before he'd married her. She'd been exactly the wife he'd needed, as much as the lover he'd wanted, and the best friend he'd ever have.

She grilled me when it was good for me. She held me when I woke up sweating. She wanted strength and perspective from me, and help with the outside world.

Work mostly. Competitors and friends. The politics of academe.

And now it's time to go to bed.

Remember to call Richard, and tell him about Carl.

Ben crushed his cigarette out in the ashtray, then picked up the letter and took it to the study, where he put it away in his desk.

So how can three months feel like a lifetime and less than a minute too? A string of days in no man's land, caught between the lines.

Four

It *had* been three months earlier, no matter how it seemed. It'd been that same night, after they'd talked by the fire. Jessie had gotten ready for bed, but Ben was waiting till later – till it was time to stoke the furnace and bank it to last till dawn.

He'd been reading Ray Bradbury on top of the covers, still wearing jeans and a flannel shirt – when he'd rolled over and laid his hand on Jessie's hard warm stomach, feeling the smooth, tight-muscled skin buckle and push against his hand. 'Does that hurt, Jess? The baby's head like that?'

'It's a funny feeling, but it doesn't hurt.' She laughed at him then, at the serious look in his eyes, as she undid his shirt and kissed the ridges of his ribs.

Ben bent down and kissed her mouth for a minute, then the small smooth hollow underneath her ear, whispering, 'Better not start what you don't want to finish, because—'

'Why would you think I wouldn't? Remember our honeymoon? You had casts on your left arm and leg, and bandages on the right that—'

'Don't remind me! I can still smell the cast on my arm.' He kissed her on the end of her nose, and then said, 'Thank you for the letter, by the way.'

'It was the least I could do.'

'I got so few of yours during the war, it's good to have one like that. Why'd you write it now, though? I was only gone—'

'Things like that need to get said, and we don't make the effort very often. Most of us did during the war. That's one of the good things about danger. When life gets safer, we tend to clam up.'

'You worried?' Ben was sliding his fingers down her arm, on their way to holding her hand.

'Some. The other baby was stillborn. It makes you think about what could happen.'

'But you feel OK? Dr Boyes hasn't said there're any problems?'

'No, he thinks I'm doing fine. But *I* thought you ought to have something that tells you what I think about you after having put up with you all this time.' Jessie's shoulder-length dark brown hair was spread across a pressed white pillow-case, her long thin legs were bent toward Ben on top of the satin-covered comforter, her large blue eyes were serious but smiling as she watched Ben Reese watch her.

Sam, the mutt, long-haired and big, a Lab–retriever mix maybe, laid his cold pink nose on Jessie's arm – which made her reach over and rub his ears. 'You're a very good boy, Sammy. And I bet you want to go out.'

'I'll take him. I might as well do the furnace too.'

'I'll just lie here and watch you work.'

'At least I *can* get up.'

'*That* was a low blow!'

'True.' Ben grabbed her hand as she tried to tickle him.

And she laughed and kissed the scar bisecting his left palm. 'I'd better enjoy being lazy now, because after the baby's born, I'll be the one getting up every night.'

Ben gazed at her, in her cream-colored gown, pink and golden-skinned and fragile-looking to him in ways he couldn't have explained, with her firm rounded middle and her soft creamy breasts. She made him want to do something serious to show her how much it pulled at him, at what was deep and gentle and protective in him, seeing her carry his child.

Nothing appropriate came to mind, as usual, so he rumpled her hair and kissed her forehead, and told Sam to come with him.

It was twenty minutes later when he got back to the bedroom. Sam had bolted, and the coal furnace had taken more shoveling than he'd expected.

And he found Jess on the edge of the bed, white and worried, making herself breathe slowly.

'It's started, Ben.'

'You sure?'

'I'm not even seven months yet! I don't want to lose this baby!' Her hands were on her abdomen, covered now by a dark green jumper, dark blue eyes on Ben.

'I don't want to lose it either, you know that. You do. But the most important thing to me is keeping you safe. I'll call Boyes and get him to meet us there.'

They treated Ben like a trespasser. The older nurses were the worst, staring at him as though he were to blame, or he'd suddenly become a dim-witted child since he'd last looked in a mirror.

Dr Boyes took him aside and told him not to expect miracles with a six-and-a-half-month baby. That someday they'd be able to do better, but the time hadn't come.

Ben wanted to be with Jess while she went through it, but husbands weren't allowed anywhere near their wives, and except for when he called Richard and asked him to pray for Jessie, he'd walked a hall for six and a half hours like Ike, waiting on D-Day.

The gray door to the delivery room opened, finally, the way Ben had been willing it to, and Dr Boyes walked out looking disheveled and tired, and led Ben away from the waiting room toward the far end of the hall.

'I wish I had better news, Mr Reese, but as we suspected when we talked earlier, the baby wasn't developed enough to live on his own. There was also—'

'Jessie's OK, though?' Ben's eyes were locked on Boyes, and weren't letting him go.

'I'm sorry, Mr Reese. I really am. An unexpected complication arose, and there was nothing we could do. An amniotic embolism, a blood clot in the placenta broke loose in Jessie's blood stream, and went into the—'

Ben turned and ran, slamming against two heavy metal doors, pushing his way to the delivery room, where a nurse was taking a cloth-wrapped bundle away from Jessie's side.

Ben said, 'Put that down, then leave us alone,' as though he had to work hard at steadying his voice.

A short, pudgy fifty-ish anesthesiologist had been doing something to his equipment, and he was just starting to take his gloves off, as he spun around toward Ben. His voice was high and outraged when he said, 'You can't tell Miss—'

'Leave us alone *now*.' Ben was taller and much broader-shouldered, and he moved across the room with quick long-muscled ease, his behind-the-lines face fixed right on the doc – the face that had taken German command posts from Omaha Beach to Trier.

Boyes had walked in behind Ben, and he said, 'Let's give Mr Reese a moment on his own, shall we, Fred?'

The anesthesiologist backed toward the door, as Ben took the blanket-wrapped bundle away from the oldest nurse. She and the rest stepped through the door, and Ben laid the small still body against Jessie's left hip. He leaned over it and kissed Jessie's lips, dry now, and rougher than usual, but not completely cold.

He smoothed her damp hair, and traced her eyebrows with the index finger he could still bend, then straightened the neck of her gown.

He kissed her eyelids and the arch of her nose, while tears slid through the stubble by his mouth and dripped off his chin.

He pulled the blanket from what was left of their child, their second dead baby in four and a half years. He lifted one arm with his little finger, then touched the tiny nose.

'This one's a boy, Jess. David. Just the way you wanted.' He leaned down staring at the tiny, pale, perfectly made body, at the fragile, dry-looking skin streaked with blood and bits of afterbirth, at the elegant miniature fingernails on the smallest fingers he'd seen.

'I don't know what to do, Jess. Your hands are so cold.' He was sliding his across hers, fitting the fingers of their right hands together, touching her cheek with his left. 'What am I going to do every day, if you're already gone?'

Ben stood, leaning over like that, for he couldn't have said how long. Silent. Stunned. Wandering. His mind grinding in circles. Trying to memorize everything about her – the look, the smell, the smoothness of her skin. The shape of her cheek-bones. The curves of her lips. The feel of her hair in his hands.

Half an hour later, he was still beside her, frozen hard with his eyes closed. His lips set. His hands on her arm. Knowing it was coming. The moment when he'd have to leave with nowhere left to go. That he'd walk out into the cold. That he'd climb into his car. That he'd hold the steering wheel in his hands and have to drive on.

There was no good reason to choose one place over any other now. Or to do one thing today, or the next. To do anything, actually, ever again, there, or somewhere else.

There was no one he wanted to talk to.

No one he knew who knew him.

No one who needed him now. Anywhere.

Except Sam. Waiting alone.

Ben stood there, thinking and praying, what he never could've said to someone else – till Boyes walked in, sometime later, and closed the door behind him.

Boyes stood still, watching Ben standing beside Jessie's body. Then he walked toward him, after a minute, carrying a large brown envelope.

Ben let go of Jessie's hand, and started past him toward the hall, saying, 'Thank you for all your help.'

'I thought you might want to read an explanation of the complication that arose.'

Ben took the envelope, but didn't look at it, before he walked through the door.

He lay on their bed with his clothes on. Sam watched him looking worried, then sank down on the rug beside him, scratching his face with a back foot, rubbing his chin on the rug.

Ben pulled Jessie's pillow over and wrapped his arms around it, holding it tight against his chest. His eyes were open and he was staring at the ceiling, when the phone began to ring.

He didn't get up and answer it. And Sam stood and looked at him, hot breath on Ben's face – before he lay down, and sighed softly, and laid his chin on his paws.

It stopped. Then rang again, ten or fifteen times more.

And it wasn't even half an hour later when Ben heard someone pounding on his front door.

Sam stood up, but Ben ignored it.

Till a key turned in the lock.

'Ben? I've used the key you gave me for emergencies. Where are you?'

Ben didn't answer. Which didn't postpone the inevitable.

Twenty seconds later, Richard West filled the doorway, saying, 'Ah. Here you are. You and Sam.'

'Yes. Here we both are.'

'I'm *terribly* sorry, Benjamin. Sorrier than I can say. I phoned the hospital and was told you'd gone home. I wish there were something I could do to help.'

'There isn't.' The voice and eyes had both iced over. The mouth was tight and furious.

'No. No. I don't suppose there is.'

It was still dark out. A little after five in the morning, wind blowing hard out of the west spitting snow across pasture and frozen plowed fields.

'It's chilly in here. Perhaps I should see to the furnace.' Richard glanced at Ben again before he left the room, and was surprised to see what looked like sadness in the old dog's eyes. Brown eyes, that followed his, from a graying yellow long-nosed face Richard had generally ignored.

After he'd dug out the ashes, banked the hot coals, blown on them with the bellows, and shoveled more coal into the furnace, Richard walked upstairs to the mudroom on the west side of the kitchen.

He took the key from a coffee can at the back of the top shelf, then unlocked the closet under the upstairs steps where Ben kept his guns.

He locked the guns in the trunk of his own car. Then retrieved his old battered briefcase.

Richard sat at the table in the kitchen grading mid-term blue books from his senior-level novel course until it was almost nine. Then he looked in the refrigerator, before checking on Ben.

'You want any breakfast?'

'No.'

'It's after nine. I can call the funeral home. And I can pick a plot at the cemetery if you want me to. If you want to bury them here. In Hillsdale. If you want to take them to your family's place in Michigan, then—'

'Here. You do it. Whatever you decide is fine.'

'Sam, you want some dinner?'

Sam's tail thumped on the floor, but he didn't set foot off the rug.

Richard phoned from the kitchen, coordinating with the funeral parlor and Ben's minister, David Marshall. Who stood at Ben's door twenty minutes later with a Bible under his arm.

Richard showed him where Ben was, and went back to reading essays, hearing the murmur of voices at a distance, telling himself not to listen. Marshall had lost his first wife fifteen years before, and he'd know how to talk to Ben, if anyone anywhere could.

Richard heard Ben say, 'Thanks, David,' an hour later, right before the front door closed.

Richard walked back to Ben's room and found him in Jessie's rocker. 'Have you called Jessie's parents?'

'No.'

'I've talked to the funeral parlor and arranged for the funeral on Monday. I've called Jessie's department head, and I also left a message for your library director. I've made notes for you about writing the obituary. The newspaper wants it before six p.m. I've arranged for a cemetery plot too, but it should be you who calls her parents.'

'Later.'

'It will take them quite a while to—'

'Not now.'

'It will take them some time to make the arrangements to get here.' Richard's voice was capable of rattling windows and doors, but he was speaking in a slow, soft, subdued tone few people would've recognized. 'They lost their son on Corregidor. Losing their other child will be exceedingly painful.'

'Really! That never occurred to me!'

'I'm sorry, Benjamin. Mine was an imbecilic remark.'

Ben didn't say anything. He sat and stared at Sam.

'Make an effort for *them*, Ben.'

Ben told Richard what he could do with himself.

And Richard left him alone with Sam and went to make himself coffee.

Ten minutes later, he heard Ben walk to the bathroom and close the door behind him. He heard Sam's nails click on the wooden floor, till he flopped by the bathroom door.

Richard tiptoed up to him and listened while Ben used the toilet, then showered and brushed his teeth. But when Ben turned off the water and started toward the hall, Richard rushed to the kitchen. He was trying to look nonchalant when Ben walked in, buttoning a corduroy shirt.

Ben looked at Richard as though he hadn't been fooled, then sat in the chair in the corner and dialed the phone on the table.

Ben told Jessie's mother, Harriet Gerard, that Jessie had gone into labor and delivered a boy who was too small to live. 'The worst part, though, was the other complication. A blood clot broke away from the umbilical cord. It got into Jessie's blood stream, and ended up in her lungs. They couldn't save her, Harriet. There was nothing anyone could do . . . I know. I feel sorry for you too . . . Do you want me to talk to Phillip? . . . Right. Yes. Exactly. How will we live without her? . . . Monday. I'm sorry, I can't talk any more right now. I'll call you tonight with more details.'

Ben walked back to the bedroom, with Sam trotting behind him. And Richard began wondering what he'd do if Ben went back to bed and refused to come out again.

Then, Ben was in the kitchen, pulling a thick brown sweater down over his head. He took the hunting jacket he'd had since high school off a peg in the mudroom, and tugged a woolen watch cap low enough to cover his ears. 'There was no reason to take the guns, Richard. You ought to know that.'

'I debated the point. But you know how I am. I err on the side of caution.'

'I shouldn't have yelled at you.'

'You had every right.'

'No. I should've been thanking you for all your help.'

Ben stepped out the mudroom door, with Sam right behind him, into a cold, gray, damp winter day. They walked toward the west edge of the back field, to a farm track that bordered the west woods.

Ben started to run north, faster and faster, as Richard watched, limping in places on uneven ground, till he disappeared into two hundred acres of dense bare trees half a mile north of the house.

The woods belonged to a neighbor of Ben's (Vernon, the landlord who owned his house), and the track wound the length of it, then out to wide-open fields.

* * *

Ben and Sam were gone for four and a half hours, but Richard stayed and waited. Watching. Eating breakfast. Eating lunch. Pacing the kitchen while making soup for Ben – till he saw him at the edge of the west woods heading back toward home. Ben was holding one end of a long stick with Sam clamping the other in his teeth, the two walking side by side, carrying it together.

When Ben came in, a wall was up. A support of some kind had been pounded into place, and he thanked Richard and asked for details about the arrangements he'd made.

Ben called the funeral parlor and chose Jessie's casket. Plain. Closed. The baby inside it. Saying he'd take them clothes for her sometime the following day.

Ben drank a cup of coffee, tried to eat a piece of toast, and couldn't. And then he said, in a deep quiet voice, 'It's strange how much grief feels like fear. Physically, if you see what I mean. The kind you get used to in combat. I hadn't realized it would.'

'Ah.'

'I think I'll go in and lie down.'

He did. But he didn't sleep. He tossed and turned and sighed and shuddered, and Richard pretended he couldn't hear. He sat in the kitchen grading essays. And didn't go home that night. Or the next.

He stayed with Ben through the visitation and the funeral. But that night he packed his things. He put Ben's guns in the closet where he'd found them. Then took his clothes and drove home.

Four weeks later, Ben went to Richard's for dinner. It must have been the fifth or sixth time since Jessie had died. Though this was the night they drank two bottles of Burgundy and talked about Jessie till dawn. Sam had come with Ben, and he kept an eye on them, till Ben took him with him to Richard's spare room, where they both slept like the dead.

When Ben went home in the morning, he opened a college blue book and began writing a journal. He told himself to write it for a year, if he found that it actually helped. To put down everything he remembered about Jessie, and what the first year without her was like. He'd keep all the letters he'd written her from Europe in the same place with the journal, and the letters she'd written him over the years, with the last one on top.

Then he'd make himself stop writing.

And learn to live on his own.

Five

T he morning after Carl hadn't appeared at the concert, Ben
woke up at six with sun warming his back, and slid his
feet into the long soft wool of the sheepskin rug Sam had
thought was his.

It had taken Ben a while to fall asleep after he'd read Jessie's
letter, but he'd probably gotten three hours more, and that was
better than sometimes.

He pulled on shorts and a T-shirt, and grabbed a new
archivist journal on his way into the kitchen, reminding himself
to call Vernon again, and ask if he'd made up his mind.

He and Jessie had wanted to buy the farmhouse they were
renting, and Ben had asked Vernon the week before if he'd
be willing to sell it to him. It was a small, sturdy, white
clapboard Georgian built in the 1880s, and Ben would've
had to look a long time to find another that suited him
better.

He didn't know yet if he could swing it financially, but if
he could get ten acres at two hundred an acre, and let Vernon
farm it with the rest of his, he could see himself staying there
as long as he stayed at Alderton.

*Especially now, when I want to get another dog and give
it land to run around on. Don't call Vernon till after seven,
though. Give him time to finish milking.*

Ben made a pot of coffee, took a mug and an orange and
two hard-boiled eggs through the parlor to the front porch,
where he sat and read Romans while he peeled fruit and eggs.

He looked at the chair beside him when he'd finished, then
at the field in front of him, and decided that what he needed
right then was something difficult to do.

Transcribing Sergeant John Ordway's journal appealed to

him most at that moment, and he walked back into his study and unlocked the drawer where he kept it.

Ordway had been on the Lewis and Clark expedition, and his had been the first published account. Ben had borrowed the original from Philadelphia's Natural History Museum, and was transcribing it because he was interested (though he'd make another copy later for Alderton University's collection of materials on western expansion).

The journal was a smallish brown calfskin volume, five by seven inches, made of high-quality linen paper that had helped it survive the expedition. It was blotched with water stains inside and out – grease stains too, in even larger numbers, from gun oil and axle grease, and animal fat of all kinds.

Ben slid a piece of black paper under the page where he'd left off, and positioned his gooseneck lamp (with a full-spectrum white-light bulb he'd gotten from the Physics Department), aiming it sideways across the pages to pick out shadows from the pen and ink impressions made when the letters were formed.

It wasn't easy to decipher, ink that faded on damaged paper, and after forty-five minutes of intense concentration, Ben walked out to the porch.

He started reading an article on oil-painting restoration in his *American Archivist* journal, then looked up when he heard a car turn into the lane a quarter of a mile away. It was running east toward his house along the south edge of the ten-acre woods west of the barn.

It was Richard's old blue Chevy, and when it hit the gravel at the south end of the barn, the gaggle of barn cats sunning themselves scattered for parts unknown.

'Morning, Ben. I knew you'd be up.' Richard was clutching a wicker basket, closing the driver's door. 'I made orange muffins before the crack of dawn, and thought I'd bring you a dozen. Left to your own devices, you'd blow away in the wind.'

'You know what my dad would say?'

'How would I? I've never met him.'

'"You'd make some woman a good wife."'

'May I remind you that the majority of America's chefs are men?' Richard was on the flagstone walk by then, heading to the house from the front of the barn. 'I felt the need of a hobby. One that's less intellectual than my academic pursuits. Being a glutton led me in this direction, since—'

'Richard—'

'Since I wished for a creative and tactile enterprise with some connection to the wider world. The accumulation of adipose tissue may be a perpetual risk, though—'

'It's OK, Richard, I'm glad you cook. I'll get you some coffee and a plate.'

'I've brought pineapple too, and some wonderful English cheese, and we shall need silverware as well.'

They'd finished their first bites of breakfast, their legs stretched out in the sun on the porch, before Richard asked how well the Columbus Symphony had performed Beethoven's Fifth.

'I didn't stay to find out. Carl Walker never showed.' Ben explained about the unlisted number, and that he'd come home early and called a friend who taught at OSU to get Carl's number and address. 'I called last night till I went to bed, and never got an answer.'

'What are you going to do about it?'

'Me? Call him again, and see if he's OK.'

'What if he doesn't answer?'

'I don't know. I don't see what else I can do.'

'There may be something terribly wrong.'

'He has a brother-in-law in Columbus. Why is it my business? I hardly know Carl.' Ben wasn't looking at Richard. He was scratching the stubble in the cleft in his chin, watching the wind in the trees.

'That's not like you, Benjamin. *You* go out of your way.'

'I'm *not* like me, though, am I, at the moment?' Ben smiled, mostly to himself, and finished the last of his coffee. 'I don't like sticking my nose into other people's business.'

'I know that. But you've helped many people who needed your archivist's ability to research and make deductions, to solve mysteries of provenance, to locate and restore.'

'That's what I do, Richard. That's my everyday job.'

'The maintenance man at your church? Remember him? Who needed a used car? The Hungarian family on the Nettabittis' farm? You helped get their cousins out of Budapest. You sponsored them, and taught others who were—'

'Yeah, well, things were different then. And *that* was

different too. Soviet tanks killing people in the streets, that's a serious issue.'

'What was different? Jessie was alive? Now you can't be bothered?'

'There's a line here, Richard. I don't cross it with you.' Ben held Richard's eyes for a second, then looked back at the pasture.

'You're right. I stand corrected. I *don't* know what you're going through, and I shouldn't be telling you what to do.'

'That's not to say you haven't been helpful.' Ben ate a bite of muffin, then brushed crumbs from his lap. 'We all need a stick stuck where it will do the most good from time to time.'

'And *I* have a penchant for sticks.'

'Right.' They were both quiet after that. Eating pineapple. Slicing Cheshire cheese. Staring across at the sheep. Till Ben said, 'I'll think about it. What I'll do I don't know.'

'I understand.'

Ben looked at him.

And Richard said, 'No, I don't. Silly of me. Of course, *you* don't know everything about me either.' He was grinning then, teasing the way he normally did. '*My* past might hold a few surprises!'

'Would it?' Ben smiled and looked sideways at Richard, then leaned back in his chair. 'I knew what you were up to when I took your novel courses at IU, before *and* after the war. At least from the perspective of a student. And students, as you know, can be extremely well informed. So are there secrets I don't know about? When you were in England, maybe? You have a wife hidden away somewhere you haven't brought out in the open?'

Richard looked disconcerted, unexpectedly, and reached across for the coffee pot. 'You'll be the first to know, should I chose to make a revelation. Perhaps he had to leave town.'

'Carl? Changing the subject, are we?' Ben raised an eyebrow at Richard, as he popped another piece of muffin in his mouth.

'No. We were talking about Carl. As you well remember.'

'*Do* you have a wife?'

'Benjamin, please!' Richard's face turned even redder than usual.

And Ben Reese laughed. 'OK. So what could've happened

to Carl? This is a man who drove to the concerts from Washington, DC.'

'Precisely. Perhaps a family emergency? His parents? Or a sibling?'

'Maybe. If it was anybody but Carl I wouldn't give it a thought.'

'No.'

'But . . .' Ben swallowed the last of his second cup of coffee and stretched his arms above his head. '*If* I decide I want to get involved, there's nothing I absolutely *have* to do today after I run and lift weights. I suppose I could drop by his house. Then stop at the Columbus Zoo before I come home to work.'

'What *are* you working on at the moment? You've got the summer off, as usual. Like all but a handful of us Alderton academics who're struggling manfully through the summer.'

'You chose to, as you'll recall, when—'

'You did finish identifying the pueblo pots your spies found?'

'Yep. Ralph, the custodian, in Smith Hall's attic. I worked with a curator at the Smithsonian, and we think they're from Chaco Grand. Now I'm restoring a damaged landscape I found in the library archives, and I—'

'Then you're doing your regular work, but doing it at home?'

'I s'ppose so, yeah. I go into the office a couple half-days a week too. And I told Vernon I'd help him repair pasture fence this week or next. I'm also studying what living in the dark was like before nineteenth-century artificial light. I have to write an article for an archival journal, and I'm looking for an angle that will fit. It actually might make a readable book, though I'm not the one to write it.'

'Why? It sounds like interesting work.'

'It is. I don't think we begin to comprehend earlier attitudes to a lot of things, and living in the dark is one of them. In England, if they walked outside, or rode out at night in the country, the percentage of broken bones and death by accident is much higher than you'd think. Did you know that country people there, who went to bed at sunset, frequently got up about midnight, then worked, or talked, or visited with neighbors for two or three hours, before they went back to bed?'

'No, I had no idea.'

'I'm studying England and Scotland because of available material, and because of the people I know there who can help with the work.'

'I envy you, you know. I shouldn't have agreed to teach this summer. Though I do have an excellent graduate student, who—'

'You *love* to teach.'

'I?' Richard laughed and said, 'Yes, I do. And there are compensations. I, at least, don't have to contend with your countless alumni enquiries. Yes, and speaking of hobbies—'

'Were we?'

'Earlier, yes. What about you? You could do with a—'

'I don't have enough hobbies? Painting. Ancient-coin identification. Early explorers and wildlife illus—'

'*I* would've said that that was your work.'

'It's both, actually. Which is no bad thing.'

'Perhaps. It *can* be, certainly. Didn't Jessie tell me you were planning to get a horse?'

'I rode on the farm when I was growing up, and if the right horse turned up, I'd consider it. But I'm not making any moves. Not anytime soon.'

'Relaxing might be worth considering.'

'Maybe. Maybe I'm afraid that if I weren't up to my eyebrows in work that takes intense concentration I wouldn't get out of bed.'

'Ah.' Richard looked taken aback, before he finished his coffee. 'I must run.' He was up then, picking up his picnic basket. 'I shall be at the office most of the day. Let me know what you learn about Carl. *If* you decide to get involved. The rest of the muffins are on the kitchen table.'

'Thanks, Richard. They'll keep me going all week. I'm sorry I said that.'

'What?'

'About getting out of bed. I never whine to anybody but you. Why do I inflict it on my one close friend?'

'Perhaps it's a sign you're human.'

'Maybe.'

'Call me.'

Ben stood and watched Richard drive off. Asking himself what he was up to. He. Himself. Ben Reese. Why he was

putting off looking for Carl. Why had he bothered late last
night, and didn't want to now?

It'd gotten him out of the concert. Out of the line of fire.
Away from the eyes of strangers who didn't know her, or him.

*The people last night meant well. Even if there was morbid
curiosity in there somewhere too. Humans goggle at car
accidents. Everyone wants to watch the bereaved. I'm being
hypercritical. Which doesn't come as much of a surprise,
since I'm human too.*

He knew he cared what happened to Carl. But he didn't
have the energy. Once he started sleeping again things might
look different.

He had enough energy for work. For dead objects, made
by dead people. For growing strawberries. For feeding barn
cats.

*Not for people who have feelings. Who want what I can't
give. Not with Jessie dead. When God's not talking.*

He knew good could come out of it. For him, or somebody
else. He'd probably see the significance later. It'd happened
more times than he could count. But it wasn't much consolation yet. It didn't make him want to pick up his feet, or
take up another day.

*That's because we don't like pain. I know I learn from
suffering. I've watched with everybody else. I just don't want
it to be me now, or anytime soon.*

*So I talk about work, and keep my head above water. But
I'm not ready to feign interest in Carl. Not me at the moment.*

It was probably something ordinary that kept Carl from the
concert. A blow-out in Arkansas. A rear-ender in Akron. A
case of flu in Kalamazoo that kept him off the road.

So where'd the snotty sense of humor come from?

*An inability to look at something serious and act as though
I care.*

*What if there's something you're intended to do, and you're
just throwing a tantrum? It wouldn't be the first time. And it
won't be the last. And I won't be the first to know.*

Ben had been stacking the dishes to take to the kitchen,
and when he got there, he saw a magazine on the counter
lying next to the sink.

It was an old *Life* that wasn't his – May 20th, the first Vertijet
on the cover – with a torn slip of paper sticking out the top.

He set the dishes down and picked it up, opening it up at the marker. It was a several-page article with black-and-white photos on a cannibal tribe in a jungle in Ecuador, on Elizabeth Elliot and the rest of the widows of the missionaries who'd been murdered by that tribe a couple of months before.

The women were still there in the jungle, their own children with them, trying to reach their husbands' killers, who were now actually choosing to listen because they'd chosen to stay.

Ben sat in the rocker and read it through twice.

Then got up and got in the shower.

Six

B en pulled into Carl's drive an hour and a half later, in the 600 block of Hester Street a couple of blocks east of Worthington's main street, a few miles north of Columbus.

It was a small white Cape Cod clapboard on a city-size lot in the oldest part of town – with no car in the driveway, or in the unattached garage, and no answer either when he knocked on the front and back doors.

Ben was standing in the front again, getting ready to look through the small paned windows on either side of the faded black door – when a young woman rode up on a bicycle, and braked by his '47 Plymouth.

She asked if she could help, as she set the bike on its side stand, her chin-length, very curly, light-brown hair blowing across her eyes. She pushed her sunglasses up on her head, using them to hold her hair back, as she squinted up at Ben.

He told her who he was, and what he was doing there.

And she said, 'Oh, I wondered who Ben Reese was. I'm Beth Morland. Carl was supposed to come for dinner before the concert last night, and he didn't show up or phone.'

'That's odd, don't you think? Especially for Carl?'

'Yes. Even though I wouldn't say I know him terribly well. I taught high school with Carl's sister, Evelyn, and she used to invite him, and me, and several others for dinner before the concerts. Not as a couple, of course.' Beth had looked away by then, and was resettling her sunglasses on her narrow nose.

'Was she older than Carl?'

'Fifteen years, I think. She passed away last fall. So now I invite her husband and Carl, and a widowed friend of Evelyn's for supper before the symphony, even when I can't go. I'm working on my master's, and I don't have extra time.'

'No.' Ben had been dangling his sport coat across a shoulder,

and he opened the driver's door and dropped it on the seat.
'Wait till you start your dissertation.'

'I don't have to get a PhD. I like teaching high school.'

'Does Carl accept when you invite him to dinner?'

'He's come every time, right at the stroke of six. He doesn't
do much socializing, and Evelyn thought it was good for him
to get out and see people, so I've kept up the tradition. Carl's
a real stickler for etiquette, and not phoning's completely unlike
him. I called last night, and came over here at seven, and
about ten too. I called first thing this morning, but he didn't
answer then either. The telephone company said the phone
was working, last night and this morning.'

'They told me that too.'

'I'd heard Carl mention your name in the past, Mr Reese,
and then earlier in the week he mailed me a letter to send to
you.'

Ben was staring at her, shading his eyes with his hand.
'That's odd. That he'd ask you to mail it to me.'

'*I* thought so. Should we go inside and look around? Carl
gave me keys, in case of emergencies, after Evelyn died. I
only live two blocks away, and he travels a lot in the summer.'

It was stuffy inside, in the small barely furnished rooms,
as they walked from one to the other looking for signs of life.
Or death. Or action having been taken.

Beth studied what there was inside Carl's refrigerator, while
Ben looked in the milk box on the back stoop. There were
two glass bottles of curdled milk, and Ben asked Beth when
Carl's milk got delivered.

'Monday, Wednesday and Friday. We're on the same route.
I don't know how much he gets, though. That could be from
Wednesday *and* Friday, or maybe just from Friday. I can't tell
much from the refrigerator. He says he lives on V8 and peanut
butter. He eats at the Captain's Inn fairly often, where a friend
of both of ours cooks.'

'How much does Carl travel when he's not teaching?' Ben
was smelling the first of two thermoses he'd found sitting in
the sink. It was half-filled with water, but smelled slightly of
coffee. The other had a faintly sour odor, as though it might've
held milk.

'I'd say two to three weeks a month. Four days one time.
Maybe ten days another. There's not a real pattern to it.' Beth

was walking through the living room into the front hall, where she started up the L-shaped stairs. 'He doesn't talk much about where he goes. Not with me anyway. I have the impression that he'll study the history of an area, and then spend a few days there. I told him about a place I own in Black Mountain, and he—'

'North Carolina?'

'Yes. He said he'd like to go there sometime, and spent a week last winter reading up on the history of the area, from there over to Asheville. He likes rustic inns. Log cabins. Places in the country. One thing he said he liked about mine was it doesn't have a phone.'

'Tell me about the letter.'

'I got it a couple of days ago, and when I opened it there was a note to me, and a sealed stamped envelope for you. Your name was on it, and Hillsdale, the city, but no actual street address. He asked me to find that out, and mail you the letter right away. He said he was leaving town that minute, and didn't have time to do it himself. That he'd see me Friday as usual, and thanks for helping him out. You should get the letter today, or Monday at the latest.'

'What day did you get it?' Ben was staring at Carl's neatly made bed, at the half-open closet door, at the unzipped empty athletic bag sitting on a straight-backed chair.

'Thursday. My mail's delivered in the afternoon, and I got your address right away, then took the letter to the post office so it would go out that night. I called information for your phone number, and asked for your address.'

'Carl could've easily done that. But maybe he *was* just unusually rushed, and it's nothing more than that.' Ben set the bag back on the chair, then studied the closet floor. 'When was it postmarked, and where?'

'I don't think I looked.'

'Could you? Sometime today? Or did you throw the envelope away?'

'It's probably in a wastebasket. I'll check when I get home.' Beth started by staring at Ben's back – the broad shoulders and strong arms half-covered by a short-sleeved shirt – then followed the long slicing scar that twisted around his left arm, before sliding under his sleeve.

'Were the addresses handwritten or typed?'

'What? Sorry. Mine was handwritten. Yours was typed. I handwrote your street address in between his typed lines.'

The medicine cabinet stood open, in a meticulously neat bathroom, and everything you'd expect was there – toothbrush, toothpaste, shaving equipment, comb, brush, deodorant.

Nothing caught Ben's attention in the guest room.

Or the small attic next door, where two suitcases sat against a wall on the far side of a thin layer of fine gray dust.

They were walking back down to the study, when Ben said, 'What do we know for sure?' His eyebrows seemed to be mulling that over while the rest of his face studied her.

'Well . . .'

'He doesn't like clutter. He doesn't spend money on anything but books and records. He's been gone long enough for milk to curdle in the milk box. There's an athletic bag on a chair in his room, though I doubt that's where he keeps it. His closet door was half open. The medicine cabinet was open too. Unlike every other drawer and cabinet in the bedroom, kitchen and study. His toiletries are where they belong, and both towels in the bathroom are dry.'

'So—'

'Did he leave town, taking only that bag, and then come back and put his things away? Only to leave his house again, unexpectedly, or in a hurry? Before he had time to replace the bag and close the closet, and the cabinet in the bathroom. He doesn't play sports does he, or go to a gym?'

'Carl? Not that I know of. He's not what you'd call athletic.' Beth was looking at Ben's hair. It was almost the color of hers, which didn't happen often – a light shiny caramel brown getting bleached by summer sun.

'So did he intend to leave town again and repack the bag? But got interrupted before he could?'

'I don't think we can tell.'

'Exactly. And I'd still like to know why he didn't look up my address when he mailed you the letter. It seems out of character to me. He's a very methodical man.' Ben was sitting in Carl's desk chair in the study by then, opening drawers, glancing through papers, his gray eyes focused intently, his lower jaw set off to the left in what looked like complete concentration. 'That's odd. Though I guess it could be over there.' Ben walked to the louvered bi-fold doors opposite the desk.

'What's odd?'

He opened the doors before he said, 'Storage shelves. But no typewriter. Not on the desk, and not here. There's typing paper. Carbon paper. An extra ribbon in the desk. He typed my name on the envelope. But there's no typewriter anywhere. And no personal address book.'

'You think somebody stole them? Or you think he took them with him?' Beth was staring at Ben, her open, guileless, good-looking face sliding toward mild-mannered worry, as she pulled her hands out of the pockets of her white cotton slacks.

'If somebody stole the typewriter and the address book, they were careful about going through the house. They had a key too, or were good at picking locks.' Ben was standing inside the front door then, gazing up the stairs.

'What do you think we should do?'

'I'll call a friend of mine at Ohio State and find out where Carl's office is there, and see if my friend can get me in. If you'll check on that envelope, I'll call you when I'm finished. Could you write your number on this?' Ben handed Beth the pocket-sized leather-bound notebook Jessie had given him for Christmas. Then he walked into the study and dialed Carl's number.

Ben got Beth to meet him back at Carl's house at three that afternoon, after he'd found nothing useful at Carl's college office – except what wasn't there. No typewriter, no address book, no explanation.

That, and the opinion of the professor next door, who'd thought he'd heard someone in Carl's office before seven that morning. It hadn't been Carl, because the professor had knocked on the door and called out to him, and whoever it was hadn't answered, when Carl certainly would have. The door had been locked too, and the professor had thought it all very odd, but he'd gone back to work and forgotten, till Ben had asked the question.

When Beth was unlocking Carl's front door, she said, 'What do you hope to find here that you didn't find before?'

'I'll look harder this time. For a safe maybe, or a cache of

some kind. When I went out to my car, when we left here
this morning, someone had been inside it.'

'Why? How would you know?'

'My passenger door wasn't closed all the way, and I know
it was when I got here. It's an old car, and idiosyncratic. It's
got what they call "suicide doors". The front one's hinged in
the front, the back one in the back, so they open out from the
middle. There's a trick to how you play with the handle to
get the front door to shut completely, and whoever shut it
didn't notice.'

'Are you saying that—?'

'I think somebody opened that door while we were here in
the house. It might not mean anything. It could've been a
neighbor kid playing around, but it could've been somebody
searching my car.'

'Why would anyone do that?'

'You could look at my car registration, and get my name
and address.'

'Yes, I guess you could. Why are they called suicide
doors?'

'I don't know. Except that the back door can get caught by
the wind, so if you opened it while you were moving maybe
it could pull you out.' Ben turned right into the study from
the front hall, telling Beth he'd start in there – when he froze
inside the door.

'What?' Beth stepped up beside him and looked where he
was looking.

'A floorboard's up. The end of it, see, under the desk? It
wasn't up this morning.' Ben pulled back the chair, then
dropped to his hands and knees close to the front of the
kneehole. He pulled the floorboard up and out, and found a
box-shaped hole underneath – maybe fifteen inches by eleven,
six inches deep.

'That was made deliberately?'

'Yep.' Ben stood then with his hands in his back pockets
staring at the bookshelves.

'Nobody else had a key. Carl told me that when he gave
me mine. So you think someone broke in?'

Ben was walking through the living room heading into the
kitchen, saying, 'Let's see what we can find.'

'Where? You mean—?'

'The kitchen door makes the most sense. Hedges hiding it on both sides of the yard, fairly thick shrubs across the back.'

Ben studied the back door, from inside, then out – staring longest at the outside of the lock, at the dull corroded metal plate around the old-fashioned key hole.

'Can you see anything?' Beth was watching him concentrate, seeing the intensity in his large gray eyes and the tightness around his mouth, looking as though she wanted him to talk, as if talking eased the suspense.

'Somebody picked the lock. There's a scratch that wasn't there this morning. Which means now we search for a safe.' He didn't look at Beth as he walked past, heading toward the study. 'That's if you have time now to hunt behind the books.'

They found nothing useful in the next hour. And that led Ben to sit at Carl's desk and call Richard West. He told him what they'd learned, and was about to ask Richard to phone a friend of his, Hillsdale's Chief of Police, to see if he'd heard anything about Carl – when Richard offered to do just that without being asked.

Ben told Beth he was about to be presumptuous and ask to borrow Carl's keys. 'I need to take more time examining the floors and the walls. Not right now, but tomorrow probably. And it also may not be the best idea for you to have the keys.'

'Why? You think I could be a target, or something? If someone were watching us here? The person who got in your car?'

'Yes. That's exactly it.'

'I'm not completely helpless, you know.'

'I didn't say you were, but we don't know what we're up against. We aren't even sure if Carl's alive.'

'I don't know what the keys have to do with it, for someone who knows how to pick a lock. But go ahead. You take the keys now, and we'll get a set made Monday.'

'Thanks. I appreciate it. Are you planning to talk to Carl's brother-in-law?'

'Roger? I probably should. I can't say I'm looking forward to it, but—'

'What's Roger like?'

'Closed off and impersonal. He's not rude, but he's not

friendly. He wouldn't even go to the symphony when he knew how important it was to Evelyn. I invite him to dinner every month, but he hardly ever comes, and he and Carl have never hit it off. Carl's quiet, but you know he likes people. Roger gives you the impression he doesn't, even when he's polite.'

'Have you seen animosity between Carl and Roger? Is there anything about Evelyn's estate that—?'

'No. Nothing like that. It's Roger being Roger.'

'Will you let me know what he says?'

'Sure.'

'I'll go home and see if the letter from Carl is there, and I'll call and tell you what I find. You'll be home?'

'Most of the time. I'll leave a few minutes before ten. I'm having dinner at the inn where my friend cooks, and we'll probably go to his place and talk, so I won't be home until twelve or so. Maybe a little later.' Beth's face had turned pink, and she looked self-conscious as she rolled up her pale-blue sleeves.

'I ought to check out the garage. You don't need to stay if you don't want to, but I—'

'Maybe I'll notice something you won't, since I've been inside before.'

There wasn't much to see, inside *or* out, in that small un-attached wood-sided garage – a push lawnmower in a back corner, rakes and clippers hanging on studs, two metal garbage cans, a short wooden work bench with a toolbox in the middle.

Beth told Ben she didn't see anything different. 'But I'm not sure I would. Anyway, I'd better go. I've *got* to get some work done today.'

'Thanks a lot for the help.' Ben latched the door and walked around the back, in the shade of the only tree there was – while Beth wheeled her bike out toward the street.

A long-abandoned flower bed wandered the length of the back of the garage – a tangle of straggling perennials invaded by ragged grass. A broken concrete bird bath leaned to the left from somewhere near the center – a round dish on a three-foot stand, the tail of its decorative fish badly chipped and cracked.

Nothing took Ben any place useful. Nothing whispered the

name he wanted. Nothing pointed to the unknown hand that had picked Carl Walker's lock and left the floorboard up.

Ben stopped by his office in Alderton's library to pick up his mail there – and found a package waiting on his desk.

Friends, and colleagues, and Alderton donors sent him things all the time to be dated, or identified, or appraised, but there wasn't a return address on this one, and 'PERSONAL' had been typed on the label.

It was postmarked 'Massillon, Ohio'. Which didn't suggest much of anything to Ben. And he put the package in his briefcase to open when he got home.

He actually didn't give it a thought, as he drove out of Hillsdale headed west toward the farm. He studied the world darkening in front of him, where leaden gray sky rolled toward him, coming in from the south-west.

Five minutes later, he watched thick shafts of solid-looking rain slant down and pound the ground a mile or more away underneath an ink-black bank of low fast-moving clouds.

He watched drizzle bleed and blow across his windshield a quarter of a mile on, and cranked up the wipers that never did much but smear the surface of the glass.

They did less the next six miles, as the rain hit harder and the wind picked up and the windshield fogged over.

Ben drove slower without much noticing, on roads, by then, where he rarely saw a car. He was beating his head against Carl's disappearance, asking what he could possibly have had that would make someone risk a break-in during the middle of the day.

He was concentrating on the letter, as he waited for the mailman to back out of his drive so he could park by the sawn-off fence pole that held his old metal mailbox. He tried to keep his window rolled high, and still fish out his mail. But he stopped noticing the rain on his face when he saw the letter from Carl – the typed name and city with the handwritten street in between.

He tore it open with his right hand, closing the window with his left, while thunder rolled and lightning flashed close above his head.

Wednesday, June 12, 1957

Dear Ben,

This letter will come to you out of the blue, with no preparation from me, or chance of explanation. I am leaving town this evening and must get this mailed with some haste.

I have taken the liberty of discussing you and your army record with an acquaintance of mine who was in Army Signals during World War II. He, and associates of his, have provided me assurances and background information which has given me the confidence to approach you in a matter of urgency and importance.

I know that you are beginning your summer schedule, and may have plans to leave Hillsdale for much of the summer. May I take the liberty of asking you not to do so in the next few weeks; not until you and I have conferred on the matter I refer to above? I do not over-state the case when I assure you that there are issues of security involved that go well beyond anything you would imagine I might be privy to.

If all goes well, I shall return no later than Friday, and very probably sooner. I will contact you as soon as is possible thereafter. If events beyond my control interfere, I will have set in motion methods of communication to replace a personal meeting. Keep this letter in an EXTREMELY SECURE PLACE; a safe, or safety deposit box.

43–24–4

Carl Walker

The signature was in Walker's handwriting. And Ben checked to see that the letter was typed on the same machine as the envelope. Then he reread the letter, and returned it to the envelope and slipped it into his briefcase.

He let out the clutch and eased the old Plymouth down the wet rutted drive, asking himself a string of questions he couldn't have asked before.

A pheasant startled in the side drive (the farm track that cut through Vernon's west woods, which were on Ben's left at that moment). And when he turned to watch the cock, he noticed what looked like fresh tire tracks stamped into the mud.

They weren't tractor tracks. Anyone could see that. Though they could've been from Vernon's pick-up. Or maybe one of his sons'.

Either that, or the other guy. Who'd left Ben's car door open. And searched Carl's house.

I've got to pay more attention, and make connections fast.

The rain was beating down hard then, when Ben pulled into the gravel beside the long west side of the barn. He parked twenty feet away, parallel to the double wooden doors, so Vernon could drive closer if he needed to get into the barn.

Ben sat for a minute, waiting for the downpour to taper off. But when it looked as though it wouldn't soon, he took off his jacket and laid it on his briefcase, on the passenger's side of the floor, and sprinted into the barn.

He turned around just inside the doors, watching the rain slant toward him as he slid them closed, one at a time, leaving a foot-wide gap.

He turned his back to the outside, then took the lid off a dented metal garbage can and reached for the bag of cat food, intending to fill the three metal bowls he kept near the right-hand door.

He stopped then. And listened. Before stepping farther from the slice of gray light that fell across the stone floor.

No cats.

Not one running up to me.

Somebody else is in here. Somebody they don't know.

He could feel it, standing there in damp dusty air, his wet shirt sticking to his back, the hairs up on his neck.

He slowed his breathing as he listened, eyes scouting the corners, the left side of the barn first, behind Vernon's corn seeder, past sacks of just-bought wheat seed and stacked bags of fertilizer.

Ben stood in the two-story center, at the edge of the right-side loft, three or four feet now from the long west wall, keeping himself in the dark, staring next at the hay and straw stored in the left-hand loft.

There was nothing strange he could see from there.

Not in the front few feet.

So he told himself to check the ground floor, then climb up to make sure.

The right side of the first floor – with the small tractor, the drill press, the table saw, the folding sheep pen, the tangle of farming and repair equipment packed close together – wasn't easy to evaluate in the dark, not from where he stood.

He was beginning to turn farther to the right, getting ready to edge his way in and search through the clutter – when he heard a noise above him that he knew came from the left.

Something hard and heavy, something with sharp edges, swung down in a wide arc and smashed into his skull.

Seven

B en came to ten minutes later, lying on his face on cold
damp fieldstone. Right arm under him. Head exploding.
Lightning flashing behind his eyes.

He could taste dirt, when he started to open them. He could
smell hay, and feed, and fertilizer, without knowing what they
were. He knew a cat was rubbing against his side, somewhere
below his shoulder. But he couldn't connect it so it made
sense and explained where he was.

When he tried to get up it got worse. So he waited a minute,
checking body parts, tentatively moving his arms and legs –
before slowly, carefully, picking his head up two or three
inches off soil-splattered stone.

He pushed his shoulders up, propping himself on his hands,
then pulled his legs up under him, shoving himself till he sat
on one hip, braced on his good arm.

Something warm was dripping in his ear.

Blood.

But not a lot. From what?

Ouch. Large lump. Just behind my ear.

What's that? Creaking.

Close by. No, wait. Up, and farther away.

He squinted, trying to clear his vision, telling himself to
overlook his stomach rolling in a sickening slide – and saw
a wooden block and tackle swinging above his head.

Used to be up. Somewhere. There.

Up where? In a loft?

Yeah. I must be in the barn.

Which loft? Right or left?

Which is right, and which isn't?

Left hand's got the scar. So . . .

Left side loft.

Wooden thing shoulda killed me.

That weight. With that much rope.
Couldn't've come undone. No. Tied up to a—
Wait. Car. Starting up. Somewhere.
Sounds like in the woods.
Heading the other way. Thank God.
Don't know what I'm doing. Don't know what's going on.

Ben stroked a half-grown kitten that had just climbed in his lap. The last of the litters there'd be, with any luck, since he'd taken Vernon's barn cats to get fixed earlier that spring.

He didn't remember that then. He couldn't have said Vernon's name. All he knew was this was a cat. He was sitting on the floor of the barn. And his head made it hard to think.

He grunted quietly as he got to his feet, standing and swaying while his head twirled. Before he carefully walked toward the doors, heading toward the car.

Something outside, something I'm s'pposed to do.
Can't remember what. Something about the car.

He was moving slowly, quietly, tentatively. Trying to protect his scrambled brain from any kind of jarring. His hands were out in front of him, as though he were trying to feel the air, or keep from stumbling in the half-gray dark.

Something's out there somewhere.
Something I have to see.
Something somewhere needs to be safe.
Stop saying 'something' now!
Have to keep something safe.

He stood by the old gray Plymouth, drizzle sliding down his face, supporting himself with his hands on the roof, trying to make himself think.

'Rats.' *I'm gonna be sick.*

He lurched over to the edge of the woods, and was, behind a wild shrub. He stood there, weaving on his feet, one hand holding a tree trunk, trying to get his bearings.

He turned his face up to the sky, letting the rain wash over him. Wanting the cold and the shock of it. Trying to jump-start his brain.

He wandered slowly back to the car, and stood there getting rained on. Till he opened the passenger door, finally, without really knowing why.

He saw his sport coat and his briefcase on the floor.

He knew he knew what they were. But not why they were there then. Or what he ought to do.

A minute went by before he picked them up and stared at them in his hands. Then he turned around slowly, feeling the weight of them, heavier than they ought to be, pulling on his fingers – and gazed at the double doors.

He took them with him, the briefcase and the coat, stepping slowly, easing into the barn, then stood there with his back to the doors, trying to decide what to do.

Car door.

Closed or open?

Can't remember anything.

Go see, and close it. If you didn't before.

Cats were swirling around his feet, eight or ten from what he could tell. And he laid his things down without thinking, and poured food in their bowls.

He stood and watched them eat.

Then sat and let them crawl on him.

Then got up to close the barn doors. And saw the car door was open.

It was black inside the barn. When he'd closed up the car, and slid the barn doors together. The only breaks in the darkness were small patches of faint gray light from widely scattered windows.

The top of one door, too. It looked like. A people-sized door. Or so he assumed. Across the short side of the barn.

He started toward it, without thinking much about it, and then went back, to find the coat and briefcase. Why, he couldn't have said. And yet he knew he should take them with him when he walked outside.

He felt for them on his hands and knees, and carried them with him to the door. He stepped out, in a softening mist, and stared across at his mudroom door forty feet away.

It was unlocked, when he got to it. Just as he'd left it that morning. Exactly the way most people would in his part of Ohio.

He knew that's how he *had* left it, without any thought or effort, and as he wiped his feet on the inside mat, he wondered why he'd remember that when so much else was gone.

He looked at his shoes and saw mud on dried dirt. His pants were smeared with mud too, matted with flecks of hay and straw. And he stepped outside and swatted at his clothes, and took his shoes off there. He carried them back to the mudroom and laid them on the throw rug in front of the sink by the washer.

Then he saw, without knowing how exactly, that something inside was wrong.

It took him a while, figuring it out. He stood there with his eyes closed and held his head in his hands. He sat on the dryer and made himself breathe more deeply than he normally would – telling himself to wake up and concentrate, and see what he needed to see.

Canned goods and tools had been shifted on the shelves. Mail had been shuffled in the basket on the wall. A cabinet drawer that stuck on itself hadn't been shoved all the way.

Ben went through every downstairs room, as well as the guest room and darkroom upstairs – and almost everywhere he turned (slowly, awkwardly, semi-unsteadily) there were differences he could see.

They probably weren't meant to be. Care had been taken. But Ben had spent too many nights analyzing the contents of German command posts not to see subtleties in his own house.

His mind was still muddled, but beginning to gear up. Not like normal. Not like before. But enough to see a chair pushed back too far, a row of books spaced differently, a stack of records by the hi-fi lined up too neatly.

Why he could remember the visual parameters of the inside of his house when so much else had been erased made no particular sense. But as he stopped and tried to think about it, standing in his kitchen, he knew head wounds were like that. He'd seen enough to be sure of that during the War.

He was sidestepping the unavoidable, though. The block and tackle hadn't hit him on its own. It'd been tied tight to a beam.

Why would someone want to hurt me? It doesn't make any sense.

Ben turned on the faucet in the old stone sink and stuck his head under a fast-running stream of icy artesian water. He had to try to clear his head and clean the wound too. But he still swore when the water flushed through it. And once he'd touched it – fingering it gently, doing damage assessment, blotting the blood with a clean kitchen towel – he went to find the peroxide, the iodine, and the gauze.

He picked up his briefcase after he'd finished, opening it up on the kitchen table, knowing something important was in there, but not remembering what.

He took out a package and laid it aside, something sent by a donor, probably, with no return address. One of the usual elderly alums asking him to research something the family had sitting around.

He read Carl's letter next, and recognized the seriousness. For he remembered then, suddenly and unexpectedly, that Carl Walker was missing. That he himself had searched Carl's house, as well as his college office. That someone else had gone through both, looking for who knew what.

Ben found himself reading the letter again without really meaning to, before the kettle on the stove got hot, holding the paper in one hand, spooning powdered coffee with the other, until he said, 'Wait a minute . . .' and reached for the brown paper parcel.

The label was typed on the same machine Carl used for the letter.

That was a relief. That he'd made a connection. That something was still in there somewhere. Carl, and Beth, and what he'd done that day were still traceable in the brain.

Whether he remembered it all, he wasn't in a position to say. Though it could've been worse, he knew that. He'd seen concussions turn Rangers into rutabagas. Wounds that looked like his.

Ben cut the string on the package, and pulled off the paper, exposing two novels by Leo Tolstoy – *Anna Karenina* and *The Death of Ivan Ilyich* – hardcover, ordinary editions. Which made no sense at all.

There was a folded piece of typing paper in *Anna Karenina* with a handwritten note from Carl that read, 'Keep everything I'm sending you in an office vault, or a safety deposit box, or another place as secure.'

There were numbers on a smaller sheet of notepaper too, stuck in the front of *Ivan Ilyich*, '23–33–180–678–374', followed by, 'Identification with photo. Passport or similar.' Written in Walker's hand.

Numbers that big aren't a combination. Not to a standard sort of safe. Although . . .

Ben couldn't finish the thought. So he sighed quietly, and sat for a minute, his hands on the kitchen table.

Someone got in my car, and probably looked through my glove compartment. Someone searched Carl's house and office. Someone searched my house too. Somebody shoved the block and tackle. So something important's at stake.

Ben picked up *Anna Karenina* and began fanning the pages, studying the printing, and the edges, and the space behind the spine – looking for signs of fore-edge painting, or a message somewhere, of some kind.

He stood up slowly, and eased himself down into the old wooden rocker, his brain beating painfully against bone, as he reached for the phone to call Richard.

It rang before he touched it – Richard calling him with news from Chester Hansen, Hillsdale's Chief of Police.

Carl Walker's body had been found by a couple of boys about six fifteen on the banks of the Tangey River. It was a spot out in Hillsdale County, eighteen miles west and twenty miles south of the west side of Worthington.

It looked like Carl had shot himself, and did Ben want to see the scene? Chester was going over, called in for consultation by the county sheriff, who was a long-time friend of both Chester and Richard.

Richard had finagled Chester's OK for Ben and him to drop by the scene so the sheriff could question Ben then about Carl not showing at the concert. Richard said he couldn't stay long, but if Ben wanted to meet him there, Richard had the directions.

Ben told Richard about the letter and the package, and heard the surprise in Richard's voice when he said he'd gotten a package too, also at his office, that he hadn't yet opened. He'd assumed it was a book he was supposed to review, and had brought it home without looking at it.

He put the phone down and went to find it. And his voice was even deeper than usual and dripping heavily with portent when he told Ben it was another copy of *The Death of Ivan Ilyich* with a note consisting of numbers – the same string Ben had received ending in 374.

They talked about what it could mean for a minute, and what they should say to the police, until Ben finally told Richard he'd rather not tell them anything then about Carl's home and office having been searched, and him sending the letter and the packages. 'He sent those to *us*, not to the police,

and he must've had a good reason. I'd like to wait till we
know more, then talk before . . .'

'What . . . ? Ben . . . ?'

'Richard?' Ben couldn't finish the sentence. His mind had
shut off like a switch being thrown, and he didn't know what
to say.

'You said, "Then talk before . . ." What? What were you
about to say?'

'I don't know.'

'Are you OK?'

'Me? Sure. Yeah. We'll talk later when we know more, and
decide what to do then.'

Richard agreed. Sounding relieved. And gave Ben meticulous
directions to a place in the middle of farmland describable only
by county roads numbered in three or more digits.

Then Ben sat with his eyes closed. Willing the headache
away. Till he took the books and the letter Carl had sent and
hid them where they'd be safe.

He put on clean cords and a long-sleeved shirt. Then made
a peanut-butter sandwich and a thermos of strong black coffee.

The rain had stopped sometime before, and he took his
dinner with him out the mudroom door and set it down on
the ground so he could fit a length of fine black thread between
the door and the jamb. He'd already put one in the back porch
door, and he moved on to the front porch and threaded a thread
through the door jamb there, before locking it with his key
the same way he had the others.

He walked along the front of the barn, watching sheep graze
in a glistening field, listening to birds in bushes, as shadows
stretched longer and lower, as pale purple and corn-yellow
sun slanted down under high running clouds, as mosquitoes
rose one by one – glowing in the iridescent light – from the
tall grass by the fence.

Ben said, 'Poor Carl,' in a low quiet voice.

Too many people were dying too young. And suicide too,
made it worse. *If that's what happened to Carl. It's way too
early to tell.*

There were sheriff cars, and an ambulance, and a Hillsdale
Police car off the edge of the road, with flares burning on the
verge.

Richard's Chevy sat opposite them, a hundred feet or so south. And when Ben parked, in the gathering dark, and climbed out behind it, his head pounding and his stomach turning, he couldn't see any houses – just tree-edged rolling fields on both sides of the river.

He stood there for a minute – his hands braced above the door, eyes closed, breathing slowly, trying not to be sick. His head felt like it'd been kicked by a draft horse, and he opened his eyes to ease the dizziness. He rubbed the back of his neck for a second, while he studied the scene across the street – then told himself to get a move on.

There were only four adult watchers waiting, parents probably, of the two young boys, who looked excited as well as nervous the way nine- or ten-year-olds do – hands in pockets, feet shuffling (raising small plumes of dust near the road) – while a deputy talked, and took notes whenever one of them spoke.

There hadn't been much rain there, not that day at least. The grass was almost dry beside the road as Ben crossed it, in the blue-gray dusk, with a breeze smooth on his prickly skin.

He walked toward Richard, who was waving at him wildly like a large exuberant bear from what looked like it might be the start of a path in a line of willows and cottonwoods.

'Ben!'

'Hey.'

'It took you longer than I expected.' Richard had already lowered his voice and was looking conspiratorial. 'Chester said I was to warn you not to touch a thing, and then bring you along. They've searched between here and the corpse. I presume that's why they're allowing us back.'

'So—'

'The river's edge here is primarily shale, with an occasional outcropping of dirt and gravel, and can't be expected to reveal a great deal. Carl's car is over there.' Richard pointed to a brown Ford (as he walked away from the willows by the road) that was pulled off on gravelly dirt, tucked behind bushes and a thick line of trees, hidden well from the road.

Ben smiled as he said, 'You look like you find this pretty entertaining.'

'Exciting, perhaps, in a modest way. Though I wouldn't wish—'

'What do they know so far?'

'I haven't the faintest idea. I've only just arrived.'

They quietly crossed several broad ledges of brittle gray shale where weeds and wild flowers, and tough shrubs and trees, grew in what cracks there were.

Carl's body was under a medium-sized maple, face down on a wide shelf of shale not far from the river's edge, right arm under his body, left arm bent to the side, legs twisted awkwardly, blood pooled under his skull – splattered too and blown across stone – back of khakis and navy sport coat largely unspattered.

A handgun lay four feet from Carl's left hand, a .45 pistol, semi-automatic – Ben could see that from where he stood – the handgun he'd carried all through the war, a Colt M1911A1. It'd been used in World War I, then become the standard issue military pistol from World War II on, found in every gun store in America – an officer's weapon Carl could have kept after World War II.

The photographer had finished shooting Carl's back, and the coroner, Bill Tate, had recorded his observations – rectal temperature, depth of liver mortis, bullet entrance below and behind the deceased's left ear – and had shoved his notebook in his pocket. Tate then turned the body over, exposing an unexpected object six feet from where Ben stood.

It had lain under Carl's upper body – metal, shiny, two feet long, a thin chrome-like rod, that made Ben step closer to get a better view.

Chief Hansen and Sheriff Hodges stood watching Bill Tate while they talked, huddled together next to the river, on the far side of the body. The photographer took his anterior shots. And then the coroner squatted beside Carl – touching, prodding, measuring, jotting notes in his notebook, examining the exit wound above the forehead, an inch or so right of center.

As he tucked the notebook away again, he said, 'Walker was shot at close range, as I'm sure you boys noticed. Can't say about powder on his hands yet. I'll start the autopsy in the morning, and let you know as soon as I can.'

Hodges asked, 'What about time of death?'

'Twenty-four to thirty-six hours. Got rained on, of course,

last night. Clothes are wet, and there wasn't much rain out this way today. That can change things. Getting rained on. Temperature. You know what I mean. Too early to say more.'

Tim Hodges talked to him quietly, taking him away from the others, and Chester Hansen came over to Richard, nodding across at Ben.

Hodges walked up a couple of minutes later and talked to Richard about county politics, as well as a charity fund-raiser they'd both started working on. It looked to Ben as though Hodges liked Richard, but might be in awe of him too.

Though he also might've been trying to humor him, the uninitiated academic at the scene of a shooting death. Because Richard did look mildly unnerved, and pasty white around the gills, when Sheriff Hodges asked them both how they knew the deceased.

A deputy took notes while Ben talked about the concerts, and about visiting Carl's house and office that morning. 'A neighbor of his named Beth Morland, who taught with Carl's deceased sister, had keys to Carl's house to deal with emergencies when he's away. She and I went in this morning, and looked to make sure he wasn't hurt or ill.'

Ben didn't mention that the house had been searched. Or what had happened to him in the barn. Or what had been mailed by Carl. And then he asked Hodges if he knew when Carl had died.

'He wasn't here Friday morning at seven. The same two boys who found him tonight were playing along here then. Boys are drawn to water like iron to a magnet.'

'Rocks must be tossed in. Stones must be skipped.' Richard shrugged, smiling self-consciously. 'Even I am not immune to the age-old appeal.'

'Will you be talking to Miss Morland, Mr Reese?' Sheriff Hodges was staring at Ben with a cool appraising expression on his long thin face.

'I thought I ought to tell her tonight. It'd be easier to hear face to face.'

'Ask her to come to the station and make a statement tomorrow. Give the deputy her address before you go too. Was she romantically involved with the deceased?'

'Not according to her. I think she's dating somebody else. At least that's the impression I got. The only link was through his sister, who died sometime last fall. He and Beth lived two blocks apart. Beth said that's why he gave her the keys after his sister died.'

Hodges asked if he believed her.

And Ben said, 'Yeah, I do. I don't think Carl had an easy time forming friendships of any kind.' Ben was staring at the shiny metal rod still lying on the ground. 'You know, you might want to have your people examine the point on that lecture pointer. Have them do it carefully, though. The surface of the metal up by the point doesn't look normal to me. It's like it's been abraded. There's another word I can't remember . . . machined, I guess, is what I meant. At least it might be possible.' Ben hoped he'd said it so it'd sounded neutral. Not as though he were telling the cops how to do their job.

But when Hodges said, 'Oh?' he looked almost amused. Good-natured, but condescending. 'Why would you think that? Why not a regular old pointer that fell outta the guy's pocket?'

'It's almost two feet long. And he hasn't taught for weeks. We can't know for a fact that Carl was here alone. Right? And the pointer's got a piece of cork on the tip, as though the point's sharp. If that's true, the regular ball-end must've been cut off. Maybe he hid the pointer up a sleeve, intending to use it as a weapon. Something like a home-made stiletto. Though I guess there could be some kind of chemical smeared under the cork. *If* he intended to use the pointer to inject a fluid substance. A poison, maybe, or a toxin. I have heard that in—'

'What kinda toxin?'

'I don't know. There're lots of different kinds. Intelligence services have been known to inject toxin with pointed objects, like hatpins, and special pens. I've heard you can kill in a couple of seconds with—'

'So you think Carl Walker woulda known somethin' about that? That he woulda brought it with him to use on somebody else? You read a lot of spy stories, do ya?' Hodges was laughing softly, looking at Richard, raising his eyebrows as he pointed at Ben. 'So this is a professor friend a yours, huh? Some smart guy who teaches college?'

'He's not as crazy as he sounds.' Richard smiled, while he pulled his pipe from his pocket. 'I've known Ben a long, long time, Tim. And he worked with intelligence over in Europe during the Second World War.'

Ben shook his head and said, 'That's kind of misleading, I was—'

'Intelligence, huh?' Tim Hodges barely came up above Richard's shoulder, but he stood military straight and very thin, as he handed Richard his Zippo, having lit his own Lucky Strike. 'You worked for OSS?'

'No, I was regular army. Nothing but a behind-the-lines scout working for army intelligence. Not Army Signals, or—'

'You were a Ranger.' Richard was looking indignant, puffing smoke toward Ben. 'You trained Rangers in England. You actually—'

'Anyway,' said the Sheriff, gazing coolly at Ben, 'you finish your statement with the deputy here, and let me know if anything else comes back to haunt you later. Any idea why this Carl Walker guy woulda wanted to kill himself?'

'No idea at all. I can't believe it, to tell you the truth. It doesn't seem like something he'd do.' Ben was staring at the maple tree next to Carl, his eyebrows gathered together half-hiding his eyes, as he rubbed the cleft in his chin. 'I didn't know him all that well, though. I probably shouldn't have an opinion.'

'Looks like suicide from here, don't it? Without something more to go on.'

'Maybe. The gun's the right distance from his hand. If the pointer doesn't have—'

'You can give your statement to Fred here too, Richard, before you get gone.'

Richard nodded, and relit his pipe with a match. 'If it doesn't matter to either of you, I wonder if I might talk to him first? I have a long-standing dinner engagement, and a chess game scheduled to follow.'

Ben had been standing with his hands in the pockets of his corduroy pants, staring at the dried blood splattered across the shale, but then he walked around the maple, looking intently at the trunk.

He turned toward the river a minute or two later, and watched the dirty milky-brown water running fast from the rain farther west. His head felt like it'd been split open with an ax, and he knew he still wasn't thinking straight. Which irritated him, and made him impatient, as he rubbed his eyes and tried to make them focus. He didn't have double vision exactly, but everything was blurred, and his depth perception wasn't right.

He'd been thinking about Jessie too since he'd heard about Carl. Seeing her in a plain wooden coffin, cried over by her parents. In a raw hole in half-frozen ground, while David Marshall prayed for him and the rest she'd left behind. Which meant that when Richard said, 'Ben,' behind him, Ben jumped before he turned around.

'Are you feeling well, Benjamin? You don't quite look like your normal self. Heavens! How did you get the gash behind your ear? And a lump the size of a plum I've only now noticed!'

'Don't fuss, Richard. I'm a big boy, remember?'

'The wound doesn't show from the front, so—'

'Good.' Ben was looking past Richard, at the coroner leaving, at the covered body on the gurney, at the eyes of the deputy walking his way, talking to Chester Hansen. 'It's been a cold spring.'

'I beg your pardon?'

'Good people keep dying.' Ben said it in a cool deep voice, and rubbed his left temple.

'Yes, of course. Yes. But it's time you explained the wound.' Richard was looking worried, biting the stem of a cold pipe, shifting from foot to foot.

Ben lowered his voice as he said, 'I'll tell you about it later. I'll call you when I get home. If you aren't home, I'll go on to bed, and catch you in the morning. What time is it now?'

'Almost nine. Aren't you wearing your watch?'

'Am I? No. Though I don't know why I'm not. It's been a long day already.'

Eight

The day wasn't over either. And Ben's wound was getting worse. It was swelling probably, inside and out, and he drove into Worthington with his head imploding. Throbbing like an ocean liner's engines had been stuffed inside his skull.

He'd been thinking about the *Queen Mary*. About sailing to England with Jessie. When they'd stood with their arms wrapped around each other, leaning against a softly thrumming door, the *Queen*'s turbines shuddering under their feet, pulsing the blood in their own bodies, while they lived inside her skin.

He told himself to forget about the *Queen Mary* (and Jessie too for the moment), and read the numbers on the old quiet street two blocks north of Carl's.

He found Beth's house about nine thirty. And asked her, when she opened the door (with a pencil in her teeth and a small black-and-white Shetland sheepdog leaning against her left leg), if she were ready for news of Carl that wasn't going to be good.

They sat in the back on a screened-in porch with a pot of tea on the coffee table, contemplating unpleasant facts, while Shep, the sheepdog, lay between them with his eyes fixed on Ben.

Beth had said, 'I can't imagine Carl killing himself,' three or four times already, but she still looked shocked and upset.

'This is a lot more complicated than that. Even if we don't know how.' Ben was speaking slower than normal, stroking Shep's head, wanting to lie down on the cold tile floor and sleep till afternoon.

'I haven't wanted to say anything, but you don't look like you feel well.' Beth's face wavered in candlelight from hurricane lamps on the table, as she stared pointedly at Ben Reese above her mug of tea.

'I think I could use some aspirin.' He closed his eyes, while he told her what had happened.

And Beth leaned over and studied the wound. Then brought him ice cubes wrapped in a hand towel, with a glass of water and a bottle of Bayer. 'You think it was the same guy who searched Carl's house?'

'Makes more sense than anything else. Carl was trying to tell me something, with the letter and the books I told you about. And wanting me to keep them safe clearly implies importance. So if somebody saw me at Carl's house, and read my address on my car registration, and searched Carl's house for what Carl sent me, it wouldn't be surprising if he tracked me down.'

'No.'

'He actually might track *both* of us down. Except that you didn't drive to Carl's, and he might not know who you are yet. But if it *is* the same guy, I'd say he'll be trying, and you're going to have to take care of yourself.'

'You think this guy's that dangerous?'

'Don't you?'

'Well . . . Yes, I guess I do.' Beth's eyes looked surprised in the candlelight. But as she drew the top of her hair back from her face, the curly chin-length thicket of it, her mouth set in a small worried smile before she looked at Ben.

'Lock the windows. Use the chain locks on the doors. Keep Shep with you.'

'I will. Yes.'

'Is there somewhere else you could stay? Do your folks live here in town?'

'Yes, but I'd rather not. I wouldn't want to bring trouble on them.'

'Still . . .'

'I'll lock everything up, and keep Shep with me. What else I can do I don't know.' She was silent for a minute, sipping her tea, staring at the flickering flames inside the tall glass lamps. 'I ought to call Carl's brother-in-law again. Evelyn's husband, Roger, and tell him about Carl. He'll have to phone Carl's parents. Oh, I meant to tell you that. I found out earlier from Roger that Carl's mother called him late this afternoon asking if he knew where Carl was. She and Carl's dad live near Stonington, Maine, and apparently Carl called them every Saturday morning at nine o'clock when the rates are low, but he didn't call this morning, and that had never happened before. So whatever it was Carl was doing this week, it had nothing to do with them.'

'Ah.' Ben had already swallowed two aspirin, and was holding the ice against the knot on his head. 'What was Carl *up* to? I don't even know what to ask!'

'The letter was postmarked Worthington.'

'What letter?'

'The one Carl mailed me with the letter in it for you.'

'Sorry. I'm not thinking straight. When was it postmarked?'

'Wednesday night.'

'So he was here Wednesday, but in Massillon on Thursday, when he sent me the package. That's the—'

'East side of Ohio?'

'South of Akron, right. Richard's book wasn't mailed from there, *or* Worthington. Washington Courthouse on Thursday too.'

'Not too many miles south-west of us here.'

'Yep. Odd, hunh? Looks like Carl was working hard to keep from being followed while he got the letters and packages to more than one person. So that if one package was taken, someone else would have the same thing? Does that make sense to you?'

'As much as anything, I guess.' Beth Morland finished her mug of Earl Grey, then poured another for Ben.

'But then what do we know that gets us anywhere? Was that all he was doing this week? Or was there another purpose to him leaving town? He could've mailed the packages to Richard and me from Columbus, without going anywhere. Did he ever talk about friends? Or other family he could've visited?'

'He had another older sister who's lived in Paris for years. Her husband works for the *Herald Tribune*. Other than that, I don't know. He didn't talk about friends. I'm not convinced he had many.'

'There was mud on Carl's car. Lots on the rocker panels, like he'd driven on wet country roads. It didn't rain around here much till today, some south of here last night, I guess, but not here. And it was gravel and shale without much dirt where the car was found.'

'I know he visited battlefields, and other kinds of historic places. He loved old cabins, like I said before. Early farm houses, that sort of thing. I suppose he could've been visiting some historic spot, down some country road.'

'But no particular place comes to mind?'

'I told you about my house in North Carolina. My aunt gave it to me when she didn't want the upkeep. Carl asked me questions about it like I said, but he wouldn't have gone there without asking. And the house doesn't have the history he liked either. It's a twenty-five-year-old wooden rectangle, pretty much like a trailer. But Bobby's house is an old clapboard cabin, right through the woods from ours. Carl could've known about his. But that couldn't be where he went. Not with the time factors, could it? When he left, and when he mailed the packages?'

'No. Though I can hardly add and subtract with my head as scrambled as it is. And what I know about Carl could pass through the eye of a . . . nuts . . . I can't think of the word.'

'"Needle". That's how I met Bobby.'

'What?' Ben was leaning back in his chair, his long muscled legs stretched out in front of him, his eyes trained on Beth as though he'd missed something important.

'Bobby. The chef I told you about who runs the kitchen at the Captain's Inn. That's how I met him. Down in North Carolina.'

'Ah.'

'*He* might know something about where Carl went. I haven't talked to him since Wednesday morning. He's been working normal hours, and catering a wedding too, so we left it that I'd meet him tonight after that was done. In fact –' Beth looked at her watch and laid her napkin on the table – 'it's time for me to walk over there. Why don't you come with me, and we can talk to him together? Bobby can be shy. His family was really poor when he was growing up, and he . . . well, you'll see. He's a very good person.' Beth said it self-consciously, looking at Ben, and looking away, as she put their mugs on a tray.

'Let me drive you. Walking around by yourself at night isn't a great idea.'

'Bobby would've brought me home.'

'I understand, but you *do* need to protect yourself. We don't know who this guy is. We don't know what he's up to. We don't *know* that he murdered Carl, but you've had keys to Carl's house. You've been seen coming and going. You've got to think differently now. Lock your car all the time. Take Shep with you when you go out, even in the car. Keep your eyes open.'

'You make suggestions too. You think of things I won't.'

Bobby Chambers sat at a table with Beth and Ben in the back of the Captain's Inn drinking a glass of iced tea, having finished his tossed salad. He'd dished that up, as well as cold beet soup, for Ben and Beth too. And he said, 'There's cold filet after this, and leftover asparagus, and a big choice of desserts.'

'So . . .' Bobby said it in a low, soft, North Carolina slide, while watching Ben across the table, his brown eyes looking wary, his shoulders hunched, his elbows on the table, his dark hair falling on his forehead, his face slick with drying sweat from working all day at a stove, 'what did you want to talk about, Mr Reese?' Bobby was staring at Ben's left hand, at the index finger that didn't bend, at the wide scar that cut across the palm, then up Ben's arm past the sleeve.

Beth told Bobby about Carl Walker's death and watched his fork freeze in mid-air, dropping a piece of beef filet back on to the tray.

Bobby said, 'Good grief! What coulda come over him? He surely wasn't the kind to kill himself. I seen him Wednesday, and Thursday too, and he was real excited, *I* thought. Like a blue-tick hound with a fox on the run.'

'Wait a minute. Carl? Wednesday, *and* Thursday?' Ben had been studying Bobby closely, considering the scar on his neck too, while he finished his glass of milk.

'Yep. More milk? Mr Reese? 'Nother glass of milk?'

'What? No, thanks. Sorry. Tell us whatever you can.'

'Well, I've made me a garden back of the inn, herbs and lettuces I can't buy around here, and I went on out in the afternoon, on Wednesday this was, to tend to it, and get outta the kitchen a while. We're right on the corner here, as you know, and I'd just set down on the back steps to rest for a minute and light up a smoke, when I seen Carl pull in a drive a couple doors down the street. I didn't notice it was his car right off, but when he backed out again and parked right across from me, facing up toward High Street, that's when I seen it was him.'

Ben asked him what time that was.

And Bobby said, 'Four forty-five maybe. Anyway, I was awaitin' on him to get out and come in, but he didn't. Nope, he sat there, holding some papers in front of him, just like he was reading something, looking at his watch once in a while, but that's not what he was doin'. Not the way it looked to me.'

'Why?' Ben was staring at Bobby with a fork full of salad halfway to his lips, his eyes part way closed too, the light from the wall sconce making his head worse.

'I was gonna go on over and say somethin', but then I got to thinkin' he didn't want to be talked to. I waved to him, and he never even looked like he noticed, 'cause he was watching this man, this dark-haired guy – a big guy – with a big head on him it seemed like. He was standing on the corner not too far from Carl's car, forty feet maybe, somethin' like that. He was talking to one of the real-estate agents, looking at the rental board with pictures of houses up around here. He was carryin' a newspaper, and a big key chain in his hand, and maybe another paper too. I can't seem to recall. So, he shook hands with the real-estate guy—'

'You know for sure it was a real-estate agent?' Ben asked, as he rubbed his forehead.

And Bobby said, 'Yeah. He comes here a lot for lunch. Anyway, the dark-haired guy walked east across High, and sat on the bench there put up by the Rotary. I went inside to see what he was up to. I watched from up in the dining room. He sat there for quite a while, reading this paper he had, smoking cigarettes one after the other, and looking across at the inn. It looked like that to *me* anyway, and I thought it was kinda strange. I mean, here was Carl, sitting in *his* car watchin' this guy I'd never seen, pretending *he* was reading something. And here was this other guy sitting on the bench, doin' the same thing, pretendin' to read, but watchin' the inn.'

'Do you think the guy on the bench saw Carl and knew he was watching him?' Ben was rubbing his temple, staring hard at Bobby.

'Don't know. Didn't think so at the time. Carl's car was in the shade of that big old oak across the way from us, and the guy didn't look like he'd noticed. Anyway, after a while, he went on into the market there, Howard's Market, right behind him, and come out five minutes later with a couple sacks of groceries.'

Ben asked if Carl was still sitting there then, watching whatever he did.

'Yep. But when the guy put the groceries in his car, it was parked just north of the bench there. When he got in and drove off, Carl started up his car too and followed him north on High.'

'That's interesting . . . Yes.' Ben was gazing at the fireplace behind Bobbie, at the old paneling and the black iron cooking arm with the pot hanging off the end, without seeing a thing. 'What kind of car was it?'

'The other guy's?'

'Yeah.'

'Ford sedan. Navy blue. This year's model.'

'Was that the last you saw Carl – Wednesday?'

'Yep. 'Bout five thirty, I'd say, when he left. But Thursday . . .' Bobby looked up and said, 'Hey, Sylvia. Why don't you sit and eat something with us? Sylvia here owns the inn.'

Sylvia Todd was standing behind Ben saying hi to Beth. She must've been in her mid-thirties, and she was very good-looking – very striking and elegantly made, thick blonde hair wrapped in a French twist, a beautiful mouth, and fine blue eyes that Ben would've said looked worried. 'I can't, Bobby, but thanks. I've got to get home. Cheryl's picking me up here in a minute. My car wasn't running right, so she'll bring Sarah and pick me up. Anyway I was—'

'Have you heard about Carl?' Beth asked in a quiet serious voice.

And Sylvia looked across at her. 'No. What about Carl?'

Bobby told her. And Sylvia sat down at the table by Ben as though the news had stunned her. 'Why? Why would Carl kill himself?'

'I don't reckon he did. I saw him watching some guy Wednesday afternoon who was sitting on the bench across the street, watching the inn here, it looked like to me. Carl followed

him when he drove off. Whole thing looked mighty peculiar.'
Bobby speared a forkful of asparagus.

And Sylvia turned toward him. 'A man here? Watching the
inn?'

'Big guy. Dark hair. Kind of a big head.'

Sylvia said, 'Hunh, I wonder why?' Then stood up, picking
up her purse, saying she was sorry about Carl, but she'd better
wait outside.

Ben asked if the description of the man across the street
had meant anything to her.

'No. Why would you think that? I just looked at my watch
and saw it was later than I thought. I'll call you tomorrow
morning, Bobby, before you're busy with lunch.'

They all sat silently for a minute after Sylvia left, heading
back toward the kitchen. Then Ben asked Bobby when he'd
seen Carl on Thursday.

'He come in for dinner. 'Bout eight I'd say. Later than
usual, and he come into the kitchen. Said he was in a rush,
and asked me to fix something in a box he could take home.
He asked me right off where Sylvia was. She usually works
the front, but sometimes she's back at reception in the inn,
and he wanted to say hi, I guess. Anyway, I told him she
hadn't come in. That was real unusual. She was always around
unless her daughter was sick or somethin', but she'd called
in and said she was takin' the night off. Thursdays are busy,
and she never done that before.'

'She say why?' Ben had finished his salad and laid his
napkin by his plate.

'Nope. But she acted funny the night before. She come into
the kitchen 'bout nine maybe, and she looked real upset. She
leaned against the wall by the big freezer, all pale and kinda
quivery, and I asked her what was wrong. She said, "Nothin."
I said, "Don't look like nothin' to me." She said, "I've had
an unpleasant shock." I asked what kinda shock, and she said,
"A voice on the phone I never wanted to hear again." She left
then. She finished up in the front, and went on home. I talked
to a waitress after she went, and Jennie told me a man had
called asking to speak to Sylvia, and she'd looked real worried
while she talked to him. It was right before she come in the
kitchen. I guess I oughta say "came" in the kitchen. Right,
Beth?'

Beth smiled, and said, 'Well—'

'So that was Wednesday night? Right?' Ben was rubbing his forehead, staring intently at Bobby. 'And then she didn't work Thursday night?'

'Yep. But she worked Friday, and tonight like usual. Sylvia's got a housekeeper who sits with her daughter whenever she's here. Cheryl, like she said. Sylvia's a widow. Husband was in the military. Died in a Jeep accident in Japan in '47.'

Ben asked Bobby if he'd told Carl Thursday how Sylvia had seemed the night before.

'I think I did. Yeah, I know I did. He left right after that, and left in kinda a hurry.'

'How old is Sylvia's daughter?'

'Nine. That right, Beth? Sarah's nine?'

'Yes. Sylvia looked pretty tense to me tonight. Especially when we told her about Carl, and the man he followed who'd been watching the inn.'

'Course she would. Anybody would, hearin' about Carl.'

Beth nodded, and ate a spoonful of soup. 'But I think it was the other man too that made her want to go home.'

Nine

'That's a handsome dog.' The man in the brown madras shirt leaned down to pet the black-and-white dog which backed away toward Beth Morland. 'What kind is he, a miniature collie?'

'No, a Shetland sheepdog. Shep, behave yourself.' Beth smoothed the hair on Shep's neck, then looked up at the stranger. 'He may be afraid of your hat.'

It was a straw hat, wide-brimmed, blocking early morning sun from a broadly smiling face. 'I'm entirely bald, and if I don't keep my head covered, my pate'll peel like an orange.' He laughed, and pushed his sunglasses up a long wide nose, while he smiled another easy, open, generous smile and pointed past Beth to the park. 'It must be delightful living near this.'

The smile had almost made Beth think about relaxing, but she was walking again, heading back toward home, saying, 'Yes,' over her shoulder.

'I'm Bob Holmes, by the way. I'll be teaching European History at Ohio State in the fall, and I'm house-hunting in Worthington. A friend of mine recommended this neighborhood. Would you say it's a good place to live? Or is there somewhere else I should look?'

'The houses are kept up. It's close to the shops. The park's a good place to walk. I'm sorry, but I have to—'

'I'll try closer to Ohio State, too. I like being able to walk to class. I'm sure I would've enjoyed living near my friend, but I'm sorry to say Carl died.' The tall man mopped his forehead, before slowly shaking his head.

Beth said, 'Carl?'

'Walker, yes. I knew him for years.' He caught up with

Beth, then, who'd been walking fast without looking at him. 'Did you know Carl too?'

'I knew who he was. Good luck finding a house.'

'Thanks. The paper implied that he took his own life, though the Carl Walker *I* knew—'

'I didn't know him well enough to have an opinion.'

'I began phoning him Friday, and got no response. I was to stay at his house, and I'd told him I'd get here tomorrow, but I was able to leave Ithaca earlier than I expected, and I drove in late on Friday. And now, to discover he's dead . . . well, it makes me terribly sad.'

'Yes.' Beth was walking steadily, wondering if she should go somewhere public, and not let him follow her anywhere near home.

'Actually, I saw someone with a gray car loitering by Carl's house early Saturday morning. I was driving around looking for real-estate signs, and passed by Carl's house on a cross street. I wonder if I should tell the police.'

'You should. Definitely. As soon as you can.'

'Which police would I call?'

'Hillsdale County Sheriff, I imagine. Goodbye. I can't be late for church.'

'I apologize for keeping you. Carl used to tell me, "Only a wife could talk more than you!" Of course, *he* was an extremely private person who never even mentioned his family. I met him in the army, and respected him tremendously. I don't expect he discussed his war work any more than—'

'Not with me. Good luck finding a house.'

'He recommended the food at the Captain's Inn, and mentioned he knew the owner. Is the food good there? Or was he simply helping his friend?'

'I don't know what he thought, but *I* like the food.'

'Thank you for your help. I hope I haven't made you late.' The man hummed something jaunty, twirling an oak leaf between his fingers, while he watched Beth lead Shep away toward the park's north gate.

Ben's head had pounded all night long, right behind his eyes, stabbing at him with quick sharp sticks every time he stirred or woke. And yet he'd slept later than normal, which he never would've predicted.

He was thinking about numbers when he surfaced, and that was highly unusual. Ideas typically woke him up and made him stare into space. Images. Dreams. Artifacts. Well-arranged words. Strange historical stories and events. But numbers? No. Never.

They did express ideas. Clearly. Complexities he couldn't grasp. Mathematicians lived where he couldn't, seeing worlds he'd never imagine.

But he knew 43–24–4 meant something. And whatever it was, was important. And then there were the big numbers. Which Ben was sure Carl had used to tell him what he was too dumb to see.

Which brings me back to 'Why me?' When he hardly knew me, for all practical purposes. And Richard he knew even less. And why'd he vet me with Army Signals? Was he trying to tell me this is military? Or was it simply that he was—

Nuts.

The phone was ringing in the kitchen. And Ben shot up and sprinted toward it, his brain rattling against his skull whenever a foot hit the floor.

It was Beth. Frazzled, worried, talking in a rush, words sticking together, as she told Ben everything she could about the man in the park.

'Did you believe him? Do you think he was who he said he was?'

Beth said she wasn't sure. That in a way she did. That he'd seemed pleasant and normal, but that wasn't all. She'd come back from early church, where she'd left Shep in the car, since it wasn't that hot and she could park in the shade. And while she was gone, her house had been searched.

Nothing had been taken, yet her things had been picked through and left disarranged enough that you couldn't have missed the differences.

Ben listened with his mouth clamped shut, then asked what the man had looked like.

She said he was tall, but she hadn't seen his face or hair very well. Sunglasses had hidden his eyes, and he'd worn a panama hat because he was bald and his head burned badly – or so he'd told her.

Ben, who'd been staring at the wall behind the stove, sighed and rubbed his forehead. 'Maybe the search was left obvious to scare you. Maybe he did that at my house too.'

Ben listened to her for a while longer, repeating herself and sounding anxious, before he interrupted and told her he thought she ought to leave town. 'We don't know what to expect. And you've been the closest to Carl, as far as the outside world would know. If this guy saw me Saturday, he could easily have seen you too, and actually gone looking for you. He may think Carl left something in your house without you even knowing. And you don't want to get caught alone with the kind of person who nearly killed me, and may have killed Carl.'

Ben told her that's what *he*'d bet happened. That Carl was prepared for some kind of confrontation when he drove to the river, and was taken off guard. 'This guy is dangerous, Beth, and something really critical to him has to be at stake. But even so, as we agreed last night, I don't want the police to know anything more than that we checked on Carl because he wasn't at the concert.'

Beth said she understood. And she'd be careful too. She didn't want to be a bother, not to him, or Bobby, neither one.

'Bobby and I fought a war, Beth. And you could be used as a hostage. Sylvia could be a target too. I don't like him having mentioned that Carl knew the inn's owner. He may've been trying to find out what you know. I'm not sure she's involved, and I'm not saying it *is* the guy in the hat, but the man Carl was watching Wednesday was watching the inn. And someone called Sylvia *there* that night, and upset her enough Bobby noticed. Whoever it was could've been connected to her taking the next night off.

'But I'm more worried about you right now. How 'bout the cabin at Black Mountain? Could you leave now, and not tell anyone else where you're going? Call your folks often enough to keep them from worrying?'

Beth said that if she did leave, she wanted to tell Bobby.

'That's OK with me. But tell him to keep it to himself, and that I'll be in touch soon.' Ben asked for his home number, and Sylvia's too, and wrote them both down, then asked for the name of her milkman. 'Thanks. So you'll leave before noon, and take Shep with you? He'll give you some kind of warning, if there's a reason to.'

Ben asked if he remembered correctly that Beth didn't have a phone at her cabin. And set up a schedule so she could call and tell them she was OK. She'd phone Ben each morning at seven, and Bobby at ten at night. Vice versa if they knew they were going to be out.

Beth agreed. And said she'd talk to the police on her way out of town.

Ten minutes later, as soon as he'd talked to Bobby Chambers, and thrown on khakis and a shirt, Ben was driving his headache to Worthington faster than he should have been on narrow, corkscrew, potholed roads that hardly saw a handful of cars from one week to the next.

He didn't want to be easy to follow, and he took a circuitous route, trying to notice what was around him, while considering Sylvia Todd. Who obviously knew more than the rest of them, which was why she'd gotten out of town.

She'd planned it well. Not telling Bobby the night before that she was leaving town, when she was actually on her way to the airport when she'd left the inn. Getting the housekeeper to drive her too, leaving her own car home as a decoy.

So Sylvia Todd was no fool. Though it *could* mean she'd had practice. That she'd run from whoever it was before. So that meant Ben had to talk to her as soon as he possibly could.

Why had Sylvia told Bobby that everyone who knew Carl needed to be careful? It might not mean she knew who it was, though. It could've just been a common-sense warning. Carl Walker was dead. Why wouldn't she say that?

It'd be nice if I could think. I can't remember, or fit facts together. The ability to come up with solutions seems almost entirely gone, except . . . Why can't I figure out the numbers?

And why am I so sleepy?

You've got a concussion, dimwit. You shouldn't even be driving. Last night especially. That was unbelievably stupid. Flying half-blind and brainless.

Turn on the radio. Crank up the volume.

Keep your mind on the road.

Ben made it to Beth's by ten thirty. He'd parked in the park and walked over, then slipped behind the Lutheran church catty-corner from her.

The church windows were open, and he listened to the sermon while he watched Beth pack her car. She made three trips hauling clothes, food, and supplies out the front, before she locked the door.

She put Shep in front on the bench seat, then walked down the drive, disappearing around the rear of the house. A minute later, she ran back, climbed into the car, and drove off toward Route 23 – with no one but Ben watching.

From what he could tell.

He'd scouted the perimeter on his way in.

He scouted his way out too. And didn't see anyone who gave him pause. Though he knew he couldn't trust himself. And it wasn't a fact he liked living with.

There wasn't much he could do about that, so he did what he knew to do. He drove to Carl's street and parked across from his house. He knocked on doors till he found a neighbor – Mrs Iris Miller, a tall skinny woman in her sixties – who'd been questioned on Saturday by a tall dark man 'who had the nicest mustache', and 'needed to know the name of the woman who had a key to Carl's house'.

He was a friend of Carl's from out of town, Robert Tipton, his name was, and he was supposed to meet Carl that night for dinner, along with that woman friend of Carl's. Carl had said he'd be driving home from out of town Saturday, and that he'd call this lady with a message for Mr Tipton Saturday afternoon, telling her where Carl would meet them both that night for dinner.

The tall man, this Mr Tipton, he'd lost the paper with her name and address while driving from his home in Minnesota, and he was hoping one of Carl's neighbors would know who the woman was, and where it was she lived.

This neighbor had known both. And the tall man with the mustache and the sunglasses had helped her water her roses, and thanked her in such a kind, shy way, that Mrs Miller had been worrying ever since how this gentleman had taken it. Waiting for hours for Mr Walker, who would never be able to meet him again, lying dead that very same day. 'Here he was, so looking forward to seeing Mr Walker. It just makes a person think. We never know, do we? You and me even, here right now. Either of us could drop dead today, and neither of us the wiser!'

'Once we do, I suspect we'll be wiser. But we don't want to think about that. Not the dying alone part. Did you see Mr Tipton's car on Saturday?'

She looked mildly taken aback, before she said she hadn't. That he must've parked it on one of the end streets and walked in from there.

She *had* noticed a black sedan on Saturday. She couldn't say what kind, but it drove back and forth two or three times in the course of the day. Morning, she thought. Though she wasn't sure. A man had been driving, she knew that, but more than that she couldn't say.

She'd seen his car too. Ben's gray Plymouth. Parked in Mr Walker's drive Saturday morning *and* afternoon. And there'd been another one too that she'd noticed. It drove by at least once in the afternoon. A turquoise car with fins. A Chevy, she thought, though she couldn't say for sure, that slowed in front of Carl's.

Ben asked, 'What about Friday? Did you see Carl, or anyone else at his house?'

'I did see Dr Walker Friday morning. Now let me think. A little before eight, I believe, though I can't be completely sure of the time. It might've been earlier. He backed out of his driveway and drove to the corner there, past his house, and turned to the right.'

'That would be south?'

'Yes. He pulled up next to a parked car. He sat there for two or three minutes too. He rolled down his passenger window, and seemed to be talking to someone in the car. As soon as Dr Walker pulled away, the car followed behind him.'

'Did it?' Ben was talking to himself, staring past Iris Miller.

'It was a dark car. I don't know what the make was, and I couldn't see the driver. There's a tree there, with a thick trunk.'

'Yes.'

'You must think I'm awful. A terrible nosey old neighbor lady, watching everyone's comings and goings. I live alone now, the last six years, and my—'

'Have you told the police what you saw?'

'Not yet. No one's come to interview me. I will, of course, when they ask.'

'You'd make an excellent witness.'

'Would I? Really?'

'Perry Mason would want you on his side.'
Iris Miller twittered.
And Ben thanked her twice.
Then climbed into his car.

He mulled over what he now knew, as he made his way west toward home. Reminding himself, when he shifted into third, to call Stan McRae.

Stan was Chairman of the Microbiology Department at OSU, and Carl might've known him. He could've sought him out if he didn't – or another biologist Stan might know – about injectable poisons.

Ben had met Stan a year earlier, and even though it was Sunday, he figured he'd find him down at the lab, where he admitted to actually sleeping on a cot more than he did at home.

An Alderton professor had introduced them because Stan had had a book he'd needed repaired – an old pioneer herbal, found in his grandparents' chicken coop stuffed behind a wall.

As soon as Ben got home, he checked the threads in all three doors, and then phoned Stan. Stan never talked much, and the call didn't take long, once Stan remembered who Ben was, and had turned off a stirrer.

He'd known Carl from faculty meetings, and Carl *had* phoned him, six months or so before, to ask if there was a very quick-acting lethal poison that wouldn't have to be swallowed. He'd been thinking of trying to write a crime novel, and needed an interesting method of murdering someone in the military who'd be difficult to subdue. He wanted a method you wouldn't find in every other book, and he was wondering if there was something injectable that would work in an innocent everyday object, something other than a hypodermic needle, like a drill bit, or a leather-working awl, or maybe even an ice pick.

Poisons weren't Stan's area of expertise. But there was one substance that had come to mind when he was talking to Carl – one found in the common mole bean that could be concentrated and experimented with, though how feasible it might really be Stan couldn't have said. He'd suggested Carl talk to Maxwell Herrington, a renowned toxicologist at the University of Michigan, who had a much deeper grasp of the subject. Whether Carl had called Max, Stan didn't know.

Ben thanked him, and got off the phone, having promised Stan that they'd meet for dinner sometime that summer. Ben was rocking then in his kitchen rocker, rubbing the back of his neck, wondering too if it mattered right then whether Carl had called Max or not.

He now knew Carl had been asking. And that was more important than what the substance might've been.

Ten

Ben's head felt as though a war were being fought there, and he got dizzy whenever he moved fast, so he told himself to eat something quick and see if that would help.

He sat down on the back porch ten minutes later, holding an ice pack behind his ear, looking at a piece of wholewheat toast covered with broiled cheese, while he fought a watery reeling stomach and a chest that felt like a metal band had been clamped around his ribs.

The band was there because his brain wasn't right. Though he had done what he'd known to do – set the alarm and get up during the night, making sure he *could* wake up, and his pupils weren't more dilated.

They were pretty much the same now, nearly a day later. The distorted vision was hanging on too, somewhat better, but not gone. Though the rest was what made Ben squirm – loss of memory, slow physical reactions, difficulty with decisions.

Elephantine ... what? ... It starts with a 'c', I think ... cognitive processes. Having to struggle to grasp implications and know what to do.

He remembered taking the envelope from the mailbox, but there wasn't anything after that till he'd walked into his mudroom. And that was followed by other gaps. How many, and where, he didn't know.

The wooziness wasn't much better than it had been the night before, and he knew he shouldn't have tried to drive. Though he had needed to see Carl's body. And watch out for Beth that morning.

He had to have missed things when he'd talked to Beth and Bobby. He couldn't put information together and know he'd gotten it straight. He even had to read things twice just to get the drift. He couldn't work as an archivist with half a brain, and he'd have to tell President White if he didn't get better soon.

He's the one college president I've met in the flesh who's a person inside the PR shell, and he deserves a competent archivist whose judgment he can trust.

My mind's wrapped up in thick wet fog. And if I close my eyes, I sleep.

Ben woke up half an hour later, and didn't know where he was.

Then he remembered Carl and the package. And told himself to call Richard. To ask if he'd heard from the Chief of Police. And tell him what had happened to Beth.

Richard had just hung up from speaking to Chester Hansen, though there wasn't a whole lot of new information. Estimated time of death wasn't any more precise – after eight a.m. on Friday, to sometime Saturday morning. Hours had passed since Carl's last meal. Only one round had been fired, based on the number of bullets in the magazine, though there did seem to be slightly more residue lining the inside of the barrel than might have been expected. Which *could* only mean that the gun had been fired sometime before without having been cleaned.

Powder burns on Carl's left hand were consistent with having fired the gun, as was the fact that the handgun was found four feet from the body. The recoil propels the gun some distance from the suicide's hand in the vast majority of cases. And it *was* that gun that killed him too – Carl's gun, registered to him.

There *had* been a substance on the lecture-pointer tip underneath the cork, but the analysis hadn't come back yet, and might take several days. The usual metal ball had been cut and filed off the tip, and the point had been sharpened and worked into something like a tiny drill bit, which allowed more material to lodge in the grooves. The reason Carl would have had it with him remained a matter of speculation. The fingerprints on both gun and pointer were Carl Walker's alone. Existing evidence taken together, the presumption of a self-inflicted wound still stood, barring subsequent revelations of conflicting evidence.

Ben said, 'Two rounds could've been fired, and it wouldn't

be easy to tell. One round that killed him, another bullet put in the magazine to take its place. The gun would be wiped, or gloves would be used, probably both today. Then the murderer would fire a second round holding the gun in Carl's hand, leaving powder on Walker's skin. They'd never find the second bullet, not with a .45, out there in the country. But there was something else I wanted to know and I can't think what it was. . . . Nuts!'

Richard told Ben to calm down and give himself a minute, which irritated Ben intensely. Till he said, 'Oh, I know. Did Chester mention any marks on Carl that didn't seem to make sense?'

Richard hadn't been told, if they had. The one fact that seemed highly unusual was that they found a small scrap of notebook paper inside one of Carl's shoes. There were four words written on it in block capital letters – 'REMEMBER KRIVITSKY. REMEMBER REISS' – in an unidentified hand. Carl Walker had written Friday's date on the other side of the paper along with the words, '*Weisberg. Tell Lennox*'. No one knew the significance of either, Richard West included.

Ben said, 'That's interesting, isn't it?' And then asked Richard to spell Reiss. He was wondering if it referred to him, without seeing how it could have. Certainly not on Friday, or early Saturday morning, if Carl hadn't written it.

Richard repeated the spelling he'd been given.

And Ben said it looked as though Carl were telling them there was someone involved besides him. Carl. That another person had written that note, that day, Friday, over and above whatever the names themselves might convey.

Richard agreed, and then told Ben he'd had an idea that morning that might be important. That in Carl's letter to Ben, the 43–24–4 could be the key to a one-time book code. Based on *The Death of Ivan Ilyich* presumably, since that was the book Carl had sent them both. Of course, the three-number string had only been sent to Ben in the letter. But that might have been Carl erecting another safeguard.

Richard told Ben it could be as simple a key as, page 43, line 24, word 4. Meaning that the first letter of that word provided the substitution in a one-time code. Several approaches were possible, depending on the code to be deciphered. Richard had looked everywhere he could think of on the paper and the book itself, but had found no code to decipher. Nothing written in invisible ink between lines of text. He'd tried using heat in various places, both an iron and a candle, but nothing had turned up. There were other approaches he could try, but he hadn't yet had time. Richard said the other string of numbers, the one in his copy of the book, were too long to be applicable. The novel was only 133 pages, so that would eliminate those.

Richard asked if Ben had studied the papers he had for invisible ink. That silly as it sounded, lemon juice might be a possibility. More complicated invisible inks relied on ultraviolet-light sensitivity. Rhodamine B, for instance, would show up in UV light and was reasonably easy to come by.

Richard thought they should probably start with heat sensitivity, with lemon juice or milk. That approach would make some sense if the information conveyed were a short string of numbers or words. If the message were lengthy it seemed less likely. *If*, in fact, there *were* such a code, which was still nothing but one possibility. Richard said Ben ought to scrutinize the two pages with numbers that Carl had sent, using an iron, and holding them over a candle, then examine them with a magnifying glass.

'So you learned something useful at Bletchley?'

Richard laughed, and replied that those kinds of approaches had nothing to do with the German Enigma codes they'd worked on at Bletchley, as Ben very well knew. The Bletchley work had been highly sophisticated, the decoding and decryption of extremely complex rotor-generated military codes, which had led to the invention of ground-breaking machines, electronic and mechanical, that performed extremely complex computations to aid the book- and code-breakers. Field operatives, however, working in intelligence, often behind the lines, were forced to use simple techniques based on whatever was at hand. Those were the methods he was considering, at least at the present time.

Richard asked Ben how he felt, and did he think he should see a doctor. Richard thought he hadn't looked well, and 'One's brain is nothing to trifle with.'

'If I'm not a lot better, I'll go tomorrow. But I don't think there's much they could do. *If* it's just a typical concussion. Thanks for the code idea. I should've thought of that myself. That could be why Carl sent the book to you too. That if mine got stolen, or lost, or fell into the wrong hands, he wanted you to have a copy, since you're the experienced book-breaker. Oh. I haven't told you about Beth and Sylvia. I'm not putting things together.'

Ben did look for signs of hidden writing when he got off the phone, and found none.

Then he called the only two car-rental companies in Columbus asking for rentals in the names of Tipton and Holmes. Neither had rented a car to anyone using those names. He asked about rentals on Tuesday or Wednesday of a navy-blue Ford sedan under any name whatever, and learned that two had been rented on Wednesday from Hertz: one to a woman from a nearby office whose car had been damaged in a wreck, who'd be keeping it for several weeks; the other to a man from California whose name was Gilbert Ross. Ross had turned the car in Friday afternoon at two. He'd rented nothing else from them. He'd rented nothing from Avis at all.

When Ben asked about other dark sedans, dark brown or black, without providing a specific name, neither rental agency was willing to give him information. There were too many to look into. And, as both politely pointed out, he wasn't the police.

Ben thanked them, and hung up, and tried to remember where he'd seen a turquoise Chevy in the last few days, like the one Carl's neighbor had seen on Saturday. He knew he had. But couldn't think where. Which disgusted him considerably.

He told himself to do something useful. To try to clean the painting in the basement, the small oil of northern California he'd found in storage in Alderton's library. He worked for half an hour, and discovered that doing close work like that made his head worse.

He went for a walk in the late afternoon, trying to clear his head. Then ate tuna salad and home-grown lettuce, and a bowl of strawberries from the patch behind the barn.

He paid almost no attention to what he ate *or* did. Which wasn't all that unusual. But this time he poked at Carl's death with what was left of his brain, looking for ways to find his killer.

There was no proof there was one. Other than the maple

tree next to Carl's body where Ben had seen missing bark on the other side – a dugout strip, four feet off the ground, that nobody had mentioned to Richard. It was a line of bark ten inches wide, with different heights of missing pieces that looked to Ben as though it'd been picked away with intent.

I s'ppose it could've been scraped off, with a chain maybe, or a rope. A rope might not do it. A chain would, but the marks would be more . . . what? . . . more pronounced, if someone had sawed it back and forth. The height of the band would be constant too. And the width of the strip would be wider around the trunk. No, it looked like someone had dug at the bark, pulling it off with their nails.

Carl's wrists had been bruised too. At least they'd looked that way from where Ben had stood. Not very obviously. And not from something hard like a chain. Something smoother and softer. Wider than a clothes line, or even a pliable rope.

A belt to a raincoat might work. A scarf, or a tie, either one. He couldn't have said what'd been used, but he would've bet Carl was tied to that tree. His arms wrapped around it, his wrists on the opposite side from where he'd died.

I think he stripped the bark off the back to tell us what had happened. Of course, with my mind the way it is, I may be overlooking something. Or overemphasizing too. Or seeing it from the wrong perspective and drawing stupid conclusions. Which is not the way I want to live.

Yeah, well, maybe it's good for me. Maybe I've prided myself on my brain, and this is a prod and reminder.

Monday, June 17th 1957

That night, shortly after one o'clock, a black car stopped two blocks away from Beth Morland's house. A man in dark clothes got out from behind the wheel, then moved quickly and silently along the sidewalk to her drive. He slipped along the side fence into the back yard and stopped under a redbud tree beside her unattached garage. He glided quietly to its side door. He opened it carefully while watching the house. He stepped inside – saw there wasn't a car – and swore under his breath.

He turned and crept toward the back of the house, toward the screen door to a screened-in porch above a square brick stoop, where a painted metal milk box sat, its lid carefully closed, a handwritten note inside:

Out of town. No milk till further notice.
Thanks, Tom.
Beth

He crumpled it up, and put it in his pocket. Then slipped out of the yard.

It was two in the morning when Ben woke up sweating, tangled in twisted sheets. He sat up fast, and shoved his back against the wall, his eyes stinging from straining while he slept, from sweat seeping in-between his lids.

The room was dark, and he knew to keep his eyes open, to keep himself from going back. Back to Malmédy, or back to Trier. Back to D-Day, or the Battle of the Bulge. Back to too many German command posts scouted in between.

Corners can't be trusted – he'd learned that the hard way. And he stared at all of them, and the windows too, at the darkness beyond the doorways, before he let himself breathe.

He'd made it home. Home to the States.

He knew right where he was.

He threw the sheet off and sat there naked, hot and sticky and wishing it would rain and wash away the heavy humidity suffocating the night. He turned on the lamp on his side of the bed, then stood up fast and found the bathroom – where he switched on the light, and turned on the water, and watched it swirl in the sink.

He was too sweaty to wash with a washcloth. He'd have to take a shower. He'd climb in, and let water roll over him till his lips weren't cracked, and his mouth wasn't dry, and he'd washed the war away.

Water felt good standing on his skin, and he decided not to dry himself off. He brushed his teeth, staring at scars that made him think of Jessie sliding her fingers across them, kissing them quick when he didn't expect it – when he was shaving, or pulling on a shirt, or bending down to play with Sam.

He looked at the smallest, his safe scars from shrapnel, the ones he'd gotten at Omaha Beach, thinking, that's what it was tonight.

Things happened in the dream that didn't on the cliffs. People were there who weren't. But that's what it came from.
   Pull on some shorts. Get a glass of water. Take your smokes to the porch.

He was in one of the twig chairs again, lighting a Camel, looking for sheep in the pasture, listening to thunder off in the distance, thinking about Omaha Beach the night before the invasion. June 5th, 1944. When he'd been attached to a Canadian Strike Force, Strike Force D2 – a hundred and fifteen commandos crammed into three subs, there to take out the German guns up on both sides of the cliffs.
   Richard had read that someone said there weren't guns at Omaha, and Ben would've liked to get *that* guy alone and tell him about midnight before the landings. Trying to climb into rubber rafts from a pitching sub in a hard-rolling sea. Trying to make it in alive with guns cutting you to ribbons.
   I'd like to see him on that beach, with body parts blowing by him. Guts under your feet. Sounds exploding you can't describe. Screaming men all around you. Trying to scale cliffs that tough to stop the guns slaughtering you. Knowing you failed, your first time in combat. You've got to see it with your own eyes to know what the numbers mean. Ninety-five per cent casualties. Seventy per cent mortality of all the guys who went in.
   Ben was standing by then, his back against a porch post, finishing the glass of water. He lit a Camel, and blew out the match, then shook his head at the night.
   The guilt of the fortunate, that's what I've got. Getting back in D-Day plus 9, instead of being mutilated, or killed where I went in.
   Later too, down by Trier, how fortunate was he then? Torn apart, with next to no chance. The way they'd treated him saved him. Guys who didn't even know him strapped him under a Piper Cub. Getting him to Paris. The doc there who got him home fast. Inventing methods overnight to fix wounds like his. A gift is what that was. Through no merit of his own.
   And what about the guys in hospitals still with wounds that made his flea bites? And all the dead left in the mud. Missed every day by their loved ones.
   There're things I'm supposed to do yet. I know that from

Trier. From being sent back when I saw myself dead. I knew it then, the second it happened, just like I do now.

But why do the dreams, surrealistic as they are, always end the way it really did with me strapped under the plane?

You're never going to answer that. So think about Carl's numbers. And what he could've meant.

Ben inhaled and sat down on the steps, letting his hands hang between his knees. Until he said, 'Geeze!' and startled two sheep.

He was in his study half a minute later dropping a map of Ohio on the desk. He shut the wooden shutters, closing the louvers completely, then took the books off one of the shelves he'd built against the long wall that backed up to the bedroom.

He fished a carefully bent wire out of the back of the overstuffed chair, pulling it up from the narrow crack between the back and the bottom.

It was 'L'-shaped like an Allen wrench, but eight or ten inches long, and he stuck the sharpened point into an almost invisible pinhole on the right side of the wooden back of the empty shelf. He worked the wire farther to the right, and pried out the back panel.

He'd made a box-shaped receptacle there, in the space between two studs, where he kept six gold British guineas he could trade anywhere in the world, plus four rare Greco-Roman coins, and a Milton first edition he'd been given by a long-dead donor.

He took out Carl's letter, and the wrapping paper and the books. And said, 'OK, folks, let's see what we've got,' as he spread the map of Ohio across the desk, and stuck his finger on Worthington.

Route 23 here, south to 33 . . . It does *go south-east to 180. Which connects . . . here with 678, then . . . Route 374 dead ends. Which means I'll see what he wants me to find when I get myself down there.*

Poor Carl had been shouting at the deaf. 'Follow the routes I've given you, you idiot.' Take 'Identification with photograph.' For a purpose yet to be revealed.

Ben asked himself why he hadn't seen it before. The blow to the head, or early senility hitting at thirty-four? Then told himself to study the books again, harder than he had already, for something other than secret writing, which seemed too much like the Hardy Boys to him.

Though you can't write anything off yet.
Speaking of lousy puns.

Ben worked at it for twenty minutes. Looking at *Anna Karenina* carefully, page by page, till he'd gotten to the back, and was holding the front cover between his left thumb and fingers, and pinching the back with his right.
It almost feels like the back cover . . . Does it seem thicker?
Some. Maybe. I wonder if Carl . . .
He had. Yes. He'd re-glued the back. He'd put a slip of paper in there, thin paper, tissue-like paper, folded in half over Carl's own handwriting:

> Ben,
> S.W. house. Structure. G.M.H. Oxford. Cloth.
> Stipple. Jessie would understand.
> Vice isn't always bad.
> Carl

Interesting. If puzzling. But progress was being made. Even if he didn't know what it meant, he knew where to go next.

Eleven

Monday, June 17th, 1957

Ben left a little before five that morning, having called Richard and told him where he was going, asking him to phone Bobby later to tell him that it was really important that he, Ben, talk to Sylvia, and would Bobby ask her to please phone him that night if she were able. *If* she actually called Bobby, the way she'd said she would.

It took Ben over an hour to get on to High Street (Route 23, in the center of Columbus), which cut straight south past OSU and a huge explosion of state government, as well as the swarming hangers-on who lived off one, or both.

It was hot and sticky by sunrise, as he crept through Columbus, stopped by one light after another in Monday morning working-man's traffic – men in the trades and truckers drinking coffee, getting up, and getting it done in the heat of another day.

Ben wiped his upper lip at a red light, thinking about Carl's G.M.H.-Oxford-stipple message. Trying to make connections, and decide how to pursue it.

He almost missed a turn because of that, and he switched to his own research on life before artificial light, contemplating where he should look for diary entries and private correspondence from resources in Britain.

It never would've occurred to him that country people could've laid down trails of lime to follow when coming home in the dark. And he knew there had to be much more to learn he'd never begin to imagine.

Especially in his present state of plodding stupidity. The headache was better, though, and the hazy, gazing underwater feeling was beginning to fade away.

It's pathetic, when you think about it. That I could know

reasoning's a gift, being able to trust your thought processes,
as well as your observations. And yet still take it for granted.
When what I should've been doing every day of my life was
thanking God I could think.

If it did come back to normal, he knew what he'd do too.
Sink back into semi-oblivion. It's probably our oldest conflict.
Petty, versus perpetual. Temporal, versus eternal. If the big
picture doesn't slap us in the face we can't wait to ignore it.

He didn't believe she was dead, that was part of it. It felt
like she'd gone off on a trip, and he was still listening for her
footsteps to cross the kitchen floor.

OK, fine. Look for the turn-off. Don't wallow in it now.

He was on Route 33 by then, running east in old Columbus.
Germantown, and neighborhoods like it. Decaying architec-
ture, congested streets, what once was thriving now turning
derelict – Route 33 crawled through it, before it turned to
farmland.

Then it headed south-east toward Athens, to rolling land,
not too far from the city, to fertile, green, wind-blowing
country, to air that smelled of earth and hay, being cut and
baled as he passed, of winter wheat about to turn golden, and
the scent of corn with the dew burning off, its leaves looking
like he'd hear them grow if he stopped and listened.

Forty-five miles from Columbus, the whole world had
changed to twisting narrow washboard roads threading through
the Hocking Hills. And there Ben stopped and got out of the
car, somewhere on Route 374 – needing to move, and wake
himself up, and get ready for whatever was coming.

He stretched his back, and jogged where he stood, then
drank a cup from his thermos of coffee, and surveyed the
green-gray world. Cooler. Damper. Rock formations everywhere. Evergreens and ferns in the rock face where trickles
of water ran.

Ben took off his belt and opened the length of it, checking
to see that the wires weren't tangled – the one coated with
diamond dust, the other smooth and thick. He patted the
pockets of his faded khakis, feeling the weight of his Swiss
Army knife, and the roll of nylon line.

It was almost nine, and he got in and drove, thinking about
what the tall man could've learned from searching his house
and Beth's.

He'd know Ben had been a Ranger. A scout who'd helped train British Commandos, then worked for army intelligence. He'd know he'd been wounded, both where and how badly. He might know where Ben kept his guns. He could've seen his work records and his personal address books, which would lead to his office and colleagues, as well as family and friends.

He'd know too much about Beth too, from her address book and personal records. Where she worked. Who her friends and family were. What her summer-school schedule was. That she owned a cabin in North Carolina, from electric bills and tax records.

Forest was all around Ben then, forest that looked a little like Appalachia's, with stretches of hard-cut field where people who knew what hardship was like pried corn and tomatoes and pole beans from rock-packed dirt.

The road curved sharply to the right, just past a sign on the left for 'The Cabins at Cedar Falls'. And when he followed it down and around, till it flattened out in a narrow valley, he could see where the road dead-ended fifty feet past a state-park sign that pointed to the right toward a cave.

Ben turned back toward the Cabins at Cedar Falls and pulled into the drive that ended by a rambling log house made of old cabins cobbled together.

There was no one in the front room when he walked in, so he rang the bell on the rough-sawn desk, smelling the scent of sassafras tea, and something sweet baking.

A wide plank door swung open, and a plump woman with dark hair said, 'Good morning, can I help you?' as she carried a plate of pale golden cookies across the room toward Ben. 'Could I talk you into an orange cookie? Help yourself to a handful. They're too small to eat just one.'

Ben said, 'Thank you,' and ate two. 'Do you by any chance know a man named Carl Walker?'

'Sure I do. He's taken cabins here for four or five years. This summer he's rented the owners' place and is keeping it till September. They've gone to visit their daughter in Oregon, and were pleased as punch he did. Gave him a good rate, 'cause they know he'll take real good care of the place. Have another cookie.'

'Thanks.'

'The Gilberts don't rent their house to hardly anybody. Carl, though, he's real persnickety. You know what I mean? Real neat and tidy.'

'Yes. So—'

'Mrs Gilbert and me, we keep talking about finding him the right kinda wife. He brings peanut-butter sandwiches every time he comes, and we kid him about it, like he can't cook nothin' else.'

'I brought one too, actually, so I sympathize.' Ben smiled, and shook his head at the plate of cookies she'd held out in front of him again. 'I'm Ben Reese, by the way, and Carl told me—'

'Oh, you're the fella we're s'pposed to be looking for. Carl told us about you last week. We aren't allowed to even go into the cabin to clean it up. No dusting, no sweeping. He's working on a manuscript and doesn't want anything touched. He said you'd be coming, if he couldn't, and we were to let you in. Told us to ask for identification, though. Something with your picture on it. He didn't want the work he's doing to fall into the hands of "an academic rival". That's what he said, and then he laughed, making fun of himself like he does. Like he knows books written by professors aren't nothin' nobody'd steal.'

'I know what you mean, but they do.'

'What?'

'Steal each other's work. You'd be amazed. How well you teach doesn't matter much today, not the way it once did. It's what you publish that counts.' Ben was pulling his passport from the inside pocket of his old navy sport coat, handing it to the short smiling woman as she wiped crumbs from her blouse.

'Yep, that's you. Benjamin Arthur Reese. I'm Hazel Shank, by the way. Pleased to make your acquaintance. Let me know if there's anything you need.' She stared at the picture, then back at Ben. 'Will you be staying the night?'

'I'm not sure yet. I need to see what stage the work is in at the cabin.'

'He left his key for you.' She'd reached into the back of a drawer and was checking the name on a tag. 'If you head back along the gravel drive on the south side of this cabin here, it's along about half a mile. You'll be in the woods right off, and it's the only house you'll come to on that lane. There's wood stacked on the back porch if you want to start a fire. Don't know if you'll need one, but they do say it'll get rainy tonight and stay that way for several days. Here,' she was spreading a napkin on top of the cookies, 'you take these with you. I've baked more than we need for tea this afternoon, and these don't freeze real good.'

'Thanks, but I won't—'

'You need some meat on your bones, boy, just like Mr Carl. Told him last week he'd been working too hard. You could tell the way he looked. You got big shoulders and muscles on you, but Carl he's thin as a bean . . . I'm sorry. I didn't mean to get personal, I just open my mouth and—'

'That's OK, that's not the way I took it. So did he come in Wednesday night, and leave Thursday?'

'He did. Got here after midnight Wednesday, so Thursday morning I guess you'd say. My husband was up gettin' ready to go fishin', and saw Carl's car drive in. Carl left Thursday morning, nine or ten I guess, something like that, after telling me either he'd be back, or you'd be over in the next few days. Let me know if you need anything. Let me know how long you'll be staying too. And what we should do about cleaning.'

In a Holiday Inn on the north side of Columbus, a tall dark-haired man stared at his face in a bathroom mirror, one side and then the other, considering the strong broad features, before he combed his hair. He parted it on the right, switched it over to the left – then brushed spirit gum across his upper lip.

He carefully removed a thick dark-brown mustache from a small leather case, and pulled out the straight pin that fastened it to a strip of cork. He arranged the net backing on his upper lip, and trimmed a few stray hairs with a pair of cuticle scissors.

He dampened his own hair and combed it straight back from his forehead, making his face look longer. He plastered it in place with hair spray, then put on a pair of heavy horn rims, and stuck a pipe in the breast pocket of a neat navy-blue jacket.

As he sat down on the bed, he pulled a list of numbers and addresses from his inside coat pocket, then laid it on the bedside table. He looked up a number in the city phone book, and dialed Ohio State.

He waited to be connected to the Theater Department, then asked to speak to whatever woman graduate student happened to be in the office.

'Hi, Janet. I'm Bernard Ziegler. I'm a private investigator from New York, and I need some female theatrical talent. It's worth a hundred bucks to me to have you phone a woman in Worthington and tell her you're one of her daughter's high-school students . . . It's nothing illegal, I promise you that, but I'm after specific information. I've written a script I'll read you in a second so you can write it down, but you'll have to improvise too. Course, you can do that in your sleep, right, an actress like you?'

He laughed warmly and easily, then asked if she had a mail slot or locker somewhere in the Theater Department where he could leave her money. 'Great! I'll put it in your mail slot by two this afternoon. OK, you ready to take this down? . . . You're to call Mrs June Morland at Garden 6–5224 and tell her you're a student of her daughter Beth's at Worthington High School. You'll say your name is Amanda Allan, and that yesterday you were supposed to have lunch with Miss Morland, but she never showed up, and you have to get in touch with her right away. You're wondering if she's out of town, because you've been phoning her in Worthington, and she hasn't answered. Her number's Garden 6–1792, in case the mother asks if you've got the right number . . . OK, good, so you got all that? . . .

'I expect Mrs Morland'll say Beth's out of town, and your job'll be to find out where. If she doesn't know, or won't tell you, you say Beth had offered to let you and your parents stay in her cabin in Black Mountain, North Carolina this coming Friday on your way to Florida. So you thought you better check with her and see if Miss Morland has gone there already and forgotten about your lunch and your visit, or whether there's somewhere else you could phone her to see if her plans have changed. She told you she doesn't have a phone there, and you need to talk to her to see if it's still OK to visit, and to get directions to the cabin . . . I'll wait so you can write that down.'

He smiled while lighting a cigarette, then inhaled intently, one drag followed fast by another, as he stared at his mustache in the mirror on the wall above the phone. 'The main thing is to find out where she is, and get an address and a phone number . . . Yeah, I'll call you at one and see if you've gotten through to Mrs Morland . . . What? I can't phone you till nine thirty tonight? Why? I'd prefer to speak to you earlier, since the . . . You mean *only* between nine thirty and ten thirty? Why couldn't I call . . . No, I don't want you to recommend someone else. No, I'll accommodate your rehearsal schedule, and make sure I phone you then. Give me the number where you'll be . . . Thanks. I've got the right woman for the role. Yeah, you're gonna make a great actress!'

He hung up, stubbed out his cigarette, picked up a brown leather briefcase, and slammed the door behind him.

Ben pulled off the mostly mud track, having driven through the ruts at a snail's pace, and parked deep in a dark green wood in front of a small log cabin.

It looked old and carefully restored, and was perched at the top of a steep hill that fell away at the back. Ben stretched his shoulders and stared at the cabin, after he'd locked the car, thinking he wouldn't mind living here a few weeks a year, with the smells of woods and wood smoke, with books and work and a dog.

The step to the shed-roofed porch was a large flat oval rock, and Ben stood on it, listening for watchers. It was highly unlikely he could've been followed, with the doubling back he'd done close to home, but care needed to be taken.

When he saw no reason not to, he stepped on to the porch and unlocked the front door, then walked into the cabin – a one-room cabin, as it turned out, with a double bed straight ahead, all the way to the back, its headboard against the left wall.

There were wide windows beyond it, looking out into densely packed treetops – but Ben stared at the desk that took up the back right corner. That was where the typewriter sat, flanked by boxes of typing paper.

Ben started toward it across the room – then told himself to take time to be careful and look around first.

He stopped by the sofa that faced the fieldstone fireplace centered in the right-side wall, and turned around toward the door, glancing at the tiny kitchen built along the front wall. He stepped through both the curtained archways opposite the hearth – and found no one in the laundry room, or the bath-room next door.

Then he walked straight to the portable typewriter, and peeled off the gray cloth cover with Royal written in the middle – and there, waiting, was a sheet of paper, carefully centered in the roller, with a message written for him.

> First, thank you for taking on this task.
>
> You will know how to stop him. Take care of your-self as you do so. He is a dangerous and deceitful man, who, I believe, has killed before.
>
> I am sorry you lost Jessie. The woman I hoped to marry was killed ten years ago. She did not love me. Perhaps she never would have. We did not have time to determine if knowing each other better might have changed her perspective.
>
> C

Ben shook his head, and said, 'Geeze, poor Carl,' as he sat down in the desk chair. *Grieving for her all those years and never saying a word.*

Ben took the lids off the boxes of typing paper – one of regular twenty-pound bond, one of very thin onion skin, one of shiny black carbon paper for sliding between the bond and the onion skin when making one or more copies.

There was a Manila folder on the desk too, where Ben found fifteen pages of lecture notes for a course on Russian-language studies that compared various English translations of Tolstoy's *The Cossacks*. A carbon copy lay under it, an eraser pencil on top.

Ben didn't find anything that looked unusual, till he'd ruffled through the box of typing paper – and discovered two small handwritten address books underneath the bond.

A fountain pen lay beside the typewriter too. An empty fountain pen, carefully washed, the nib inkless, the bladder clean, the top set off to one side, an ink bottle beside it, washed and turned upside down to drain on a folded towel.

As he started to put the cover on the typewriter, Ben noticed there wasn't a ribbon. He looked in waste baskets, in drawers, and on surfaces – then stirred through the ashes in the fireplace, where he finally found a two-inch strip of singed black and red ribbon. He sealed it in one of the envelopes he'd brought, and slipped it back in his coat pocket.

Next he took the fountain pen, eraser pencil, ink bottle, typewriter, boxes of paper, lecture notes, and address books and laid them on the front seat of his car. He pulled the spare tire out of the tire well in the beetle-shaped trunk of the Plymouth, and leaned it against a back fender. He wrapped the old towels he kept in the trunk around the Royal and the boxes of paper, and fitted them (with the rest of Carl's things) inside the vertical tire well on the right side of the trunk. He draped an army blanket over the top, folding and rounding it to look like a tire, then dropped the formed felt cover on top, and leaned the spare against a porch post.

Then he searched the cabin systematically – examining the ashes once again for unburned paper and scraps of ribbon, looking in the toilet tank, and behind prints and mirrors and every last book, in every single drawer and cabinet, and under the outside deck. He didn't find the ribbon reels. Or anything else Carl had left.

Ben drove over to the office, and brought Hazel Shank back. And when he was closing the door behind them, Ben told her what he'd avoided before – that Carl had died on Saturday, shot with his own gun.

'What?' Her face looked stuck, to begin with, stunned then, and astonished, mouth hanging open, eyebrows appalled.

'It was made to look like he'd killed himself, but I'm not convinced he did. He came here with a purpose. He wanted me to follow him, if it turned out he couldn't come back. He left several things here for me, which I've already put in the car. I need to find out from you if anything looks different. You said this cabin belongs to the owners of the inn. Is anything of theirs missing? Or is anything out of place?'

'No. I don't think so.'

'Take your time. Look around. Look in the cabinets and cupboards.'

Hazel did, methodically, shaking her head and blowing her nose on a handkerchief pulled from her skirt pocket. When she'd done everything she could think of, and was getting up from looking under the bed, she said, 'Looks just the way it was to me. I don't see nothing different.'

'What about the fireplace? Were there that many ashes when he arrived?'

'No. Now that you mention it. We'd swept it all out. Why would he make a fire? It was real hot last week.'

'He may have typed something here, or handwritten something, or brought papers with him he had reason to destroy. Maybe he copied something, and destroyed the draft.'

'Why would anybody kill him?'

'I don't know. But I will before it's over.'

'I sure do hope so. And I hope you do it quick.'

'I'll drop you back at the main building, and then I need to get going. Oh, one other thing. Could I store my spare tire somewhere that's out of your way? I'll come back for it later. I can't tell you when right now, but—'

'You shouldn't drive around without a spare.'

'True, but this time I have to.'

'I guess we could put it in the laundry room. Nobody else'll be staying here, not till September.'

'Thanks. I appreciate it. Another thing too. Don't let anybody come in here. There may come a time when the police get involved, and they'll have to investigate the cabin the same way they would a crime scene.'

'You can count on me, believe me.'

In Worthington, a few minutes before noon, a thin, agile, good-looking woman in a pink silk shirtwaist stood in the archway between her living and dining rooms surveying the tables in both with an anxious distracted look on her face.

There were four card tables in the living room – draped with white tablecloths, set with bridge pads and boxed cards, with teacups and ashtrays and bowls of pastel mints.

The dining-room table was set for lunch, with roses and crystal and china. A buffet was laid out on a high mahogany sideboard – dainty sandwiches, ambrosia salad, cold cooked shrimp on a bed of ice, white frosted coconut cake, serrated cake cutter lying in wait – everything there but ice for the tea, and ice cream scooped for dessert.

She asked herself what she'd forgotten as she untied her apron and fluffed the sides of her hair. She'd been working since five, as usual, and she could feel perspiration gathering on her upper lip. She dabbed at it with a Kleenex, being careful not to smear her lipstick, ticking off tasks on a notepad too, on the end of the long buffet.

She'd scrubbed the kitchen floor exactly the way she did every day but Sunday, and vacuumed the downstairs even more thoroughly than usual, having dusted the house, and washed down the bathrooms, before she'd finished the food preparation she'd started the day before.

She told herself for the second time that morning that she hadn't been a scrub nurse for ten years for nothing, as she gazed at the mirror above the buffet, smoothing the delicate eyebrows, adjusting the waves with a mind of their own that were winding around toward her forehead. She could see the shine on her kitchen floor as she looked over her shoulder, and she told herself with quiet satisfaction that Ralph could operate on her kitchen table if the need ever arose.

Rolls! That's what she'd forgotten. She had to get the rolls on the cookie sheets ready to warm in the oven.

The phone rang then, as she turned toward the kitchen, and she hurried to answer it in the living room, walking silently on cream-colored carpet, straightening spoons as she passed.

'Dr Morland's residence, June Morland speaking . . . Then you're one of Beth's students . . . No, I'm sorry, she's out of town . . . She's visiting her college roommate. She didn't leave a number but she calls me every day . . .' June Morland laughed, wondering why it sounded forced, and why she felt ill at ease. 'I *suppose* that would be all right. Though I'd rather speak to Beth first . . .

'Yes, I understand that, but . . . Her roommate's name is Ginnie Weiland. Her father's name is Michael . . . Wheaton, Illinois . . . But I'd prefer to give her the message first . . .

'Black Mountain? No. But it's interesting you'd ask that. I had a call this morning from a friend of ours who lives there. She thought she'd seen Beth at a vegetable stand where the . . . No, it was just mistaken identity. Estelle Stewart is one of those wonderful Southern women who love to entertain, and I think she was so hoping . . . Even if Beth *were* there, there's no phone at the cabin. I'll make sure to tell her to call you the next time she phones . . .

'I don't feel right giving you directions, not when I haven't spoken to her . . . I do understand that, but . . . Well. It's not actually too complicated, if you come in from Asheville.' June

Morland gave her directions, but still felt uncomfortable about it. 'I really would prefer that you wait until . . . I'm sorry, I have to go. Company has arrived.'

It was almost five when Ben braked at the light on Main Street in Hillsdale next to Alderton's main campus. The university was on his right, the post office was on his left, and past that, just across the side street, the Coffee Cup, Hillsdale's one good diner, took up the whole corner.

He was thinking about picking up a couple of cheeseburgers to take with him to Richard's, when he laughed, and blamed the concussion. Richard West had more spectacular food in his house at any given moment than anyone else he'd ever met.

Ben realized too, as soon as he'd laughed, that his head hadn't hurt since he'd left Cedar Falls. And he smiled at a woman on the street, who smiled back looking pleased, before she had time to get embarrassed.

When he pulled into Richard's drive, the screen door to the small white house slapped open against the front wall and a deep booming voice said, 'Ben! What have you discovered?' Richard filled the doorway, his thin auburn hair lifting softly in the breeze, his large round face turning pink with excitement as he worked at lighting his pipe.

'Settle down, Richard, I'll tell you in a minute. I've got a few things to bring in from the car.'

'I shall help, of course. You know me, the soul of perpetual usefulness.'

'True. Though thousands would disagree.'

'Do I deserve your ignoble asides? I, who feed you, and assist your investigations?'

'Maybe not. Although a case could be—'

'I do *so* wish for a code to sink my teeth into.' Richard was beaming, smoke billowing around his head, as he rushed out toward the car. 'My solar plexus is all aflutter with preliminary anticipation.'

'What's got you so—?'

'Carl's number strings. The duplicated books. They've begun to raise my hopes. They're exactly the sort of harbingers one might expect.'

'We don't even know if there's a—'

'It's been twelve years, Ben, *twelve* years this very month since I've undertaken any sort of cryptological work. I've been reduced to joining Puzzlers of America out of sheer desperation.'

'I don't think I've ever heard of it.'

'It's a national organization.'

'Yeah, well, *that* I figured out.'

'Did you?' Richard was watching Ben remove the spare tire cover while puffing happily on his pipe. 'It caters to those who enjoy crossword puzzles and brain-teasers of every type. Any sort of problem, really, based on vocabulary and syntax. Meetings are said to be extremely lively, and competitions abound. I shall attend my first meeting in September. Have you eaten?'

'No, I—'

'Sustenance, then, before we work. *I* shall manage the typewriter. You retrieve the rest and close the trunk.' Richard glowed with enthusiasm as he turned around toward his door.

'Were you bossy as a little kid?'

Richard's head craned toward Ben, and the look on his face was abject, a small boy's sudden horror at having kicked a favorite dog. 'Am I being dictatorial again? I simply don't seem to notice.'

'I'm just teasing you. I don't let you go too far. But I'd hate to see what would happen to somebody weak-kneed and indecisive who couldn't speak up for themselves.'

'Ah. Well, such a one as you describe might harbor resentment. Hidden, deep-seated, violent resentment. I might be strangled in my bed!'

'Hopefully not, though you never know.' Ben smiled.

And Richard laughed. Before he said, 'Let's put these on the living-room desk.'

'You looked at the lecture notes while I cooked, and they appeared to be perfectly normal?'

'Yes, the carbon copy too.'

'I see nothing whatever on the onion-skin paper. No invisible writing. No indication of—'

'Richard, we've hardly started. I've only gotten to the thirteenth sheet of bond.'

Richard was lying in his worn leather dentist chair, the box of onion skin settled on his chest, examining each sheet under the hundred-watt bulb of the floor lamp he'd bent above his head. 'By that you imply that my own impatience has—'

'Just a thought, just a wild guess, but why don't we both look at sheet 43 in our stacks of paper? If you're right, and 43–24–4 means page 43, line 24, word 4, referring to the *Ivan Ilyich*, maybe he wrote instructions, or whatever he's trying to say to us, on sheet 43 of the typing paper too. Maybe he'd do it to be consistent and help us save time. If we find anything, then we back up from there and check the earlier pages.'

'Perhaps. It would not be normal procedure. Though I suppose we could certainly *try* that.' Richard climbed out of his chair, and set his box of paper on the opposite end of the long oak desk from where Ben sat with the typing paper. They were both silent, counting pages, while Vivaldi's *Gloria* played in the background on Richard's newest hi-fi, the last in a long line of state-of-the-art improvements – the one indulgence, after food and books, on which he spent money.

'So,' Ben said. 'Sheet 43. Let's see what we can find.' He held it up to the old pharmacy lamp Richard used as a desk lamp, and began to examine the front. 'Richard . . . look at this. Do you see anything? Or am I imagining it? Sort of a puckering on the paper in a couple of places, as though it'd been wet and then dried?'

Richard shot along the length of the desk, faster than one as tall and heavy as he might be expected to, and ripped the page of typing paper out of Ben's hand. 'My! . . . Yes! Benjamin, yes, very faint, as you would expect, very faint indeed, but . . . I shall light a second candle.'

It was a pillar candle, made of beeswax, which burned cleaner than many, and Richard held the sheet a few inches above the two flames, sweeping it back and forth. 'No. Nothing. Heat isn't doing a thing. I could try an iron, but if the candle won't do the trick, an iron won't reveal much either. It could be a chemical-reaction ink. Copper sulfate, developed by sodium iodide. Iron sulfate, developed by sodium carbonate. It could also be one of the fluorescent types revealed by ultraviolet light.'

Ben was rubbing the scar that cut across his palm, watching Richard West. 'Wasn't there something else you mentioned before, a chemical that—'

'Rhodamine B. Yes, used in dilute solution. Rhodamine B is a harmless dye, relatively easy to procure, used for all sorts of applications in medical and scientific laboratories, though its most interesting property, from our perspective at the moment, is that its presence will be revealed by exposure to ultraviolet light. There are many other substances as well that become legible under UV light, though most would be harder to procure I expect, and be somewhat more—'

'Where can we get a UV bulb? The hardware store closes at six, and it's gotta be after—'

'If I'm not very much mistaken, I have two in the bowels of the basement. One never knows when black light might come in handy.' Richard grinned over his shoulder at Ben, as he thundered down the hall toward his basement door.

Twelve

Richard shouted, 'Keep your fingers crossed!' And then looked taken aback. 'Why would I admonish you with a meaningless superstition? It may have more interesting beginnings, possibly even Christian, though . . .' Richard's mouth snapped shut as he laid the sheet of what he hoped was an encrypted message under the UV tube lamp he'd set at his end of the table he used as a desk. 'Ah!'

'Well?' Ben was at the other end watching Richard closely.

'Nothing. Drat!' Richard drummed his long banana fingers on the scarred oak tabletop, while he glared at the piece of paper. 'It doesn't respond to UV light, and I haven't the reagents one needs to reveal the chemical-reaction inks of the sort I described earlier.'

'What about something simpler, like you said before? Carl would've known we wouldn't have the sophisticated resources real labs would have. Maybe he used something we'd be able to develop more easily.'

'Heat-developed techniques would be the simplest. Lemon juice, vinegar, milk, substances of that sort, which is why we began with those. We *could* try the oven, I suppose. That might give a better result than we managed with the candle. That's all I can think of to do tonight.'

It was fifteen minutes later when Richard, using kitchen tongs, pulled sheet 43 from the box of bond out of his smaller oven. 'Ben!'

Ben was coming through the kitchen door carrying the box of onion-skin paper, saying, 'I don't think there's anything on this, though you may want to check it again.'

'The oven's done the trick! The paper's turned slightly yellow, and there's a lighter grid made by the rods in the racks, but there is visible handwriting, a very light caramel brown. See?'

'Wait!' Ben was looking around Richard's arm, trying to read the words.

'I suspect he may have used milk. If memory serves, there are those who think it works more effectively than lemon juice.'

'There was a thermos in Carl's kitchen sink that smelled like it might've held milk. He could've taken it to write with at Cedar Falls, then rinsed it out at home. There wasn't a milk bottle at the cabin, but—'

'I've preheated both ovens. We can put several sheets on two racks in each, and hasten the developing. Depending, of course, on how much text there is. They'll have to be watched very carefully and moved from place to place on the racks. Thank God it's gibberish!'

'What?'

'Look. Nonsense!' Richard was staring at the sheet, holding it under the brass chandelier he'd hung above his center island. 'A code, Benjamin. A code to be decrypted! To have the pleasure of another is . . .' He was talking over his shoulder, carrying the sheet of spidery tan writing toward the front of the house.

'Is what?' Ben smiled at Richard's broad back. As Richard began giving orders.

'Keep the temperature at three hundred and fifty degrees. Wait two to three minutes at least to determine whether there's writing on a page, though it may take five or more to develop the text fully.'

Ben had followed Richard into the living room in time to see him pull a legal pad from his desk drawer and sink into the wooden chair he'd found outside a warehouse.

Ben asked how he thought Carl had done it. 'Did he type this out at the cabin, whatever it is he's written to us, then copy it out by hand with invisible ink, and burn the typescript in the fireplace? He wouldn't have wanted it typed out ahead of time in case it fell into the wrong hands. And he wouldn't want it left around for anyone else to read.'

Richard said, 'That's intuitively obvious,' then reached for a well-chewed pencil.

'I'm still not back to normal, you know.'

'Yes, I can see that.'

'So how will you start?'

'I shall copy the letter strings on to another sheet of paper, then begin looking for patterns.'

'The old "E is the most common letter"? So if you see a lot of—'

'Something of the sort. Bring me whatever else develops as speedily as you can.'

There were seven more handwritten pages, 44 through 50. Those were followed by fifteen more that revealed nothing whatever when exposed to heat in the oven.

Ben had no intention of overlooking anything, so he went on anyway, arranging sheets of paper on the four metal racks – and was rewarded eventually when another twenty-eight pages of gibberish appeared starting on page 64 in a stack of a hundred and one.

He could fit six pages on every rack, and with two racks in two ovens, it didn't take terribly long. He carried them to Richard as soon as they developed, then rushed back so nothing burned.

Richard had been mumbling to himself earlier, but when Ben brought in the last batch, Richard sneezed three times, the explosions sharp as rifle shots in that silent house. 'Dratted allergies. I'm not bothered on the coasts. Wind off the oceans tends to blow the . . . Oh. Too bad.'

'What?'

'It's child's play. The code on the first seven pages couldn't be simpler, and I don't mind telling you, it comes as a great disappointment. Once one has tackled really difficult work which affects the outcome of a desperate war, racing daily against time—'

'Richard—'

'You *do* know the difference between a code-breaker and a book-breaker?'

'Well, a code-breaker—'

'A book-breaker breaks the language strings. A code-breaker works with the numbers. The distribution of—'

'Would you please get to the—'

'I was only one of the plodders slogging away on the Red Key, though that was still—'

'The Red Key was the—'

'The particular German Enigma code that communicated solely with the Luftwaffe. Each arm of the military had its own code. Even so, they did need my sort as well as the geniuses. In addition, of course, to the mathematicians, Turing and the rest of them. He was absolutely brilliant. In a league of his own, I gather, though I thought him a rather sad man. Terribly unkempt. Filth under his fingernails, that sort of thing. Of course, finding the navy Enigma machine—'

'*We're* racing against time too, you know.'

'Are we? The stakes are appreciably lower.' Richard was grinning at his papers, wiggling his eyebrows like Groucho Marx.

Ben smiled as he threw an eraser so it bounced off Richard's arm. 'The point isn't to amuse you, and the stakes aren't inconsiderable.'

'No?' Richard looked up and laughed. 'You should be able to manage the first seven pages, leaving me free to tackle the twenty-eight.'

'You'll have to tell me what to do.'

'Well, if you'll look at what I've done, you'll see that the string of numbers is indeed the key to a one-time book code, just as one might've suspected. Page forty-three of *The Death of Ivan Ilyich*, in this particular edition, line twenty-four, word four, turns out to be the word "not". That indicates to us that "n" is to be substituted for "a" in the alphabet.'

'So you wrote out the alphabet, showing that "a" is equal to "n", "b" is equal to "o", "c" to "p" and so on. And then when you got to "n" and ran out of letters—'

'"N" became equal to "a", right on to "z", which therefore equaled "m". You'll also notice that the coded message is divided into five letter strings, arbitrarily breaking up the actual length of the English words in the original text. Yes?'

Ben had time to look at the first three lines, before Richard grabbed the paper.

qrneq eernf rnflb hxabj
vsvas npglb hnere rnqva
tguvf yrggr . . .

'Which means,' said Ben, 'that even though it's a simple code, if someone had stolen the letter with the list of numbers that gives the key, but didn't have the book, they couldn't have decoded this.'

'Precisely.'

'Or if they'd gotten *Ivan Ilyich* without the letter I got, they couldn't have decrypted it.'

'You'd have the list of route numbers in *Ivan Ilyich*, which would confuse you if you had the book, and were expecting a one-time book code, but not the information you needed.' Richard had already pulled out his pipe and was fumbling around for a match.

'So Carl set it up well.'

'He did. He increased the chances of leading *you* off in the right direction by spreading the information between the two of us, while making it hard for anyone else to amass what was needed, once Carl had removed his papers to a safe and distant location. I never imagined him as a book-breaker, but now that I think of it, his linguistic abilities were just the sort required. We *will* have to make copies of both Carl's documents. The developed ink will fade rather quickly, and working with more robust script will save time in the end. Are you ready to proceed?'

Ben had taken the first page from Richard and already started to work.

A little over an hour later, Ben had finished decoding the shorter message, the seven pages in large painstakingly handwritten script, and read it out loud to Richard, who'd finished copying the longer document, and begun to look at the code.

Wednesday, 12 June, 1957

Dear Ben,

As you know, if, in fact, you are reading this letter, I have gone to great lengths to keep the accompanying information from falling into the wrong hands. I am depending on you and Dr West to uncover and decrypt these pages.

There is much you must know and little time to communicate. I am passing on information to you in this, and in the longer document, which I swore when in the US military I would never reveal. Circumstances have led me to believe that it is now my duty to do so, after having had you well vetted by my former colleagues in army intelligence and the FBI, as well as what was once

OSS. It is a tack I chose to take after having learned from Dr West of your activities during the war.

I would not choose to reveal this information if I were not (1) convinced of the ethical necessity of bringing a traitor and murderer to justice while the opportunity to do so exists, and, (2) aware of the danger I now face in this attempt.

He is beyond the power of due process. The legal system in this country (for many complicated and con-voluted reasons, including policy decisions made by those more elevated than you or I would ever aspire to be) cannot prosecute him as he deserves.

During, and after, the Second World War, I was involved in decrypting a Soviet military/embassy/espionage code under the auspices of the US Army Special Branch, which was then a part of the War Department's Military Intelligence Division. Versions of the code were used by the Soviet army, navy and 'diplomatic corps', a branch you may rightly take to mean a KGB-operated espionage network working in, and against, the United States, as well as Great Britain.

I am aware that the self-aggrandizing behavior and the many unsubstantiated claims of Sen. Joseph McCarthy might make the statements I have made above, and those I shall make shortly, look suspect to any without the information to which I have long been privy. I assure you that incontrovertible evidence exists for the claims I shall make. Sen. McCarthy and the investigative committees of Congress were intentionally kept un-informed, as they still are today.

The Soviet espionage network I referred to above worked hand in hand during the nineteen-thirties and forties with the American Communist Party, largely directing the operations thereof. I can assure you that such was the case even when the Soviets were our allies during the Second World War.

Surprising as it may seem, the Soviets communicated with their agents in America by way of telegrams, even though they knew very well that wartime telegrams were censored. They did so because they were thoroughly convinced their code was undecipherable, and telegrams were far less expensive than all other means of swift, long-distance communication.

The code was virtually an unbreakable one based on one-time code pads using random-number sets. However, for reasons no one understands (perhaps because of the difficulty the Soviets have generally had managing the production of materials of every sort), they ran short of pads in 1943 and chose to reprint and reuse one pad for a period of several months. This enabled American code-breakers in the course of the next few years to decrypt many of the telegraphic communications that were written during that specific period – that period alone.

The US and Britain, working in concert, came to call the encryption 'the Venona code', selecting the term at random; a code you will find described in some detail in the accompanying encrypted document.

An American citizen who was a Soviet agent first revealed to the Soviets in late 1947 that America and Britain had recently begun to break the code, thereby leading the Soviets to abandon Venona altogether as soon as was practicable. (Since only the messages from '43 were breakable, they did not need to change the code overnight.) This same agent also informed the Soviets, probably in '47, that many of their conventional lower-echelon military book codes used in radio transmission had been broken by us as well. If he had not done the latter, we would have learned of Stalin's massive arma-ment of China and North Korea, as well as their secret plan to invade South Korea in time to foil their surprise attack and possibly prevent the war. The agent respon-sible for those leaks to the Soviets is now here in Columbus. Whether or not he is still an active agent I have no way of knowing.

I have made it my business, for personal reasons as well as public, to attempt to uncover his whereabouts since 1949, and have recently been rewarded for my efforts. I do not believe he is yet aware that I am here. But I can assure you, Dr Reese, that a meeting will shortly take place.

I am placing in your hands the means of discovering the damage he and his confederates have done individual citizens, as well as American society – damage the US has not made public for a host of security and political reasons. Our Venona work still goes on – the decrypting of those intercepts from 1943 when the one-time code was reused daily – which has ferreted out the identities of, as well as some of the actions taken by, more than three hundred Soviet agents in the US during the thirties and forties, several of whom were in top positions within the Roosevelt administrations (Harry Dexter White, Laughlin Currie, Alger Hiss, Laurence Duggan, to name only a few).

A promise was made by J. Edgar Hoover when the Venona decryption project began to bear fruit, that information gathered from the decryptions would not be used to prosecute those incriminated. With very few exceptions, those guilty of spying against us (unless significant non-circumstantial evidence unrelated to Venona existed that would be conclusive in a court of law) have had to be left unexposed and unpunished in order to preserve the secrets of our decryptions concerning KGB agents and espionage against us. (Soviet agents have code names, and many agents have yet to be identified, since external corroborating evidence is almost always required. Many text strings have yet to be broken, and we do not want the Soviets to learn what we know, and what we don't, now, or in the future.) The decision not to expose and prosecute hundreds of internal agents, both foreign and domestic, sticks in the craw of many of us who have seen at close hand the damage they have done; damage that includes the passing on of our atomic energy work, enabling the Soviets to develop an atomic bomb years earlier than they otherwise would have.

I have never been trained in, nor involved with, US counter-espionage of any sort. I was merely a book-breaker. I am now nothing more than the language professor I am seen to be. But I have witnessed more than I can overlook. I find myself under moral compunction. If I am killed, or cannot bring William Weisberg to justice, please take on the work yourself.

He is now using the assumed name of Richard Samson (which I determined by phoning the realty company from which he rents his house in Worthington). I know it may seem an impertinence for me to involve you in such a task and ask you to face danger of any sort, but it is a task worthy of anyone's time and effort.

I am including Dr West in the undertaking because of his experience as a book-breaker who worked at Bletchley Park. The code I have used is simplicity itself for someone of his experience, but time is of the essence.

Sylvia Todd is acquainted with Weisberg. He may well place pressure upon her. She is the reason he has come to Columbus, and is in a vulnerable position. You may discuss my knowledge of Weisberg with her. She does not know of Venona, and must not be told. She worked as a secretary at Arlington Hall (where the Venona work was done), but left Arlington in 1945 at the end of the war in Europe, after having been assigned to sections there where other 'problems' (the Japanese and German codes) were worked on during the War.

She never met me at Arlington Hall. Her closest friend did, and has helped me follow Sylvia across the country as she fled from Weisberg. Sylvia Todd is not her real name.

Sylvia may not wish to cooperate for reasons of her own. She may also need protection, though she has long protected herself, and I have some confidence she will do so fairly effectively still.

I hasten to assure you again that I am in no way a trained intelligence operative. I am well aware that I am 'in over my head'. Your background will serve you better with Weisberg than mine serves me. I was sent to work on the codes immediately after basic training, and had no combat experience.

If you are reading this, I haven't survived my confrontation with Weisberg. You, therefore, need to be aware that I have told him that the search for him will not end with me. I will have told him that I have passed on evidence which proves his actions as an enemy agent and implicates him in a murder that took place in 1947. I will not identify you, but I will have told him that the person to whom I've given this information is far more capable than I, and will not let the matter rest. You must,

therefore, take precautions, Dr Reese. Do not under-
estimate Weisberg. He became an American citizen, and
was in the American military, though never in combat
as far as I know. There is some reason to believe he may
have been trained as an agent within the Soviet Union,
though that's unsubstantiated. He will be desperate to
retrieve the photographs and other materials I have
preserved for you.

　　May fortune smile upon your efforts.

　　Carl Walker

Ben looked at Richard.

Richard looked at Ben.

Ben shook his head, and said, 'What's he gotten us into?'

'Us?' Richard was lighting his pipe, his eyebrows raised
innocently. 'The letter's addressed to you.'

'Very funny, Richard. What photographs?'

'Yes. Interesting man, Carl Walker.'

'Though I may know where to look. Remember the message
in *Anna Karenina*?'

'Remind me.'

'I think this is verbatim. "Ben. S.W. house. Structure.
G.M.H. Oxford. Cloth. Stipple. Jessie would understand. Vice
isn't always bad. Carl." '

'And you have a glimmering of what that could mean?'

'Maybe. You should too.'

'Should I?'

Ben laughed and said, 'You're the English professor.'

'And?'

'Who were Jessie's favorite poets?"

'Shakespeare. Rilke. T. S. Eliot. There was another too.'

'G.M.H. Gerard Manley Hopkins. The poet who went to
Oxford. Who became a priest. A man of the "cloth". Who
wrote a poem that starts, "Glory be to God for dappled things
– For skies of couple-colour as a brinded cow; For rose moles
all in *stipple* upon trout that swim." Remember that?'

'*I* have never taught poetry, as you'll recall, but yes, vaguely.
What are the implications?'

'Well, I think Carl's talking about something at his house.
South-west of his house there's a garage. The "structure" he
could be referring to. I'm hoping the references to "stipple"

and "vice" will become obvious when I look for them. Though I do have an idea about both.'

'Do you? Then I conclude your mind's coming back to you. Despite my jibe at you earlier.'

'Some of it. Yes. For which I'm profoundly grateful.' Ben yawned and rubbed his eyes. 'So why hasn't this guy Weisberg come after me again?'

'*That* I couldn't say.'

'We know from Carl's letter that he's told Weisberg he's passed the information on to someone who'll be prepared to pursue it. Weisberg must've figured out I'm as good a choice as any for the person Carl would've given it to. He searched my house. He's seen my army papers. He's—'

'That may be why he hasn't. Wouldn't he prefer a less experienced opponent?'

'Yeah, but he must've talked to professors at OSU, to ask about Carl's friends. He's questioned Beth. He may've talked to Sylvia, which is probably what drove her out of town. He'll know Carl didn't have a lot of friends to choose from. He'll try to get whatever it is Carl had on him, that's for sure, and I suspect he'll conclude it's probably me. Which makes me wish I knew a lot more about him.'

'He may not approach you directly. He might exert indirect pressure.'

'That's why I wanted Beth out of town, once the tall guy in the park, whom I assume is probably this Weisberg person, knew who she was.'

'When is she to call in next?'

'Tonight, to talk to Bobby. But what we need to do next is decode the other document.'

'At least one good thing's come out of this.' Richard smiled puckishly as he sucked on a cold pipe.

'Yes?'

'You've been out of your house more in the last four days than you have in the last three months, and you haven't been as morose. I don't intend that as a criticism. Certainly not! How could I? And yet, I do believe it's done you good to have had a compelling and worthwhile project to take on as a distraction.'

Ben didn't say anything, but he looked at Richard as though it might not be a bad idea for him to shut his mouth.

'That's not the form in which I should have expressed it. You know my methods. Excessively blunt and heavy handed. I'm simply pleased that valuable work needs to be done to help other people, and you've taken it on.'

When Ben still didn't answer, Richard took his pipe out of his mouth and looked at him almost meekly, the feisty, teasing expression on his face bleeding away in uneasiness.

'I know what you mean, Richard, but let's not beat it into the ground. If Weisberg tries to get into my house he's not going to like what he finds.'

'No?'

'No. Because Vernon's granddaddy built the house with doors that open out.'

'The import of that is what?'

Ben told him.

And Richard laughed. 'Are they loaded?'

'What do you think?'

'With you I couldn't say.'

'True.' Ben grinned, and then yawned again, before he rubbed his eyes.

'You've left cracks he can peer through?'

'Yep, that looks accidental. Are you ready? Shall we get to work and get this done?'

'The second document will take considerably more time. It's much longer, and a far more complicated code, for which I'm exceedingly thankful, by the way. It's based on the same book-code substitution, "n" for "a" and the rest of it, but additional safeguards have been added, which I won't take time to explain. You're welcome to stay here in the spare room, if you're too tired to drive home by the time we've finished.'

Richard was standing by the front window stretching his arms out to the side as though his shoulders ached. 'There's a car down the street that's been parked there for several minutes. Someone is sitting on the driver's side, though . . . No, now it's moving off. Turning around in Fenton's drive and heading the other way.'

'I hate to do this to you, Richard, but I need to lie down for half an hour. You promise to wake me up?'

'No, I shall let you sleep.'

'You *have* to wake me up. There're things I've got to do tonight.'

'Very well, Benjamin, if you insist. Have I told you about the turquoise Chevrolet that was seen at the crime site?'

'No!'

'Chester Hansen mentioned it to me this afternoon. The father of one of the boys who found the body remembered seeing a new turquoise Chevy drive by slowly on Saturday morning when he was working in a field that overlooks the road.'

'What did the police make of that?'

'Chester didn't say.'

'Rats.'

'Pardon me—'

'I know I've seen a Chevy like that somewhere in the last few days, and I can't remember where.'

'I know something else you don't, as well.' Richard was grinning, waiting for Ben to beg.

'Would you mind speeding it up here, Richard? I think you could say I've got a right to know.'

'The police noticed marks on Carl's wrists, and found bark embedded under his nails, and though I haven't been given any further particulars, Chester did leave me with the impression that the police are beginning to consider murder a possibility.'

William Weisberg, in a dark hooded jacket and black pants, stepped out of the west woods heading for Vernon's barn, where he walked quickly around the back corner toward the rear of Ben's house.

There were lights on inside the house, faint lines of low light just visible inside the windows behind some sort of obstruction. Curtains, perhaps, or window shades, or some type of blinds.

He walked to the mudroom wing first, and found the door locked. The window was latched too, and there were heavy wooden shutters fastened across the inside.

There was a gap between two louvers, a crack just wide enough for him to see inside. And the second he'd leaned over and looked through the gap, he stepped away from the glass.

A shotgun was pointed at the mudroom door – a big-bore over-under braced between two wooden chairs, with a wire running from the trigger around the back of the chair's corner post, fastened tight to the doorknob.

If he'd picked the lock and opened the door, which opened out like a public building's, he would've been gut-shot before he could blink.

He ran next to the back porch, where (standing up on the porch chair) he could just see enough through a gap at the side of one broken louver to make out another shot gun – a side-by-side, wired the same way, aimed at the kitchen door.

There was less of a crack in the louvers inside the window on the front porch, but by crouching and leaning he still saw a rifle, a .30-06 it looked like, propped, wired and pointed straight at the front door.

He heard a car driving up the drive, while he looked at his watch and considered what to do. And it made him sprint around the house toward the back of the barn.

A medium-sized, gray-haired man in a black shirt and dark jacket, carrying a stack of five or six books, walked up to Ben's front porch and knocked on the door. He waited, and knocked again. Then sat in one of the bent-twig chairs on the narrow plain-pillared porch.

He ripped a page from a small spiral pad he'd pulled from a pocket of his sport coat, then stared across the pasture for a minute before he started writing.

When he'd finished, he slipped the note in the top book of the stack he'd set on the table so half the paper could be seen.

It was still twilight, a deep summer half-light, muggy and close and beginning to be buggy, bringing bats out of the woods, and flushing a flock of lightning bugs, one at a time to begin with, that floated up from the fields. They blinked on and off above the flowering alfalfa like tiny yellow lamps. And the man walked over and leaned on the pasture fence, watching the fireflies, talking to the sheep – the two who were standing the closest, who considered him with very little interest other than wary concern.

He was wearing a clerical collar, and he ran his index finger back and forth inside it as though it were hot and uncomfortable. Then he hummed something quietly to himself and walked back to the car he'd parked in front of Vernon's barn.

After the swish and crunch of gravel had faded off in the distance, there was silence for a minute, except for the bats and the chatter of birds settling down for the night, before

Weisberg came out from behind the barn and ran to Ben's front porch.

He picked up the books and read the note, and dropped them back on the table, then stood still beside the door, leaning against the clapboard.

There wasn't much time before he had to call the actress. But if he could stand off to the side and pick the lock at arm's length (which wasn't an inconsiderable 'if'), he should be able to turn the bar-shaped door handle and push the door out with something from the barn (a hoe, a pitchfork, a shovel) – letting the rifle round fire safely so he could search the house.

Someone still might come to check on Reese, though. Hills and woods screened most of the views, and neighbors might be closer than they seemed.

It wasn't hunting season, so a shot might draw attention. Though this was the middle of nowhere, and farmers probably had to shoot varmints at all times of the year. Weisberg had lived in cities all his life, and wasn't sure what to expect.

But he knew he *had* to get into the house – and that *if* Carl's evidence was there, he'd be able to find it. If Reese had hidden it in his library archives, Reese would have to be forced to retrieve it, and that wouldn't be easy.

He could've hidden Carl's materials in the barn too, and searching that would take more time than Weisberg had then. He needed to phone the girl soon. And Reese might be home any minute. There was no reason to think he'd stay at the fat guy's all night.

Windows were his best bet. And he grabbed the flashlight from his coat, and hurried around the house, testing one locked window after another. Only to find that the louvered wooden shutters had been bound shut with heavy wire, in addition to the inside catches.

He couldn't see the upstairs windows well – the two in the front, the two in the back, the ones that were large enough to climb through. He could see there were louvered shutters, but not whether they'd been locked and wired.

If the guns were loaded, Reese had to get in some way, and the upper back windows were the place to start, since they weren't visible from the drive *or* the barn.

Weisberg needed a ladder. And the barn made the most sense.

If it hadn't been for the do-gooder with the books I could've been in the house by now, with the list and photos in my hands.

At least watching the friend's house had paid off. And Weisberg smiled at the stupidity of women. Secretaries. Librarians. College cleaners. Volunteering every sort of information if you looked benign and smiled.

The fundamental decision he'd reached already made what to do next largely procedural. He wasn't prepared to meet Reese face to face. But when the time came, it would be on his own terms. Benjamin Reese wouldn't walk away whole, and Weisberg would have what he came for.

Weisberg froze by the mudroom window on his way to the barn's side door. He could hear another car coming. And he swore lengthily, under his breath, as he ran to the rear of the barn.

He edged along its back wall, then stopped at the northwest corner, where he glanced quickly around it once – in time to see a beat-up pick-up slide to a stop in the gravel.

He ducked his head back and listened – as the double doors were rolled open and hard-soled shoes hit stone. A light came on inside the barn, and he could hear something being dragged across the floor and thrown on to the truck bed.

There were many more trips to and from the barn, many more bags of something solid landing in the back of the truck, while two men talked tediously about baseball, then switched, finally, to the Salk shot for polio coming out that fall.

The light that slipped through the cracks in the siding was snuffed out suddenly. And the sound of the barn doors sliding shut was followed by the pick-up truck starting down the lane.

Weisberg looked at his watch and cursed in four languages, before he started running toward the overgrown track in the west woods where he'd left his car.

It was nine-twenty already. And he had to get back to call the actress before ten thirty.

Depending on what she's learned, I have to be ready to leave tonight, now that Susannah's gone. I don't have any other choice now, through no fault of my own.

When Ben left Richard's, he drove to Alderton's library and let himself in by the back door. He used the school's first

Xerox machine, just installed the first week of June, to make copies of the coded documents and the two decryptions.

He took the originals to the muniment room in the Administration Building, where the university's founding documents had been kept for a hundred years. He squirreled them away where no one could find them, in the midst of board notes and legal documents, since he, as Alderton's long-time archivist, had the only key.

It was after eleven thirty when he parked on a side street two blocks from Carl's house, and started sidling, quietly and carefully, through one dark patch to the next – from the shadows of houses to the shadows of shrubs, from hedges to high trees – till he'd woven his way into Carl's backyard. There he stood, watching and listening, his back against the wall of the house, his breathing slow and steady.

When he was sure he saw what there was to see, he slipped across to the garage and unlocked the small side door. He closed it silently behind him, then felt his way toward the workbench on the right-hand wall.

He took out a pencil-sized flashlight when he'd reached the far end, where the vise was bolted to the bench, keeping his body between the light and the small-pane window.

It was a large, heavy cast-iron vise, and he studied the outside and saw nothing that helped. He turned the long metal handle, feeling the weight and the smoothness of the rod, as it spread the tightly clamped jaws.

He couldn't see anything on either jaw plate, and he carefully worked his fingers across both – till he felt a slick patch on the iron surface that faced the back of the bench.

Black electrician's tape was stuck across something, and Ben pried the tape from the plate. A small brass key was stuck to the sticky side, the kind that fits a jewelry box, or small metal cash box. He peeled it off and slipped it in his shirt pocket, buttoning the flap across it under the black hooded sweatshirt he'd grabbed from a hook in his office.

He found a shovel, and turned off the flashlight. Then walked outside, and around the garage, till he stood in the center of the overgrown garden that stretched the length of the back.

He walked first to the bird bath that was leaning sideways in the middle, the one with the concrete fish tail sculpted on the flat round dish so it'd look as though the fish were diving when the saucer was full of water.

He examined it in a patch of filtered moonlight that threaded down through the branches of the oak tree – then took the top off of the pedestal base and set them both on the lawn.

He began digging where the bird bath had stood.

And ten minutes later hit something metallic.

He went to work with his hands.

But only found the corner of a box when he was ready to give up and go back to the shovel – a small green cash box that Carl Walker's key unlocked.

It held a packet of papers and photos, wrapped together in cloth, covered in sheets of plastic – several layers taped together, one on top of the other.

Thirteen

B en got home from Carl's a few minutes before two that morning, and was halfway to the mudroom before he remembered the extension ladder he should've gotten from the barn.

He laid it down near the mudroom step, then checked the windows and doors.

He'd sprinkled talcum powder on the porches, and he smiled to himself when he saw the footprints. Large feet, doing back-and-forth debating. Two sets of shoes on the front porch, one that belonged to David Marshall, based on the note he'd left with his books.

Ben leaned the ladder against the back of the house, cloth-wrapped feet set on flagstone to keep from leaving unintended information, and went in through the guest-room window – the one he hadn't locked, with louvers he hadn't latched.

He pulled the ladder up and locked the window, yawning as he started down the stairs, rubbing his left temple as he walked to the half-lit kitchen.

He poured himself a large glass of water and drank it in the rocking chair as he reopened the buried packet, and began reading the letters Carl had included with the photos.

One was a note written to Carl in Russian on a small sheet of tissue-thin paper in a hand Ben hadn't seen before. It was signed by Miriam Gold, and (according to the translation Carl had written on a sheet of plain paper) it appeared to be a list, written in short synoptic phrases, of acts taken by Weisberg that she herself had witnessed, as well as an explanation of who was in the photos and what she thought they meant. There was a longer letter, also in her hand in Russian, on both sides of the same tissuey paper, with more writing, perpendicular to the rest, to fit more words per page.

There was a note to Ben too, written by Carl, explaining that Miriam had left the letters with the photographs in a box of books by Carl's apartment door hours before she was pushed from her third-floor window in December of 1947. She'd hidden the writings, the negatives, and five small photographs – black-and-white, two inches by three – between the back lining paper and the hardback cover of the *Anna Karenina* Carl had sent Ben. The end paper had been glued with some sort of cement that would allow the sheet to be peeled back easily to get at the photos inside.

On the night Miriam died, Carl's neighbor in Arlington, Virginia had heard Carl's phone ring several times between seven and eight, and it was Carl's opinion that Miriam had been calling to explain where he'd find the photographs and what they were of. He believed she'd known her life was in danger, and was trying to give him the evidence of Weisberg's guilt so Carl could help stop Weisberg, even if she were killed. There were references in her note to other copies she'd made of the photographs, but they'd never surfaced, and Carl believed Weisberg had found and destroyed them.

Until that spring, Carl hadn't noticed anything unusual in the back of *Anna Karenina*, though he'd glanced through it, along with the many other books she'd left the night she died. The note she'd pushed under his door had said she was moving to a smaller apartment and needed to give away some of her books. It was only this past May, when he'd been rereading *Anna Karenina* in Russian, and had taken down Miriam's English translation to check that particular translator's choices, that he'd noticed the thicker back cover and found a corner of the lining paper curling away from the edge.

What he'd found under it gave him the proof of Weisberg's espionage he'd been looking for for years. It made Carl even more determined to make Weisberg pay for what he'd done. His betrayal of Venona at the very least, since he couldn't prove he'd murdered Miriam.

Ben laid Carl's letter down and looked at the photographs under the floor lamp by the rocker, referring to Miriam's list to understand what he saw. The photos were in reasonably good shape, though dry and cracked with age. Two were perfectly photographed, one was underexposed, two others were overexposed, bleached by bright sun.

One of the overexposed was of a large man in an overcoat sitting on a park bench laying an envelope on the bench between him and a smaller man. Both of them were wearing hats – the smaller man a homburg, the taller a hat with a wider brim. Neither was looking at the other. They were staring away in different directions as though they were nothing but strangers. The larger was William Weisberg, according to Miriam's note, and the smaller was Yuri Bruslov, a long-time Soviet agent. Carl's note identified Bruslov as Weisberg's contact later too, in southern California where Weisberg was finally implicated under another name for passing information to the Soviets from an engineer in an aeronautics firm working on military jets.

The next photograph was of the same two, Bruslov sliding a second envelope across the bench, a darker envelope that was also smaller, both the men still looking away, though Weisberg seemed to be talking. The clothes looked like the forties, especially the coat and shoes of a woman walking away in the distance.

Miriam's note said she thought Weisberg had worked for money (the contents of that envelope, she believed), as well as ideological reasons, unlike most of the American agents in the thirties and forties who'd worked for political ends alone.

The third photograph was of Weisberg again, slipping something under a garbage can in what looked like an alley between two brick buildings. It was harder to make out. The scene was darker, as though the picture had been taken after dusk, or early in the morning, when available light was limited to a street light several feet off.

The next to the last photograph was of Weisberg on a street corner climbing through the passenger door of a dark Packard sedan driven by a man identified by Miriam as an underling who worked for Anatoly Gromov at the Soviet embassy.

The last shot was different. It was a handwritten series of Russian words that, according to Miriam, were Russian names written in Weisberg's handwriting, for five high-grade machine ciphers that had been solved at Arlington Hall and at the navy's equivalent, the Signals Intelligence Service on Nebraska

Avenue. Those words told the Soviets which of their ciphers had been broken, and needed to be replaced.

Weisberg fitted the description Ben had been given by Bobby, and Carl's neighbor, too. The size matched the man who talked to Beth in the park, though her description wasn't as helpful, because of the hat and dark glasses.

Still, progress was being made. And he told himself not to make prints that night. That he needed to get some sleep. The headache was back. And a slow, dull, listless fogginess that made it hard to concentrate.

Ben put the photos and letters in his bookshelf safe.

Crawled into bed five minutes later.

Set the alarm for five thirty.

And slept long enough to turn it off.

He made toast with peanut butter and a bowl of strawberries, and took them, with a mug of coffee, into his study, in order to type a synopsis of what they'd learned from Carl's longer message (the one in the harder code), as well as Miriam's notes with the photos, and Carl's accompanying letter.

Ben had too many other things he needed to do that day to worry about organizing the synopsis perfectly. So he sipped coffee, finished his toast, and popped strawberries in his mouth, while he punched the worn keys of his old Smith-Corona.

- When Carl worked on book-breaking on the Venona-coded telegrams starting in '42, Miriam Gold, a linguist and gifted thinker, was secretary/assistant to Carter Clarke, the head of the Army Signals group in charge of all the code-breaking being done at Arlington Hall in Arlington, Virginia.
- Miriam typed up the decrypted Venona messages for Carter Clarke, plus other decrypts from other sources. She spoke and wrote Russian, German, Italian, French, Yiddish and English, and was invaluable to him.
- Meredith Gardner, primary book-breaker (language expert, not mathematician), decrypted the first Soviet Venona message in '46 (one which indicated that the nuclear-bomb work done at Los Alamos was being leaked to the Soviets).
- William Weisberg – American army officer and linguist,

born in Russia like Miriam, worked at Arlington Hall after the war as a linguistics consultant working with several code-breaking groups, among them the Russian Program, which included all kinds of coded materials (legit diplomatic, military traffic, some police interceptions). Venona was taken out of the Russian Program after the war, but he'd be asked for help on specific phrases or syntax. His position gave some knowledge of Venona work, but wasn't privy to much that was learned. W. not assigned any one place; roamed from group to group in Arlington Hall, cultivating people with access to sensitive material, trying to get a broad perspective on all work being done. When Gardner decrypted the first important part of Venona code in Dec. '46, Weisberg was in the room, looking over his shoulder. Gardner had asked his input on Russian syntax.

- Weisberg chatted up the women who worked at Arlington Hall. Most code-breakers were women; the rank and file who scanned the thousands of coded telegrams all day long, as well as many of the higher-level book-breakers. Weisberg created opportunities to make himself charming with his 'consciously cultivated charm'.
- Weisberg arrived spring of '46, began dating Susannah Adams (Sylvia Todd today) by early fall. Susannah (Sylvia) at Arlington Hall from '43 through end of '45. Left after the end of the war to work for National Geographic. Weisberg introduced to her by friend of Susannah's at Arlington Hall named Patricia Bennett.
- By late summer of '47, Weisberg had observed the organization at Arlington, and began pursuing Miriam Gold, carefully keeping his relationship with her hidden from Susannah, and vice versa. Miriam wanted marriage, not an affair. Eventually succumbed to Weisberg's pressure. Convinced he intended to marry her and was beyond reproach of any kind.
- Fall of '47, October/November, Susannah walked into Weisberg's apartment, found him with Miriam. Told him in front of Miriam that she (Susannah) was pregnant, and warned Miriam of Weisberg's duplicity. That

if he would treat her as he had, with the promises he'd made her, yet take up with another, he'd do it to Miriam too. Told Miriam to ask herself what Weisberg was after, and had she been as scrupulous as she should be with classified information? Susannah was very beautiful. Miriam was quite plain. The point made was obvious.

- Susannah disappeared the next morning. Weisberg tried to track her (while working at Arlington 12 hours a day), but couldn't. He questioned Susannah's friend, Patricia Bennett, repeatedly, but Patricia told him nothing. She never phoned Susannah from her apartment; only received letters from Susannah at her uncle's house in Great Falls, etc. She and Susannah vigilant and clever, communicating without being traceable.
- Miriam began to be uneasy about Weisberg's interest in her work. She hinted that to Carl Walker who was deeply in love with her, and who had been courting her in a tentative way before Weisberg came on the scene. Miriam only hinted at Weisberg's activities, and wouldn't say more till she was convinced by evidence. Regard for intellectual honesty said to be her strongest trait.
- Miriam followed Weisberg out of a restaurant when he placed a call on a street payphone and overheard snatches in Russian. Conversation not incriminating. Made her uneasy because he hid it from her and lied later. Followed him another night when he used payphone in lobby of her apartment building at 3 a.m. She (in hall outside her door) again heard Russian phrases. Weisberg lied when she asked why he'd gone out. She started noticing more deliberately after that than she had before.
- Her parents were Jewish Bolsheviks who fled Russia before the Revolution. Raised her in New York City. Poor, struggling, non-practising Jews, father worked as cobbler, later started own shop, mother sewed for Jewish matrons in neighborhood. Both active in American Communist Party in NYC. Miriam observed them and their friends for years. Disturbed by differences she saw between what

they said they believed in – fairness, equality, concern for all – and what they justified (exterminations in USSR) and did themselves (treacherous and duplicitous acts she observed here).

- Studying Communist Russia on her own, reading the writings of Malcolm Muggeridge after he'd come back from Russia in '33, M. sought out refugees who'd fled Soviet Union, and saw it for what it was despite her parents perspectives, or what was written by Duranty, the New York Times' Russian correspondent, who lied deliberately about conditions there – labor camps, extermination of whole classes and populations, genocide in the Ukraine, lack of every freedom, unimaginable persecution throughout whole regime. By 1940 even Time magazine was reporting on the concentration camps, and Miriam watched her family and their comrades refuse to believe the truth, and/or justify the actions that were taken.

- With that background and perspective, Miriam is appalled by what she thinks Weisberg may be doing, acting as a Soviet agent reporting on the work at Arlington. Consequently she starts following him, and then finds list of Russian high-grade machine ciphers that had been decoded at Arlington in a coat lining and photographs the list. Sees him push papers under a garbage can in alley below her apartment at 4 a.m. (thinking she's safely asleep). She follows second time, gets a photo. Sees him pass documents on a park bench, and get paid in return. Sees him get picked up in a car driven by an embassy thug. She knows W.'s a traitor, and has to turn him in.

- M. tells Carl Walker she has something very important to tell him, but must choose meeting time carefully. M. trusted Carl and respected him. Had also seen his feelings for her and didn't want to hurt him (or so Carl believed).

- Earlier that week, M. told C. they needed to meet before the date they'd set for Friday. Sounded worried and upset the day before she died when telling him she'd get back in touch and pick an earlier time.

- M. died the next night. C. learned the following morning

that Miriam had tried to find him at his office at Arlington Hall, right after he'd left, saying she had to see him that night. Carl had gone to a lecture in DC after his afternoon meeting, but nobody at the Hall knew where. When he'd gotten home, a box of books was by his door with a note saying she was moving to a smaller apartment and cleaning out her shelves. That she'd call him later to tell him more about the books.

- Miriam died a couple of hours later. Carl never believed she'd jumped. Weisberg left Arlington Hall five days later, after police accepted suicide theory. W. claimed not at her apartment that night. Left without talking to Carter Clarke (his boss), or leaving forwarding address with police or Arlington Hall. Surfaced in California year or so later and was identified late in '48 by an American engineer in a high-security airplane manufacturer who fingered Weisberg for the FBI as the Soviet agent he'd passed information to, and was paid by for that material.

- W. refused to answer a grand-jury subpoena, and was sent to federal prison for one year for contempt of court.

- As far as anyone can prove, he's never returned. Was supposedly seen in Moscow in '51. Was reportedly seen later in Egypt by a British MI6 agent stationed in Alexandria.

- Day after Miriam died, Carl Walker told Carter Clarke, director of Arlington Hall, what Miriam had hinted to him of her concerns about Weisberg's loyalty, but as far as Carl knew, she had no real proof. Carter Clarke set an investigation going, working in conjunction with an FBI agent named Lennox, virtually the same day Weisberg left Arlington after Miriam died.

- Weisberg continued to try to find Susannah Adams before he left the country. Susannah had changed her name to Sylvia Todd, but kept in touch with Patricia Bennett. Patricia trusted Carl; knew he thought W. had killed Miriam, and wanted to help him prove it.

- Patricia never told Susannah/Sylvia she was talking to Carl because she didn't think Susannah would approve; she'd be afraid of information getting out to Weisberg. But Patricia thought Carl could help protect

Susannah by keeping an eye on her while looking out for W.

- Susannah/Sylvia hadn't known Carl at Arlington. He'd arrived in '42; she'd arrived '43. Security was very tight. They'd been in different buildings, and in different sections, and never met. The Venona Project, where Carl was, had been the highest security area at A. Hall; at a different level than any other department. ONE reason was that the USSR had been an ally late in the war, and investigating their communications was controversial with some outside Arlington.

- Susannah/Sylvia had gone to Richmond, Virginia, where she knew no one, taken an assumed name (from obituary in DC), calling herself Sylvia Todd. Took job as a waitress, became manager of the restaurant, told everyone her husband (in the army in Japan) had been killed in Jeep accident fall of '47 when she was pregnant. She stayed away from her family because that's how Weisberg could find her. She believed him to be a traitor (Patricia B.'s info regarding his departure from A. Hall, and his jail sentence in Calif.); didn't want him near her daughter, never wanted to hear from him again.

- Carl Walker would visit the places Sylvia lived (observing, never being seen, never introducing himself) – Richmond, then Middleburg, Virginia, when she moved there to manage the Middleburg Inn. When her mother died, she inherited money under her assumed name, and decided to buy an inn. She was from Ohio, and wanted to go back, since buying a business there would be cheaper than Virginia. Didn't want to go back to Dayton, thinking Weisberg might keep an eye out there, knowing that that's where she came from.

- When Carl learned Susannah/Sylvia had left Middleburg and bought inn in Worthington, he applied to Ohio State. He'd left Arlington in '48, and had been teaching at the University of Virginia. His sister lived in Columbus, and that was an inducement too. He might as well move there as anywhere and keep an eye on Sylvia. He couldn't believe that Weisberg wouldn't come after her. W. definitely obsessed with her – the beautiful woman who left him (most women fell at his feet). He'd want to see his daughter too, Carl presumed, thinking there'd be the ego irritation for W. of having his daughter (something that 'belonged to him') taken against his will.

- CRISIS FOR CARL – It was only this May when C found the photos that he had proof Weisberg had been passing information to known Soviet agents when at Arlington Hall. CARL AFRAID TO SIMPLY HAND THAT EVIDENCE OVER TO THE GOVERNMENT for fear they wouldn't prosecute for political reasons – and wouldn't investigate Miriam's death further.
- FINDING THE PHOTOGRAPHS MADE CARL CERTAIN WEISBERG HAD KILLED MIRIAM, and he wanted to make absolutely sure he didn't escape retribution. CARL CLEARLY WANTED TO CONFRONT WEISBERG HIMSELF.
  Did he want to:
  Catch him and force a confession?
  Take him to Lennox, hoping there was enough evidence to prosecute?
  Kill him himself with the gun, or with the toxin on the pointer?

THEN HE SAW WEISBERG ON THE CORNER ACROSS FROM THE INN.

- Carl had kept in touch with Lennox, who'd been the FBI agent who'd worked most with Arlington Hall in investigating the agents in America the decrypted Venona intercepts referred to.
- Lennox – one of few FBI personnel who worked well with the code-breakers. Honest, intelligent, not brash and overbearing like some FBI, Lennox did most of the identification work on the three hundred plus Soviet agents in the US mentioned in the decrypted codes. The decrypted messages were only a fraction of the messages sent and received during 30s and 40s. Only a fraction of the agents referred to in those messages who were working against us internally have been identified. Among those identified were top people in FDR's

administration working covertly for Stalin – Harry Dexter White (#2 in Treasury Dept.), Laughlin Currie (FDR's trusted personal assistant), Maurice Halperin (head of a research section at OSS – our foremost intelligence organization) – who turned over hundreds of pages of US secret diplomatic cables to the KGB).

– The infamous Kim Philby, British Soviet agent, leaked our Venona decryptions to the Soviets AFTER Weisberg, in his role as liaison between the Brits and our intelligence people here starting in '47. His info confirmed for them what W. had said.

– Lennox helped match the coded names Venona used for their agents, with the identities of the real people, cross-referencing all the particulars in personal history, etc. Lennox did the work needed to prove that 'Antenna' and 'Liberal' were the code names used at different times by the Soviets for Julius Rosenberg when communicating to, or about him – though that Verona-based proof was never revealed at his trial.

– Many of these spies held on through Truman's administration, till finally, in '47, after much pressure from those who impressed upon him the importance of the Venona findings, Truman instituted an executive order, strengthened by Eisenhower in the early fifties, requiring that US government employees undergo loyalty-security investigations, which vastly improved the situation.

– Now . . . to the present situation . . . On Wednesday Carl saw Weisberg outside the Captain's Inn and followed him to his rental house. Carl phoned Lennox that night, found he was out of the country, left message for him to call back. C. called Patricia Bennett that night too, learned her uncle's house had been broken into the week before and his papers searched. Her address in California apparently uncovered, since her house was searched a few days later while P. out of town. The assumption was Weisberg had done both, and had finally gotten Susannah's new name and address from what he found from Patricia's things. (P. phoned Sylvia that Tuesday, as soon as she got home, heard from her uncle, and saw her house ransacked.)

- Why had Weisberg waited that long to search her uncle's house? Maybe W. was newly back in the States? Maybe he had only just found P. had an uncle and learned where he lived? She'd married in '48, changing her name to Morris, and had moved all over since. She would've been hard to find. And why would he zero in on the uncle, except that he lived near Washington when she'd been nearby in Arlington?

IMPORTANT POINT IN UNDERSTANDING CARL: Because they knew from Venona that Alger Hiss, the Rosenbergs, and others had all given atomic secrets to Stalin, those who knew had had to watch the misinformation in the news, and the wholesale withholding of evidence by the government in the trials that actually took place in order to keep the details of what we knew through Venona from the Soviets. If what was really known about Hiss et al had been publicly revealed there'd have been no question of their guilt. (Carter Clarke, J. Edgar Hoover and many others hadn't wanted Mrs Rosenberg executed because of her children, and her lower-level espionage involvement. She helped her husband, but was never a useful spy in her own right, partly because of ill health.)

- The Venona insiders also knew that McCarthy, who was right in claiming that the US government had been widely infiltrated by Soviet agents, was wrong in many of his accusations. Carl and other Venona insiders believe that him conducting the investigations with his self-publicizing flamboyance did damage in the public eye so that an accurate presentation of the seriousness of Soviet espionage here became less likely to be taken seriously by the public in the future. That was a real ongoing, growing frustration for Carl and many others.
- WEISBERG. Not much known. Born Odessa 1908. Parents Marxist revolutionaries. Left Russia 1912. Probably because of czarist Jewish persecution and fear of political retribution. Bill four when moved to Alexandria. (Nobody knows why Egypt.) Moved to NYC with parents in '25. Father clerk/bookkeeper

first in oriental rug firm. Later owned jewelry store in NY. Had been jeweler in Alexandria. No evidence parents involved with Communist Party USA. Bill spoke/wrote Russian, German, Arabic, English, Yiddish. Before he enlisted in army (not willing to do so till after the Stalin–Hitler pact collapsed when Hitler invaded Russia) he's thought to have worked in Chicago. Applied for government position there in '38, never completed interview process. Served as signals clerk/translator in army in N. Africa & Italy before being sent to Arlington. Not thought to have fired a shot in army in anger.

- Lennox, the FBI guy, told Carl he's convinced that W. hated jail far more than most inmates, and would do anything he had to do to keep from going back. Why, Lennox didn't know. Other than his love of wine, women, gambling, and gourmet food, which is prodigious.

Ben stopped typing, telling himself that that was enough, even if it wasn't organized well. His head hurt again, and his eyes felt as though grit were grating his eyeballs every time he blinked. He ignored both, and drank a glass of water, staring out the kitchen window.

First he'd copy the photos. Everything was ready in the dark room, so that wouldn't take long. He'd handwrite margin notes on the synopsis too, to help him find what he needed fast. Then he'd Xerox everything – Miriam's letters, Carl's explanations, his own typed synopsis – and hide the originals (including photos) in the muniment room, and stash the copies in the safe in his study.

Taking photos of Weisberg to the real-estate office had to be a priority too, because even though Weisberg had probably left long before, looking through his rental house might still turn up something.

The car-rental places had to be worth a shot. If Weisberg had actually rented a car, it could help Ben piece his movements together. The turquoise Chevy, he couldn't forget that either. Though it still didn't make much sense.

Why would anyone rent a car like that? It'd be too easy to remember. Unless you wanted to incriminate someone who had a car just like it.

He needed to take Weisberg's photograph to the neighbor who told him where Beth lived, and Carl's department at OSU. And also spend time with Bobby too, so whenever Sylvia was expected to call, Bobby could hand him the phone.

Why can't I remember where I've seen a turquoise Chevy? I bet I saw it just before, or after, my head got smashed in the barn.

Give Bobby another hour, then call and see what Beth said last night. And if Sylvia called this morning.

Fourteen

Bobby Chambers rolled over and stared at the ceiling, shoving his hands under his head, stretching his legs out in a wide arc, taking in every sensation. It felt so good to lie between sheets. Soft. Clean. Cool. The scent of ironed cotton. Combat had made it matter. The feel of skin sliding across smoothness.

The comfort too of coasting into quiet settled across him, making him smile. That, and being away from the uproar of cooks in everyday crisis, made him hum something old and ordinary they'd sung at home before the war.

Bobby hardly ever got to slide into the day – to drift along from one thought to the next, remembering a piece of a dream, revisiting home in the mountains in the morning, considering chicken and tarragon, and how to add a new twist.

He never got to bed till one, and then had to be at the wholesalers by six to get the pick of the day. When he found a good sous-chef work would get easier, though inns are trickier than restaurants. Three meals. Every day. Sunday morning off, for him. A chance to sleep in Tuesday – 'Don't anybody call before eight,' repeated till he could count on having the dawn to himself.

Though he still loved to cook. Restaurant work had started sounding good to him years before with his grandma, watching her cook for the big houses, west a ways in Asheville. Being fed in France, too, before he got hit, at a real small farm where they'd lived off a garden, had showed him there was more to food than he'd ever thought to imagine.

He'd promised himself he'd get back to France – someday soon, in the next couple of years – and learn more about how they cooked. And what they grew in the ground too, that he'd never seen here. French sorrel. Leeks and roquette. Truffles dug up by big old hogs.

Beth wanted to see Europe too, now that it was back to normal. They'd talked a lot about where she'd go, after she'd finished her master's.

Bobby could see Beth right that second, watching his pa years before the war, when she was just a little squirt down with her aunt from up north, watching his dad try to build him a shed with the short corner poles down the slope a ways, and the long poles up on top.

Beth said maybe he should switch them to make the roof flatter, and right then – as Bobby lay there staring at his ceiling – he could still feel how furious he'd been, when his dad said right in front of her, 'You got you a good eye for bidness, girl, a whole lot better'n mine.'

Bobby couldn't have said why it'd bothered him so bad. Except that her dad was some big doctor up north, and his never went to school. Never had him a job but field work during harvest, or watching somebody's cabin. He felt like she'd been wrong to suggest any kind of thing at all to any grown man, and his papa had had no call to sound so weak and feeble.

Then Bobby pictured Beth, coming into the dining room with Reese Saturday night, pale and grave and older in some way. Excited looking, and worried too. As though she could use an arm around her shoulders, making him want it to be his.

Bobby's smile slipped as he thought that. And he rubbed his eyes and whispered, 'You gotta do what you know is right, and stop being so weak.'

He had to. Soon. It wasn't fair to her to let anything more go on. She didn't see the situation half as clear as he did. She could afford to be a romantic, with her family, and her education, and what her future could be.

Me, I got to see the world real cold-blooded for what it is when I was just a kid. I seen what folks thought when I'd nod to 'em on the street. 'Fit to come in by the back door, if he wipes his feet good. Fit to help his grandma wash up after she's cooked for a party. Fit to pick our corn and beans, but not to sit down to supper.'

You get to feeling stupid and dirty, and that makes you hoppin' mad. And then you start lookin' to start up a fight, like a stray, bristling down the back. I am not *gonna be the cause of Beth learnin' what it's like.*

If I don't make a move here soon, it'll be too late for me too. I'll go and do what I want to do, and that'll be the ruin of us both.

He'd seen it happen before. An educated woman, a school-teacher, a daughter of a judge, married a dirt-poor farmer and moved to a patch of dried-up hardpan, where she pecked at her husband the rest of his life. Corrected his language. Mocked him to the kids. Acted shamed in front of folks. The whole county laughed behind her back, 'cause she married him for his looks, they reckoned. Plain old Alice Raney lusting for a dirt farmer no better off than a sharecropper. Married to better him, and drove him to drink. Turning the kids mean and crazy, both of them parents together.

I gotta stand up and tell Beth the next time I see her. Either that, or move on myself. Find me a job in some distant city. Though I can't walk out on the inn now, not with Sylvia gone—

He heard it then. And couldn't believe it. Somebody pounding on his door.

He decided it must've been the downstairs apartment. The house was old. The brick walls thick. It probably sounded closer than usual with Ted and Paula off at work and the rooms closed and quiet.

The hammering started again. Louder. More impatient. And he swung his feet on to the floor and grabbed his jeans from a chair.

'Yes?' Bobby had opened the wooden door, and was looking through the screen, squinting out at the wood-railed landing shaded by a tall old oak, at two closed-faced deputy sheriffs – one large, one small, both staring at him.

'Mr Chambers? Mr Robert Chambers?' It was the larger of the two asking, huge hands hanging at his sides, dark-gray uniform with razor-sharp creases, buttons carefully polished.

'What can I do for you? Here, come on in.' Bobby pushed the screen door open and backed out of their way.

'We'd like to ask you a few questions.' It was the smaller one talking, stepping in first behind Bobby.

'Sure. Though I can't think what this could be about.'

'Carl Walker's death.' It was the larger one this time, taking off his visored hat. 'I'm Deputy Fuller. This is Deputy Johnson.'

'Make yourselves at home, and I'll brew up some coffee.'

'Don't bother for us. We're real rushed for time.'

'OK. Like I said though, can't see how I can help.' Bobby sat in an overstuffed chair that had once been Beth's mother's, while the deputies sat on both ends of his couch and stared straight at him.

'How well did you know Carl Walker?' It was the smaller one asking, notepad and pencil in his hands.

'Not real well. Counted him as a friend, though. He come into the Captain's Inn a good deal, and we had friends in common. We'd chat when he come in for dinner. He'd stop back in the kitchen, and shoot the breeze. Asking what he oughta order that night, that kinda thing. Ordinary talk like that.'

'You know where he lived, do ya?'

'Yessir. Hester Street. Two blocks over from a young lady of my acquaintance. I've been by his house many a time, but I never had call to go in.' Bobby was reaching for cigarettes on the coffee table, feeling his face turn pink.

'That would be Beth Morland?'

'Yessir. Known her since we was kids. Not real well till recently, but a good long while.'

'You own a 1957 turquoise Chevrolet?' It was the short one, Johnson, still looking at his notepad.

'I do. Bel Air Sport Sedan V8. Top's white. Bottom's turquoise. Why would you wantta ask me that?'

'Where were you Saturday?' It was the bigger one asking. Fuller. Laying his hat on his knees.

'Morning or afternoon?'

'Both.' The two of them said it together, neither looking at the other.

'Well, pretty much where I always am, only more this last weekend. Up at the inn, cookin'. Got there before five a.m. Had a wedding we was catering, plus the regular work.'

'You sure about that?'

'I am.'

'You never left? Not all day?'

'I don't b'lieve I did. Let me think though. Let me make real sure.' Bobby stared across at the screen door and slowly shook his head. 'No, that's right. All day. You can ask the kitchen help. I was prob'ly only alone there from a little before five till six, when the breakfast crew come in. What's all this about? I don't see, for the life of me, where I could fit in.'

'You know where Mr Walker died?'

'Not for sure, no. South-west of here somewhere, according to Mr Reese, down along the river. Don't know how far. Or right where it was.'

'The reason we're asking, Mr Chambers, is a car like yours was seen at the scene of the shooting Saturday morning.'

'Wasn't me, you can bank on that. Wasn't me, *or* my Chevy. I don't loan it to nobody.'

'Not a real common car.'

'Common enough. It's a popular color this year. That's what they said at the dealer's. First new car I've had.'

'You had no other dealings with Mr Walker?'

'None but what I told ya. He was a quiet guy. Shy, I guess you'd say. I liked him fine, though, and I looked forward to seeing him when he'd stop in for dinner. Said he wasn't much of a cook, and we was real convenient for him.'

'There weren't any hard feelings between the two of you you'd like to mention?' It was Deputy Fuller this time, staring hard at Bobby.

'Nope. What could there be for us to quarrel over?'

'Miss Morland.' The smaller one, Deputy Johnson, glanced at him, before he made another note.

'There was nothin' between them but being friends. Beth had worked with Carl's sister, Evelyn, before she died. Beth and Carl used to have dinner at Evelyn's house before the symphony concerts, and Beth kinda felt sorry for Carl, and kept on with those dinners, inviting other folks along. Carl give Beth a key to his house too, after Evelyn was gone, 'cause they lived so close, and he traveled so much in the summer. But that's all there was.'

'What about you and Miss Morland?'

'I don't mean to be disrespectful, but I don't see why that's your concern.'

'Don't you?' The bigger one, Deputy Fuller, laid his hat on the sofa and gripped his knees with his hands.

'You sayin' Carl didn't commit suicide?'

'That's what we're trying to find out. Where were you Friday?' It was Deputy Fuller staring sideways at Bobby, sliding Marlboros out of his shirt pocket. 'Mind if I smoke?'

'Nope.' Bobby was lighting a cigarette of his own, and he held the match out for Fuller. 'Worked all day. Getting on to the wedding. Started the cake that morning real early before the breakfast crew come in. Used the prep room next to the kitchen for doing a lot of it, so we wouldn't be falling over each other up at the main prep station.'

'Can anyone vouch for your whereabouts? Staff there at the inn?'

'Yeah, sure. Like I said. Somebody'd remember. Why do you care where I was Friday?'

'Your car was seen Friday afternoon at the scene of the shooting. Friday was when Dr Walker died. It was seen Saturday cruising by Carl Walker's house. Two times, maybe. Seen by a couple of neighbors. Out by the river too, right where he was shot.'

'Wasn't me. I can swear to that. And if I was up to no good, why would I do that? Car like mine stands out. If I was doing something I shouldn't a been, I woulda borrowed a car or something, or rented something plain.'

'Maybe.'

'Why would I want to hurt Carl? I liked him real well.'

'That's what we have to find out. Don't leave town without informing us, Mr Chambers.' Fuller stood up, cigarette still in his mouth, staring down at Bobby, sitting in his faded tan chair. 'Call the County Sheriff. Ask for Fuller or Johnson. Number's on the card.'

As he handed Bobby the card, he said, 'We'll be talking to you again. Nice apartment you got here. Like to see old houses fixed up. Too many falling apart in town.'

'Suits me just fine.'

Bobby stood on the landing once they'd left, gazing down at the cool green lawn, thinking about calling Ben, hoping he'd figured something out that made sense of Walker's death.

Mark Meyer at Worthington Realty recognized the man in Ben's photo. He'd rented him a furnished house at 433 Fairview. Mr Samson had returned the keys late Friday morning, however, saying his plans had changed unexpectedly. There'd been a family emergency of some sort, and he wanted his month's deposit back, since he'd stayed there only two nights.

Mr Meyer hadn't agreed. It had only been because the owner had died suddenly and the heirs were uncertain what they planned to do that they'd agreed to rent the house on a month-to-month basis. Mr Meyer couldn't let Mr Richard Samson renege simply because it became convenient.

Ben nodded, and thanked him.

Then drove to Weisberg's house on Fairview, where he picked the lock on the back door and stepped into the kitchen.

He didn't find anything inside that could help anytime soon. Though he did lift three fingerprints from the kitchen and the bathroom with the talcum powder and Scotch tape he'd brought for that purpose. They'd be useful if he found a match somewhere else that mattered – like Carl's, or his, or Beth's house.

He stuck the tapes with the prints on the sticky side to three-by-five cards, then sealed them in the envelope he'd brought, and slipped it into the inside pocket of the sport coat he'd worn for its pockets. He was standing in the middle of the kitchen's cracked linoleum staring at a butter-colored wall, asking himself what to do next to look for William Weisberg.

He couldn't hit every motel in town. That's what the police were for, mass sweeps with manpower. And now that he knew what Carl knew, he sure couldn't leak it to them. No, the FBI guy was the one to give the prints to, so he could run them through their files.

Why would Weisberg rent a house for a month, and then want out of the lease? If Carl was right, he came to find Sylvia. So if he'd hoped to stay long-term, motels would've been too expensive.

Once Carl had traced him to the house, Weisberg would've wanted to get away from it. He would've hidden his tracks, and moved from place to place. From one motel to the other, probably. Even before he murdered Carl.

That's if I'm looking at it right. I still may not be. Even though my brain's gearing up.

Ben didn't like doing it, making up a bald-faced lie, but there wasn't any way around it. And he told the middle-aged woman at Avis that an uncle of his with a terminal condition had suddenly left his home in St. Louis and was thought to have flown to Columbus where he'd lived as a boy. They had reason to believe it was a pilgrimage of sorts, before he took his life.

The Avis woman recognized Weisberg from the photograph as Richard Samson from Minnesota who'd rented a navy blue

Ford on Wednesday that he'd unexpectedly turned in Thursday, after saying he'd keep it a month.

Ben gave the Hertz man the same story. But no one working at Hertz that day recognized Weisberg from the photo. No one named Samson had rented a car. And though there were many dark-colored cars out at that moment, there was no good way to check on an individual without an accurate name. Mr Reese could check back the following afternoon when others on the staff would be on duty. Maybe his uncle would've turned up by then, and would make the search unnecessary.

'I hope so. If they'd put our pictures on our driver's licenses finding people would be easier. Right? We couldn't fake identities.'

'Why would you be thinking about false—?'

'What about a turquoise Chevy? Have you rented any of those?'

'If you'll wait a moment I can check.'

There had been one rented. Friday at noon. Returned Saturday evening. 'Mr Russell Abernathy. Santa Barbara, California.'

'What was his local address?'

'476 High Street, Columbus.'

'Thanks. You've been a real help.'

'You think that's your uncle, using a phony name?'

'Don't know, but it could be.'

'Your uncle likes turquoise?' He was gazing at Ben with a speculative eye and beginning to look amused.

'Not exactly, it's that—'

'Let me get this straight. You think he'd want a particular color? Someone suicidal?'

'It's just a wild guess on my part. It's the car he owns at home.' Ben smiled, and got himself out the door before he had to tell any more lies to cover his retreat.

He drove to 476 High Street. And found the Char-Burger, a small grubby diner that catered to college kids, where a waitress named Vi ruled the roost.

She was six feet tall, and powerfully built, and her skin was a deep rich brown. She wore large unmatched Christmas balls for earrings – one blue, one purple (the same dark electric shade as the apron over her uniform). She kept her pencil

where she knew where it was (stuck through the strands of
her skinned-back hair above the bun at the back of her head)
– and she hooted at Ben's photo of Weisberg when he asked
if she'd seen that man.

'Once. And, honey, he ain't my type. No, sir, no, he ain't!'

'Why? Is he—?'

'Thinks he *real* cool. You could see that right off the bat.
Thinks every woman on the face of God's green earth oughta
fall right down at his feet. Yeah!'

'Why am I not surprised?' Ben was smiling at the shrewd-
ness on her face, at the amusement too in the large dark eyes
evaluating him.

'He ain't that good-lookin', and that ain't gunna be
happenin' here. Seen *way* too many cats like him, *way* too
many, let me tell ya.' She was leaning on the counter, looking
up at Ben, her large red-lipsticked lips curled in a wide grin.
'He give you this address?'

'Yeah.'

'This SOB here? Like this was where he was livin'?'

'Yep.'

'He pullin' your leg, boy. He pullin' your leg *real* hard.
Pick up your char-burger!' It was shouted loud enough to
wake the dead, and four or five college kids leapt out of their
chairs, then dropped back as soon as they saw Vi point to a
mousy-looking girl in black framed glasses, who stood up
looking startled as though she'd been stuck by a pin.

She trotted to the counter, pulling money from her purse,
while Vi tapped her foot on the floor to tell her she had better
things to do than stand there waiting on her.

The girl pushed a bill across the counter and picked up two
white pottery plates, seconds before Vi said, 'I'll bring you
folks your drinks in a sec.'

The girl said, 'Thanks, Vi,' and turned toward the table with
the plates piled with food: two bacon cheeseburgers, two chili
dogs, mounds of crisp-looking fries.

Vi had started waving her arms from one side to the other
to Ray Charles' 'I Got a Woman' blasting out of the jukebox
– when she stopped dead, and twirled around twice, before
pointing two long index fingers (nails painted candy-apple
red) at the table where the dithery girl was just sitting down.
'Tell me now if you want more fries, I'll serve you real quick,

if you tell me no lies!' The arms flashed straight over Vi's head as her hips pumped to the music.

The four at the mousy girl's table said, 'Yeah, Vi, more fries!' as though this were a well-known ritual.

Ben laughed, and then thanked Vi, who winked at him, unexpectedly, as he turned toward the door.

'You come back now, ya hear? We got us charcoal-broiled burgers! We got us the best fries any ol' white boy ever did eat! We got us our chocolate milkshakes, honey, that a spoon'll stand up in straight! It'd do me good to see a man 'round here, 'steada all these sweet little boys!'

A refrigerator-sized college kid in an OSU T-shirt who could've been a lineman for Woody stood up and said, 'Wait a minute, Vi, who you calling a boy?' He was grinning across the packed tables.

And the other two waitresses laughed with Vi, who was shaking her head to make her earrings dance.

Ben bowed to Vi from the doorway, and smiled as he straightened up. 'All I can say is you made my day. I'll thank you again, and be on my way.' He stepped out fast as Vi laughed and slapped both hands on the counter.

Sylvia had told Bobby she'd phone him at three. And shortly before that, Bobby took Ben to the drug store down the street from the inn, where they both finished coffee ice-cream sodas while waiting for the payphone in the last booth to ring.

Bobby talked to Sylvia first, and persuaded her, with considerable effort, to talk to Ben Reese.

When Ben got on the phone, he didn't mention Venona, or the nature of the work at Arlington Hall. He told Sylvia he knew who she was, and where she'd once worked. That Carl had worked there too, and had known Patricia Bennett, that Carl had been tracking Weisberg for years. That Weisberg was implicated in Carl Walker's death, and they needed her help to find him.

She asked Ben questions. She extracted several promises.

Then, finally, she told him that Sunday, after she'd learned of Carl's death from Ben Saturday night, she'd called Patricia Bennett. Patricia admitted that she'd kept Carl informed whenever Sylvia had moved over the years. But had been afraid to tell Sylvia about Carl – afraid she'd run off and drop out of sight, when Patricia claimed to have known in her bones that Carl could be trusted. She'd watched him closely after Miriam died, and she wanted him looking for Weisberg, and keeping a protective eye on Sylvia and her daughter too. She hoped Sylvia would understand she'd done it for their good.

Eventually Sylvia had said she did. Once she'd had time to think about it, and realize how judicious Carl had been in the way he'd treated her. She'd liked him too, as a person. And then she saw the difficult choices Patricia had had to make.

As a result of those considerations, she'd agreed to talk to Ben. But she didn't see how she could help.

He asked if she'd seen Weisberg in Worthington, and she told him Weisberg had come to her house Thursday night, telling her he wanted his daughter, and some kind of life with both of them. He'd called her first at the inn the night before, telling her he knew where she lived, and if she wanted her daughter there when she got home, she'd better agree to see him.

She'd sent Sarah off the next day to stay with friends so she wouldn't be there when Weisberg arrived. And she'd talked to him for an hour or so, telling him she'd have to think about letting him meet their daughter, but there would be no question of a life together, not Sylvia and Weisberg. That she'd say Weisberg wasn't Sarah's father, and there was no way he could prove otherwise.

He told her he'd never been an agent, but that he had passed on sensitive information that he'd thought ought to be shared with the Soviets, and still believed he was right to do that, though he knew she'd disagree. He'd served his time in federal prison. He was a free man, not being hunted by anybody, though he had changed his name to make life easier in the US.

He had a responsible job working for a well-known businessman and international investor. But he'd arranged to take a full month away to get to know his daughter and restore his relationship with her too. She'd managed eventually to get him to tell her that he worked for Armand Hammer, entrepreneur and Soviet supporter, financial backer of the Kremlin, for whom he had real respect.

She saw Hammer very differently, and she'd told Weisberg she'd want to confirm that he had a job and wouldn't try to leech off her in Worthington, and he gave her the name of an import–export firm owned by Hammer in DC.

He'd denied killing Miriam. He admitted that he'd been there, but said she'd fallen accidentally when they'd been arguing by the window. He'd threatened Sylvia, subtly, in very deliberate and careful terms, assuring her he'd expose her lies about her daughter's parentage, if Sylvia wasn't willing to acknowledge him to Sarah and let him see his daughter in the coming years.

She'd left it that she'd talk to him on Sunday. That she needed to think what best to do. She would want time to prepare her daughter, *if* she decided to introduce them. That *if* he wanted her to believe they could work out a reasonable arrangement anytime in the future, he had to prove to her, to Sylvia, in the course of the next three days that he could act in a trustworthy manner. He had to leave her alone, and not watch the house, and act like a normal person.

He'd phoned her Friday and Saturday, and she'd agreed to meet him late Sunday afternoon, knowing when she talked to him that she'd leave Saturday night.

Ben asked if she believed that he'd killed Miriam, and she said she wasn't sure. He was such a consummate liar, she wouldn't want to guess.

Ben also asked if she'd seen his car, or managed to notice the license plates.

Sylvia said he'd parked out of sight and walked to her house in the rain Thursday night. And she had no idea where he might be staying.

It was not going to be easy for her to hide from Weisberg this time. Not when she owned her own business. She'd be tied to that, to the bank and monthly creditors, so the time had come to make Weisberg stay away, and how to do that she didn't know. What she'd done was give herself breathing space, running away this time. What she ought to do next, though, she still didn't know.

Ben asked if he could explain about Weisberg and Sylvia to Bobby. Sylvia didn't answer for what must have been a minute. Then she said, 'No. Not now. I'll tell him myself later. When I've thought everything through. I have your word, do I? That you won't tell him yourself? Or anyone else either?'

'Yes. I promised you that already.'

* * *

Bobby had asked Ben to walk back with him to the inn, and when he'd sat on the kitchen steps and pulled out his Camels, he told Ben about the cops.

Ben was standing with his hands on his hips looking at the vegetable garden, when he turned and stared at Bobby. '*That's* where I saw the turquoise Chevy! It must've been yours, parked here Saturday night. I saw it when Beth and I were climbing these stairs. I couldn't remember till you mentioned it.'

'Concussions can be real weird. You never can tell what you'll recall. What do you think'll get the cops off my back?'

'Finding the real killer.'

Bobby stopped rubbing his eyes and studied Ben, his black hair falling in his face, his wide dark eyes uneasy. 'That wasn't a real big help.'

'Sorry. I didn't mean it to sound that flippant. The cops'll talk to the night clerks and the cooks at the inn, and that'll make them look elsewhere.'

'I'd like to think so, but I seen worse.'

'You heard what I said to Sylvia on the phone? About Carl working in Washington after the war, at the same place the guy Weisberg worked?'

'Yeah.'

'I can't say much about that, but I'll tell you what I can.' Ben told him that Carl thought Weisberg had killed a woman in DC in '47. That there were issues involved that had to do with military information. That Weisberg had known Sylvia years earlier, and she wanted nothing to do with him. 'And if Weisberg thought Carl could prove what he did to the woman in Washington, or that he hadn't handled information during and after the war the way he should have, he'd have had very good reason to want Carl dead.'

'Man!' Bobby didn't say anything else. He stared at Ben and shook his head.

'Not what you expected, is it?'

'You can say that again. Not with shy old Carl. You wouldn't expect him to be part of anything that big or important. So this Weisberg's the guy who phoned Sylvia here? And she left town to get away from him?'

'Yep. And Weisberg's a dangerous man. You and I need to remember that. Will you call me after Beth calls tonight? I'd like to know how she's doing. I've been phoning her mother all day without getting an answer. I want to find out if anyone's been calling, or snooping around them. If I don't get her mom by eight or so tonight I'll drive over to their house and leave a note asking her to call me.'

Ben didn't get an answer the rest of that day, and at eight forty-five that night he was driving toward Beth's parents' house on a cool, shady, prosperous street of solid brick houses built in the teens and twenties.

There was still no one home. And he left notes on the front and back doors asking Mrs Morland (or Dr Morland, either one) to call him, no matter how late it was, when they got in. He was a friend of Beth's, and Carl Walker's, and he needed to speak to one of them as soon as they got home.

Fifteen

A premonition of impending danger might've helped that night. Though being warned and worrying about it could've made it harder too. Either way, for better or worse, Beth Morland wasn't given one. And after she'd phoned Bobby at ten, from a gas station in the valley, she'd settled-in in her living room in the glow of a kerosene lamp.

She'd left the front windows shuttered so the house looked empty from the road, and she sat on the sofa and sweated, sipping iced tea and staring into space, with *The Federalist Papers* unread in her lap, while she thought about Bobby Chambers.

It was hard not to on Black Mountain. She saw him everywhere she looked. Clearest of all when he was fourteen, when he'd glared at her with fury on his face because she'd suggested something to his dad that'd embarrassed Bobby terribly.

Beth had been crushed by his anger, and then had to suffer three whole weeks when Bobby wouldn't look at her, because she'd talked to his father the way she talked to her own.

She knew now it'd been unbearable for Bobby – seeing her, in front of all the kids, correcting a man who had nothing she had. No education. No public standing. No easiness anywhere in life. No pride to fall back on, except that he 'never took nothing that weren't his, and never'd take charity from nary a one, not as long as he lived.'

Those weren't inconsiderable accomplishments from Beth's perspective, then *or* now. But Bobby thought she'd shamed him by acting as though she knew better.

His dad hadn't seemed to see it that way. He'd been a soft-spoken, easy-going man who loved his life on the mountain – the woods, the wildness, the look of the land, the animals all around him. He hadn't felt the need of cash money, he'd said it to her more than once. Not if it meant living in a city with crowds and noise and misery around him. Not when he could shape his own days on his great-great-granddaddy's land.

Beth, on the other hand, had never had to struggle. Her parents had, to get an education, to make ends meet for years on end. But Beth had lived her entire life without having to worry once about putting food on the table.

Neither did she give a thought to what people had, or did. Not in the sense of liking the person because of either, or respecting them more (*or* less) depending on if they had weight in the world.

That might've been a luxury too. She saw that when she thought about it, being able to feel secure enough – or distanced enough from the fray, maybe – to not care a lick.

Though nothing in life *is* secure, from one day to the next. A lesson Beth had grasped intellectually, but knew she still had to learn where it hurt. When something substantial's at stake.

She saw differences the way anyone would. Her father was a surgeon. Bobby's father hadn't had a job, or a car, or an indoor bathroom. But he'd known things she'd wanted to know. And he'd had what her father lacked – the time and inclination to actually raise his kids.

Bobby's dad had made a life that satisfied him right where he was, growing vegetables, making his own medicines, raising chickens and salting pork – caring for his family with his own two hands. He'd let them read to him whenever they'd wanted. And he'd beamed at them, and roughed up their hair, letting them know how proud he was they could do what he couldn't.

Beth's father had worked round the clock at Columbus's most prestigious hospital, and was usually too tired, and too self-absorbed, to spend time with his daughters. He had two Cadillacs, and a membership in a country club Beth couldn't stand to set foot in, where he seemed to like watching the waiters kiss his shoes while he ate.

She knew there were explanations for that. He'd come from the backwoods of West Virginia. His parents had died when he was twelve. He'd stayed there alone on the farm, then fought his way, hard-eyed and desperate, through years of silent deprivation into a brand-new bright shiny place where patients and nurses had to bow and obey.

He'd ended up taking credit for every talent he'd been given, with the sin of the self-made man. It was *his* intelligence, *his*

self-motivation, *his* self-discipline, *his* hard work that had
pulled him up by his bootstraps.

He didn't have a gift for life, though. Not like Bobby's
father, who'd tapped on Beth's window screen at five one
morning, whispering to her to get up right quick. 'I seen bees
dancin', and I'm fixin' to take y'all back to the hive.'

He'd led her, and all the kids but Bobby, halfway round
the mountain to a bee tree where he gathered up honey, bringing
everyone home again unstung and sticky, giving her her favorite
memory from when she was small.

Beth had tried to help Bobby understand all that, in the last
two years in Worthington. After worrying about him all through
the war, when she'd tried to keep up with where he was
stationed by writing his sister, Cassie, when she couldn't make
herself stop.

No matter what she did, he saw her as being above him,
even though the very idea made him froth at the mouth.

Beth sat on the sofa and asked herself again whether Bobby
would ever get over that and see her as a person. *If he can't
stop feeling furious and inferior, I'll have to find a job somewhere else.*

*I hope I'm not just attracted to the challenge. Of a strong
man who runs the other way. Women have been, since the
dawn of time, like bulls to red flags.*

*Of course, knowing Bobby, he probably thinks he's being
noble when he pushes me away.*

Shep was staring at Beth, leaning against the sofa, humming
softly, willing her to notice, looking as though he were worried.

'*You* know, don't you, Shep, whenever I start to feel sad?'
Beth rubbed his ears, and patted his head, before she asked
if he wanted to go out. 'I'll have to put you on the chain
again. I don't want you in poison ivy, giving it to me. Tomorrow
we'll take a really long walk before it gets too hot.'

Shep stood up and stretched, shaking his thick black-and-
white coat, fanning it out around his back, before he walked
to the cabin's only door and tapped it with his paw.

Wednesday, June 19th, 1957

Ten minutes later, just after midnight, Weisberg cut the engine
and coasted on to an overgrown track, an abandoned red-clay

lumbering road, halfway up Black Mountain. It was one of the landmarks he'd known to look for, from the directions the actress had gotten from Beth's mom. And it turned out to be just what he'd hoped for – a place to hide his car.

He'd gotten into Asheville about four, eaten fried chicken in a diner there, then slept in his car at the train station. He'd driven all that day, and most of the night before, through drizzle or fog or pouring down rain, and he'd needed to sleep before he dealt with Beth.

The drive hadn't been easy, coming south on Route 23. And after he'd cut the engine in the lane, and reached for his thermos of hot strong tea (Russian tea, steeped the way it should be), he thought again, for the twentieth time, that for such a decadent country, the highways in the US were an absolute disgrace. Eisenhower claimed he was going to build a four-lane network connecting major cities. But Eisenhower was a liar and a fool, and if he did it would be the result of nothing but pork-barrel politics.

Weisberg picked up the sandwich, wrapped in wax paper, he'd bought at the Asheville train station. Ham and cheese, and who knew what else, on white bread made from sawdust. It was dry, stale and constructed with Velveeta, and he chewed glumly, swallowing tea between bites, wiping his mouth with a paper napkin, seeing the mountains in front of him again that had made the trip exhausting.

Seventy miles of hairpin curves in the thickest fog he'd ever seen. Trucks fighting to make the grades, nearly invisible in front of him. Cars behind him, coming too fast, not seeing him any better. Cars in his own lane, heading straight at him, sheer drops on his side, high cliffs on the other.

Then would come the painted scrawls emblazoned across the rock face. REPENT SINNER! JESUS SAVES! PREPARE TO MEET YOUR MAKER!

The type of person who'd write that drivel is crying out to be neutered in the interests of all mankind. The archetypical backwoods American. Superstitious. Feeble-minded. The result of incest in remote communities.

He'd seen them in the service stations. Toothless, filthy, spitting tobacco, the type to believe any kind of nonsense, and take it as a raison d'être to lecture all mankind.

It'd made Weisberg even more anxious to get home to

Washington, to fine restaurants and urban sophistication. To what there actually *was* of that on this side of the Atlantic. To women who talked about issues of importance, and made themselves attractive.

Unlike Miriam Gold. The embodiment of the unattractive woman, with no ability, and little intention of improving the situation. She was smart, he had to give her that. Intelligent, but deluded. Repudiating her people. Rejecting her upbringing. To swallow whole every indigestible morsel of anti-socialist propaganda.

He didn't relish the part he'd played in her demise. Miriam had been disarmingly childlike, and she had aroused paternal feelings. But the conflict they'd been engaged in had had to take precedence. He couldn't have let himself be exposed by an inexperienced shrimp of a girl, no matter how accomplished.

Compare her to Marta of the silken skin. Of long-legged, languid grace. Of shining hair and liquid lips. Whom I shall phone from somewhere near here before I start for DC.

He'd arrange a room at the Willard, with dinner reservations there as well, booked too, in the name of Armand Hammer to ensure the sort of preferential treatment Marta clearly enjoyed.

Armand's tastes were what she aspired to. Those of a world-renowned connoisseur, who, unlike the stereotype, considered the common man in whatever he planned and accomplished.

Few men of business had recognized the atrocities inherent in the capitalist system nearly as clearly as he. Even fewer labored as tirelessly to bring about change.

Why shouldn't he pamper himself and indulge his aesthetic passions? He could afford to expand his collections. He was able to squeeze substantial profits from whatever schemes were in hand.

He was certainly obsessed with 'the hunt'. And yet the desire to possess each piece appeared to trump the rest. And that, of course, provided opportunities as he came to rely more heavily on Weisberg for managing each acquisition.

Weisberg told himself this wasn't the time to dwell on Armand Hammer, that he needed to evaluate Reese, and whether his guns had been loaded. Did he light the rooms and arrange the louvers, to use the guns for deterrence?

Or did Reese intend for him to get shot without a qualm or a quibble?

The doors had been locked. A casual visitor wouldn't have been injured. Though Reese would've had to get in too, and Weisberg still had to assume he'd have used an upper window. Either that, or the firearms weren't loaded, and he'd have entered at will.

It wasn't an unimportant issue, for Weisberg was far from taking Reese's measure. Even considering the impressions of the several women Reese worked with, Weisberg needed whatever details he could force from Miss Morland.

I shall not be thwarted in this. I shall acquire the materials Carl left. I shall not endure again the manifold miseries of a US prison. The execrable food. The constant degradation. The mindlessness of the animals one contends with. The numbing effects of a lack of stimulation, intellectual and sensory. I shall not submit to it. Now, or in the future.

Weisberg felt the bottom of his shirt pocket, as though checking the contents. Then stuck his left arm out the window, as he breathed in earth-scented air, hot and damp and heavy with leaf mold, as well as the buzzings of bugs.

I am, of course, in excellent company. Philby shares my horror of incarceration. And as the KGB's most famous double agent, he basks in the Kremlin's limelight today in luxury and honor.

He's bored, though, I suspect, finding himself on the shelf. Kim and I share a need for challenge, as well as collegial bonhomie. To be 'in the business' and work where it matters offers real satisfaction. To know precisely what's being done, when and where it counts.

Still, watching from the sidelines had certain compensations. Such was the advantage of working for Armand Hammer. Consulting from one remove, giving aid without risk.

He slapped at the mosquito biting his neck, and reached to roll up the window, telling himself to concentrate, and prepare to deal with Reese.

An unfortunate ally for Walker. Requiring proper pressure if he's to be managed well. This is the logical location, however. There're few here to see and report, and that's an obvious advantage. Though once the preparation's done, flexibility's key.

The girl had been a good choice for tightening the screws. Unless he learned something when studying the land that made him alter his plans. The actress had been more useful than one might've expected too, getting the name of the woman in Black Mountain who said she'd seen Beth, enabling Weisberg to question her before he left Ohio.

If the pear-shaped friend came with Reese, the approach might have to be different. Still, care, planning, knowing more than they did, would pay off this time as it had in the past.

Then he'd hunt Susannah. Running away with the girl again, lying to him to his face, that had been the final straw. He'd endured more from Susannah than any other woman he'd known, and that had now come to an end once and for all.

Now that he knew she'd kept in touch with Patricia Bennett, Susannah would be easier to handle. Even if she cut all ties to Bennett, pressure could be applied by manipulating Susannah's affection for darling little Patricia.

Sometime, after I've managed this situation, when I'm holding a knife to Pat Bennett's throat, and Susannah learns that when phoning the inn, Susannah will come running.

This is not the moment for distraction, however. It's time now to investigate the mountainside between here and Miss Morland's.

Weisberg retrieved a paper bag from the glove compartment and pulled out a Colt semi-automatic, the same model that had killed Carl, though this had a specially machined barrel, a longer barrel threaded on the end, to fit a German silencer.

He screwed the silencer into place, shoved the magazine into the handgrip, set the safety, and slipped the Colt into the left-hand pocket of his hooded windbreaker. He zipped a second magazine into his right hand pocket, then opened the trunk and grabbed an army satchel, dark khaki, stained in places, made of heavy canvas.

He looked at the contents with a narrow-beam flashlight, added two lengths of rope from the trunk, then slid his arms through the wide webbed straps and shrugged the pack on his back.

The cabin wasn't easy to see, when you were looking for it for the first time, he knew that from Mrs Morland. Not with clouds as heavy as these, or with the moon a pale white sliver – for the house sat tucked back behind a thicket (a heavy fringe of hardwoods and evergreens, with shrubs and vines entwined) that was thicker than most of the woods he'd pass on his way to the cabin.

There were trees along both sides of the road – a red clay and gravel road, dried into hard-packed ruts, that climbed around Black Mountain. He walked along the road's right edge, the valley somewhere below him on his right, on the far side of a shelf of land – a flying buttress covered with woods and tangled undergrowth that hid all but the berm.

He kept close to the brambles and the dusty leafed trees, ready to fade into them if anyone came near, stopping to listen every so often for someone coming on foot.

The mountainside climbed hard on his left, on the other side of the one-lane road, where the line of trees was narrow and patches of clay and outcropped rock could be seen growing up vertically.

He spent an uneasy minute or two thinking he'd gone too far, that he must've missed the lane on his right side, a turn-off of some sort cutting toward the cabin.

Then he saw a shallow clearing, and after he'd walked past it, and turned and looked back, he saw the end of a small wooden cabin the size and shape of a trailer, angled off deep into woods on the right edge of the clearing.

There was no car parked by the wooden steps. And the solid outside shutters were closed across the windows. The door was shut behind a screen. And he couldn't see any lights.

Then a dog barked from the far end, in the trees somewhere beyond the cabin – and Weisberg stepped into the woods, heading back the way he'd come, windbreaker sticking to his hot prickly skin, sweat running down his ribs, while the dog barked again.

A woman's voice told it to be quiet. And Weisberg heard a screen door slap against a wooden frame as he worked his way through blackberry bushes along the edge of the road, feeling them tear into his clothes and prick the skin on his shins.

He trudged past them into the trees, toward the back of the long narrow cabin, and saw a faint yellowish light in the middle of that long north side.

He edged closer, moving slowly, listening for sounds from the cabin, hearing an owl in the distance, and something scrabbling under the bushes, close by on his right.

The dog barked once, and he headed toward it, away from the road, toward the edge of the mountain – deciding the dog must be close to the cabin, tied, most likely, since it stayed where it was and didn't come looking for him.

He walked on past the weathered wood house, staying twenty yards or so away, pushing through the woods toward the west, heading out to the edge of the mountain, having seen a path near the front of the cabin that led that way through the woods.

He needed to know what else was nearby. And five minutes later, eighty yards past, straight west of Beth's cabin, Weisberg saw a much larger clearing, a vegetable garden, and a wide patch of land with another house on the far edge that seemed to look out and down off the mountain, for there he could see lights in the distance beyond and below the open land.

He stepped back deeper into woods, headed around toward Beth's land again, listening to the dog bark, thinking it sounded unsure of itself, and noticeably less alarmed.

Two minutes later Weisberg was north of the cabin close to the west end, and the dog was barking as though he knew his business, and now considered it serious.

Weisberg pulled the Colt from his pocket, twenty feet from the west end of the cabin, hearing the woman on the south side somewhere tell the dog to be quiet. She'd opened and closed the screen again, and it sounded as though she were standing on the porch. He heard her say, 'I'll get you in a minute. You better not tangle with the raccoons, 'cause if you do you'll regret it,' before she went in.

There hadn't been a car on that road the whole time Weisberg had been on the mountain, but as he stepped around the back of the cabin – the dog barking louder and faster, lunging against his chain – a car, or a truck, with the radio blaring, pulled around the curve by the cabin climbing up Black Mountain.

The Carter Family had just started singing, 'May that circle be unbroken, by and by, Lord, by and by', when Weisberg shot the dog in the chest, and sprinted around the cabin's north wall heading toward the east end.

The sound of singing had gotten faint and thin, something you'd have to strain after, when Weisberg heard the front door open and Beth Morland say, 'I'm coming to get you now.'

She screamed 'Shep!' a second later, and ran to where the dog lay dead – as Weisberg slipped through the screen door into Beth's living room.

It was lit with a kerosene lamp (even though he'd seen electric wires strung up from the road), and an old wire fan blew at the sofa, where a book had been laid face down and ice tea sweated in a glass.

He could hear Beth crying, two minutes later, stumbling back toward the cabin. He was listening in the guest room, squeezed under a narrow bed built tight to the floor, hidden too by a long denim dust ruffle that spread across the rug. He'd flattened his pack, wedging it between his shins, and he waited, breathing slowly, smiling in the dark.

Sixteen

B eth Morland had carried Shep into the tool shed near the west end of the cabin, and laid him on a tarpaulin. She'd stroked his ears, and kissed his forehead – then sprinted across to the house.

She was in shock, she knew that. From grief. From horror. From the sickening and surreal fact that Shep had been shot.

She couldn't make herself stop crying as she locked the front door and ran across the living room to close and lock the back window.

Questions she couldn't answer hammered at what was left of her brain – Who could've done it? Weisberg, the guy Ben named that morning? What would he do to her if it was? Where was he right then, whoever it was who shot Shep? – till she crushed her lips together, finally, to keep herself from some pitiful sound that made taking control even harder.

Tears had started sliding off her face as she rushed into her bedroom to lock the back window there. And when she stood in her living room again, back against the outside door, she felt more stranded and defenseless than she ever had before.

She knew that the guest-room window that faced the road was shuttered on the outside already, so she didn't need to worry about that. She'd kept it closed, and parked at a neighbor's so no one would know she was there.

The back windows in the kitchen and the bath were already closed and locked. The front window in the kitchen was shuttered on the outside. Nobody could get in that way, kitchen *or* bath.

Not unless they broke the glass in one of those back windows. And if they did, the sound of that would at least give her some warning.

Though what would she do if someone got in? Somebody

armed and experienced? A killer like this William Weisberg Ben said had murdered before.

Beth sat on the sofa, gulping air and shivering, gripping her elbows to keep her hands steady – seeing Shep with his chest blown apart, blood splattered on the shed, asking herself time after time how someone could be that cruel.

She told herself she was shaking at the viciousness, at the cold-blooded shooting of an innocent. But she knew it was fear too, beating in her bones, bringing her back to Weisberg.

Ben thought Weisberg was the man in the park. The one who'd searched Carl's house, and may actually have killed him. Who also might want her as a hostage, if he thought Ben had Carl's papers. Ben had told Beth he couldn't say more, to protect her from Weisberg. Making her feel completely cut off without enough information.

But how could Weisberg have found me? And what if he's here now, watching in the woods? What if he got into the house while I was in back with Shep?

Please, Lord, don't let it be that! I wouldn't know what to do.

Beth told herself she should've thought of that before. Though where he could've hidden she certainly didn't know. When there weren't closets or cabinets, only pegs and open shelves.

She told herself to think about the options. Including the one she'd been avoiding because of the dreams when she was young.

There'd been too many, for too many years, of teeth-rattling terrors hiding beneath her bed. Escaped murderers. Strangers trying to kill her. Why the dreams had had such power, Beth had never understood.

But she walked back to the bedroom anyway, heart shuddering in her throat, and turned the light on fast – just long enough to force herself to look under her bed with nearly the same bone-crumbling dread she'd felt when she was four.

The relief of finding no one there took her into the living room again, where she told herself to start with the guest room, then move on to the bath.

What could she do if he was in the cabin? All she had was a butcher knife. No phone. No gun. Though that might be a good thing. She didn't know how to use one, and it could've been turned on her.

She couldn't go to Bobby's mom and bring trouble on her. And if this guy was inside, he'd stop her anyway before she could get through the woods.

Go on and get it done. It's better to find him than let him surprise you, but take the knife too.

That could make it worse, though. It must be hard to stick a knife into someone, and get it past the bones. What if she couldn't even try? Weisberg could use it on her.

Go before the panic gets worse!

Beth still didn't start toward the guest room. She pushed her hair away from her face, then exhaled raggedly and leaned against the front door, covering her eyes with her hands. She couldn't risk barging in again, the way she had her bedroom. And she grabbed the flashlight off a hook by the door, then blew out the kerosene lamp, telling herself to picture the guest room, and think before she made a move.

It was even smaller than her room. Eight by eight at the most. Three empty corners, with the bed pushed tight against the fourth.

Behind the door, that's a possibility. That, and under the kid's bed. Though Uncle John built it so low no grown man could fit under there, or stay for more than a minute.

She couldn't think of anywhere else. And she stood beside the guest-room door – off to the left, close to the knob – and slowly pushed it open.

She swept the light around the room, craning her head to look around the door frame – seeing plain bare studs and old pine floorboards looking the way they should.

She took a deep breath, and stepped around the door – where no one was waiting. Then closed it quickly behind her, and looked behind her own bedroom door, before she walked through the living room toward the kitchen beyond.

She held her breath, as she swept the flashlight around the small stud-walled kitchen, standing carefully on the left side of the doorway, seeing what she expected – white sink under the window, tiny stove and refrigerator, no counters of any kind, old wooden table used for cooking and eating.

No one was hiding there. For which she thanked God.

Nothing was out of place.

And she walked through to the bathroom, which looked perfectly normal. Very hot, like the kitchen. Very muggy. Very still. Windows closed and locked.

The everydayness was comforting. The warm silent sense of security that made her feel safe enough to turn on the light – which was when she saw blood on her hands.

It was smeared on her arms. And her blouse, and her shorts. And she wondered why she hadn't noticed sooner, as she washed her arms off in the bathroom sink, and slipped on the gown she'd hung behind the door. She plugged the sink and filled it with cold water, and dropped her clothes in to soak.

She walked back to the living room, and lit the kerosene lamp. She liked the light of the old brass lantern, the soft, glowing globe in mid-air. The smell she didn't, so she lit a home-made candle Bobby's mother had scented with mint.

Beth sat on the sofa, drinking the last of her lukewarm tea while the fan blew on her face, wishing she'd locked the outside shutters across the back windows. They were solid wood like the ones in front, made for winterizing the cabin, so they locked on the inside.

She knew she couldn't do it in the dark. She'd have to take the wooden screens off the outside, raise the bottom windows and lower the tops (which wasn't easy when the wood was swollen in the summer), then lock the shutters on the top and bottom from inside the house.

They'd make it stifling. Horrible if it got to a hundred again. Better than being easy to attack, though. That went without saying. She'd have to do it in the morning after she'd talked to Ben, and had time to bury Shep.

Whoever shot Shep should be shot himself.

Except that he was still a human being. Even if there was no excuse for the viciousness of what he'd done.

How was she going to defend herself when she left to call Ben in the morning? She couldn't take time to bury Shep. It didn't make any sense.

She needed to get out of there as soon as it was light, when folks on the mountain started going to work. But how could she get to her car, half a mile up the mountain? He had to be watching the cabin, and he'd know how to stop her.

When I get home to Worthington, I'm going to learn to

*shoot, or study self-defence of some kind. I don't intend to
feel this helpless ever again.*

She told herself to get some sleep. But she still wasn't ready
to lie down. So she read for a while, *The Federalist Papers*,
trying to take her mind off Shep, and calm her body down.

She found herself thinking about him anyway. The rainy
night he arrived, a scruffy-looking half-grown dog standing
on her porch, with a sense of who he was already she could
see right in his eyes.

*He saw himself as a working dog. A dog about town, who
took responsibility. He liked me a lot, and was glad I took
him in. He obeyed my rules, but he wasn't a bootlicker. And
I'll never have another dog I love as much as Shep.*

Beth's chin trembled first, and then she started crying.

But she brushed her teeth at the kitchen sink.

And went into her room.

A few minutes before two, when she was in between her
sheets with an oscillating fan blowing across most of her –
she thought she heard a noise somewhere in the front of the
house.

She pulled the top sheet up to her chin, listening hard in
the darkness, then turned off the fan, straining every possible
nerve to hear what she couldn't see.

There . . . somebody's in the house.

Where, I can't tell. Though . . .

The doorknob turned. She recognized the click.

Then the hinges squeaked – right before the ceiling light
went on above her head.

It blinded Beth for a second, then left her squinting at the
tall man who'd talked to her in the park. Without the hat now.
Without the sunglasses. Broad features, icy eyes, thick dark
hair falling on his forehead – large square hands aiming a
handgun right at her face.

'The dog was the protective type. He wouldn't shut up.'

Beth didn't say anything. She lay where she was and stared.

'Get up.'

Nothing changed in that hot, still room.

Bill Weisberg stepped to the bed and ripped the sheet off
her body. 'You and I need to understand each other. I'm not
playing games. My life is at stake, and I need information
I'm going to get from you now. You can tell me what I want

to know as soon as I ask, or you can waste my time, and suffer because of that. I won't tell you what to do twice, and every wrong choice you make will bring consequences that hurt. Do I make myself clear?'

Beth nodded.

'Say it.'

'Yes.'

'Get up and walk to the kitchen.'

Weisberg shoved her when she got to the bedroom door.

And as soon as he told her to stand still in the kitchen, he bound her wrists behind her, then pushed her down in a wooden chair drawn up to the kitchen table, and tied her arms to the frame.

He pulled a hand drill from his army pack and drilled two holes in the studs above the shower tile – one at the foot of the six-foot tub, the other above the shower head.

He screwed two ringbolts into the holes, the bolts already fastened to two heavy chains. He undid the ropes tying Beth to the chair and grabbed her by the upper arms, her hands still tied behind her back. He dragged her into the bathroom, pushed her into the tub, then wrapped the chains above her elbows, fastening them together with a combination lock.

'Don't move.' Weisberg laughed, apparently at the fact that she couldn't. And then said, 'I'll be back.'

He pulled a chair in from the kitchen and set it in the bathroom facing the tub. He took off his black windbreaker and threw it through the door on to the kitchen floor. He wiped his face with Beth's used washcloth, after dipping it in the sink.

He leaned back, in his cane-back chair, and smiled an easy, self-satisfied smile as he pulled a pack of Chesterfield's out of his shirt pocket. 'Do you have Carl Walker's papers?'

'I don't know anything about them.'

'And you'd tell me if you did?' He was still smiling, a cold sharp predatory grin, when he blew his match out with a stream of smoke, before he inhaled.

'What choice do I have?'

'*That* was an excellent response. The next answer's equally important. Who has them now?'

'I don't know. I really don't. Why did you put me in the tub?'

'It'll keep the bathroom neater. I hate to make an unnecessary mess. That's a lovely gown, by the way. Egyptian long-staple cotton is the finest in the world.' He'd leaned over into the tub and was rubbing the fabric of the front hem between his thumb and forefinger. 'I'd say this is Egyptian. The sheerness, the softness, the fineness of the weave. Cotton was more valuable than silk *or* wool through much of world history. Most people here don't know that. Insular. Cultureless. Modern America. The land I know too well.'

'Why do you live here if you hate it that much?'

'I've had work of importance to do. For *that* one endures deprivation.' He paused as though he were expecting her to speak, then continued when she didn't in a low languid voice, while he scratched his left armpit. 'Yours is a shallow, self-satisfied nation without intellectual curiosity beyond the activities of getting and spending. There's an almost unwavering conviction that the rest of the world is of little importance. It's arrogance to an unprecedented degree. I take it you agree?'

Beth shook her head, but didn't choose to speak.

'Baseball cards. Backyard barbecues. Cars the size of aircraft carriers intended to scream "money". The adulation of sports figures. American television's mewling mediocrities. Music of cretinous barbarity. A view of the world based largely on advertising. These are not admirable accomplishments in the eyes of the world's wiser nations.'

'There're plenty of people here who have other interests. You don't want to be objective.' She was facing the outside of the tub, her arms drawn behind her, her gown pulled tight across her breasts.

Weisberg sat quietly staring at her calves and ankles, at the contours of her thighs too, underneath the sheer gown, smiling at the spaghetti-strapped bodice, while he tapped ashes off his cigarette on to the bathroom floor.

He stood then, still smiling, Chesterfield dangling from his lips, looking directly into her eyes as he slowly ran his hands down both sides of her body, letting his thumbs press against her breasts, tracing the ridges of her ribs, grasping the wings of her pelvis, clasping them tightly in his hands. 'So.' He laughed quickly and sat down again, leaning his chair back as he gazed at her neck. 'How long have you known Carl?'

Beth's breath had caught in her throat, and she couldn't make herself speak. When she saw him start to stand again, she managed to whisper, 'Not very long. And not very well.'

'Be specific. I told you that before!'

'I don't know. Something like three years.'

'How long precisely?'

'Since he moved to Worthington. I think it was the fall of '54. I want you to keep your hands off me.'

'Do you?' He smiled at her, scratching his heavy, black, two-day beard along both sides of his chin. 'That's not the usual reaction I get. And you're not in a position to bargain, are you? What did he say about his past?'

'That he's from Maine. That he studied languages in college. That he was in the army during World War II, and had a desk job in Washington.'

'Tell me precisely what he said about his work.'

'Nothing. That it was anything but exciting. That he barely got through basic training, and was glad to get out of the army.'

'What did he say about Sylvia?'

'Nothing much. That he liked the restaurant. He only met her through his sister, and she died last year.'

'That's all?'

'Yes.'

'You're sure?'

'Yes! He barely mentioned her name.'

'What do *you* know about Sylvia?'

'Nothing much. She's hard-working. She's a conscientious mother. She runs the inn really well. Bobby likes working for her. We talk about food and the weather. About books we've read, and movies we've seen, and that's pretty much it.'

'What has she said about her daughter's father?'

'He was a career army officer who was stationed in Japan. They had one last R and R visit together the September before he died in a Jeep accident in Japan. I think in '47. That she was pregnant with Sarah when he died.'

'It's a lie, of course. Intended to preserve her good name.' Weisberg blew smoke out in a long thin stream, tapping ash beside the chair. 'But then you guessed that.'

Neither of them said anything as he dipped the end of his cigarette into the water in the sink and dropped it on to the floor.

'I'm the father. And Sylvia's real name is Susannah Adams. I had to leave her shortly after the war, for reasons I couldn't control, and I've been looking for her for years. She was paying me back for leaving her, and she's kept me from knowing my daughter, though that's now come to an end.'

'She left *you*, is what you're saying.'

'No, that's not what I said.'

'She's left you this time.'

'What happened is that—'

'The fact that you murdered Carl, and are tormenting me, makes it look like she had a good reason.'

'Don't talk about what you don't know! You have no reason to say I murdered Carl. Tell me where she is.'

'How would I know? Why would she tell me?'

'*You* know. She would've told that chef you like so much.'

'She didn't! She went off without telling anyone. She's got a business to run. She can't disappear.'

Weisberg was lighting another cigarette, moving his chair toward Beth, when he said, 'Ah, yes,' as though he'd remembered something he wished he'd thought of earlier. He picked up his army pack, and pulled out a silver flask. 'Single-malt Scotch from the Isle of Islay. You know where that is, do you?'

'An island off the—'

'West coast of Scotland. This is a fairly peaty whisky. That's what the Scots call it, of course, whisky, not Scotch. This one's much regarded in the most discerning circles. It's time now, sweetie-pie. I gave you a breather. Tell me how Susannah gets in touch with the inn.'

'All I know is that after she left she called a real-estate company, or a hardware store, or some place like that, and had them get a message to Bobby. Now she calls in to payphones in different places at specific times that change every day. She hasn't told Bobby where she is, and says she doesn't intend to. I don't know where all she's called him, and it wouldn't matter if I did, because it changes all the time.'

Weisberg was leaning forward with his elbows on his knees, grinning slyly at Beth, his pale-blue shirt yellow under the arms, his throat wet with sweat, the sour sharp smell of him infecting the stale stuffy room. 'What did Carl say about me?'

'Nothing. Not your name, or anything about you. I never

knew you existed. I still don't know who you are, or why you're doing this to me.'

'He must've talked about the war.'

'Only that he got stuck in Washington in some kind of bureau and never saw action. I told you that already.'

Weisberg put his flask on the edge of the sink, raised the hem of her thin batiste gown, and squatted down by the tub. He licked the front of Beth's thighs. Then straightened up, smiled at her, and lit another kitchen match, which he blew out a second later and laid on the skin next to her spine beside her left shoulder blade.

Beth gasped and stared at him. The smell of him, when he'd reached around to get at her back, made her feel sick.

Then he licked the delicate skin underneath her armpit, and pinched her left nipple hard enough to make it hurt. 'Where are his papers?'

'I don't know! I told you!'

'You can do better than that! You know you can. Come on, Beth, don't make this hard on yourself.' He took the end of his cigarette, tapped the ash on to the floor, and touched it to the inside of her left elbow close to where it was bound by the chain.

She screeched before she could stop herself.

And he leaned behind her and kissed the skin he'd only that second burned. 'Come on, sweet pea, talk to me so I can let you go.'

'All I know is that Ben Reese was looking for papers at Carl's house, and didn't find anything. He went to his office too, and didn't come up with anything there either.' Two tears had started toward her chin, and she was hoping he hadn't noticed as she sighed and gritted her teeth.

Weisberg didn't say anything more. He sat down in the chair. He drank from his flask, and gazed at the tile up above the tub. He leaned his chair back, balanced on two legs, and smoked intently for a minute or two, one puff followed fast by another – till he crashed the chair's front legs down on the heart pine floor. 'What about the fat guy? What do you know about him?'

'I don't know who you mean.'

'The friend. The professor. Reese's buddy in Hillsdale.'

'I don't know him. I've never met him. I've never—'

'You know something!'

'Nothing I can think of. Why would Ben Reese tell me about him?'

'What's his name? You know that.'

'I don't. It's the truth! I don't know anything about him.'

Weisberg stood up, leaning toward her, the smell of his body twice as strong as his cigarette – and then he rolled the burning tip of his unfiltered Chesterfield across the back of her knee.

'*No!*'

'No?' His eyes forced hers down, as his hot damp sweet-sour breath settled across her face.

'How can you do this to anybody?'

'You don't like it? You're sure?' He was kissing the back of her thigh, sliding his tongue up the quivering flesh, standing then, kissing the front of her neck, licking the skin stretched between her breasts.

'The only friend of Ben's I've heard about *is* a professor, but I don't know anything about him except that he was in the army during World War Two. Carl told me that months ago. That a professor friend of Dr Reese's had worked somewhere in England. Is that the one you mean? I don't even know his name.'

'Richard West. Does that ring a bell?'

'No. I don't think so . . .'

'What did he do in the war?'

'I don't know. Carl never said.'

'Where was he in England?'

'I can't remember the name.'

'But you've heard it?'

'Carl said it. Park something, but—'

'Bletchley Park?'

'Maybe. Carl mentioned it a long time ago.'

'And you know the significance of Bletchley, do you?'

'No. I could see Carl thought it was interesting, but I never—'

'The truth has yet to be revealed to the public, but the British broke codes and ciphers there with American help. The Germans transmitted military messages all over the world, different code versions for different branches of the service, different codes every day, by generating random-number codes on rotor-based machines the Allies called "Enigmas". Being able to break the codes was one of the two or three most critical factors in enabling the Allies to win the war. I'm not overstating it, by the way. You can take that as read.'

'I don't know anything about it.'

'Would you have studied it if the information had been released?'

'I don't know. Probably not.'

'No curiosity, is that it? No intellectual interest in the forces that shape your world? I suppose I shouldn't be surprised. You are, after all, a Midwestern American. More concerned with making "bread-and-butter" pickles, and watching Milty on TV.'

'*My* area of interest is the eighteenth century. The Founding, and the writing of the Constitution. Living through the Second World War is something I'd rather forget.'

'So, there *are* history teachers in this country with a modicum of interest in the subject? That *is* more than I expected. Perhaps I've underestimated you. Though, with the level of education here, your attainments are bound to be modest.'

'I'd say we're holding our own.'

'Would you? You've fallen behind in the space race. We'll see where you are in another twenty years. You're entirely too comfortable, and much too sentimental. It leads you to lower standards, and prevents you from placing sufficient pressure on students to make them perform. Take your attitude to immigration. You've consistently allowed large numbers of foreign nationals across your borders whose stated purpose is to destroy your political system, and yet you—'

'What foreign nationals?'

'Have you read about espionage in America in the course of the twentieth century? Japanese? German? Soviet?'

'Not much.'

'You offer your enemies asylum, and are surprised when they take advantage. It's a charmingly naive attitude. One which many have used to advantage.'

'At least people want to come here. We don't get murdered by our own government while trying to escape, like Russians, Hungarians, East Germans, and Czechs.'

'That's a predictably superficial riposte. But what can one expect?' Weisberg smiled, but didn't say more. He crushed his cigarette under his shoe, settled his arms across his stomach, and told Beth to be quiet, that he needed a short nap. 'But first, I shall ask a technical question. When I hid myself while you searched the cabin, and I let you get into bed and relax, thinking yourself safe for the present, did that make it more alarming when I appeared afterwards?'

'Why do you want to know?'

'Answer the question.'

'Maybe. Where were you hiding?'

'Maybe?'

'Perhaps.'

'Answer me!'

'Yes, I suppose so.'

'That was my working thesis. I like to evaluate these decisions once they've been put into effect.' Weisberg slid his chair sideways, closer to the sink, and leaned back, his head against the end of a pine stud. He turned off the overhead light, locked his arms across his chest, closed his eyes, and exhaled slowly, settling himself in the chair.

His mouth fell open a few minutes later, while Beth Morland, in a stifling room, shivered in the tub. From fear, from shock, from what was in front of her making her feel sick.

Nothing had prepared her. She'd never seen evil like this, much less thought she'd be touched by it. She hadn't watched anyone close up who enjoyed intimidation the way he did, or took such pleasure in inflicting pain. Not in her civilized secure life in small-town Ohio, where the people she knew, and passed on the street, said, 'Please,' and 'Thank you,' and smiled at small children, and petted other people's dogs.

But what if she'd done harm? She didn't know enough not to say the wrong things. Ben had been right not to tell her what he knew. It'd made her mad that morning, and yet now she could say, 'I don't know more,' and Weisberg could see it was true.

It's the eyes, when he's touching me. I watch him waiting to do more. He's turned himself into something vile, and he's proud of what he's become.

He's going to keep hurting me too. Regardless of what I do. He likes it too much to stop.

But what he'd do when he was done with the questions and hadn't gotten what he wanted – those possibilities turned her bones to water. Death. Rape. Mutilation. In descending order of horror. Making her pray harder than she had since Bobby Chambers was in combat. For wisdom. For safety. For strength. That she'd be kept from saying anything she shouldn't. That Ben would be able to stop him. That he and Bobby, and Bobby's mother (who was not much more than a hundred yards from Weisberg), would be kept safe too.

The burns burned. Her shoulders ached. And as she stared at Weisberg in the light from the kitchen – at his broad head, hanging on his chest now, at the square hands clasping his elbows, at the big bones and broad shoulders and powerful-looking legs – she made a sound she couldn't call back, something like a soft quick groan.

Weisberg's head jerked up – and the fury in his eyes seared hers. 'You couldn't shut up for fifteen minutes?'

She almost apologized. Then stopped. She forced herself to straighten her shoulders and stare over his head.

He picked up his flask, then lit another cigarette, and pushed his hair off his face. 'You think I can make you wish you had?'

'What?'

'You heard me. You ready for what comes next?'

'I'd like a drink of water.'

'Whose house is this?'

'Mine.'

'Not your mother's?'

'My aunt gave it to me. My father didn't want my mother to have it.'

'Sounds like a reasonable man. Doesn't want some shabby hovel that he has to pay to keep up. Where's the closest house?'

'Behind this, through a section of woods, farther away from the road.'

'How do you drive back to it?'

'You can't. There's a walking path through the woods.'

'You're not telling me the truth.' He was blowing smoke rings and playing with a match, keeping his eyes on her face. 'You aren't fooling me, sweetie pie. You know what I need to know. Staying alive will get considerably more painful if you don't cooperate soon. Let's try again, shall we? Let's start with something simple. Who lives in the house down the path?'

'Bobby's mother.'

'She live alone?'

'She used to. As far as I know she still does.'

'Good. You can do this. You can keep yourself from getting hurt. How old is she? And does she have a car?'

'She doesn't have a car, and I'd say she's in her late sixties. Could I have a drink of water?'

'I don't know. Maybe. Sure. I'm not such a bad guy, am I? I don't want to hurt you.'

'I'd say you enjoy it.'

Weisberg laughed as he held a glass up to her lips and let her take two small sips – before he drank the rest of the water, and dropped the glass on the floor. 'Oh . . . now, see what I've done? I should've been more careful. It's so easy to cut yourself, or somebody else.' He laid the point of a broken piece near a vein in Beth's right arm below the inside of the elbow, and pushed it in slowly, cutting a narrow gash. 'Oh, look at that. See, I was right. I should've been more careful.'

Weisberg walked into the kitchen, and Beth could hear him opening drawers as though he were looking for something specific.

He came back with a butcher knife and laid it on the edge of the sink. 'I want you to listen to me very carefully. You must tell me now, *right* now, what it is you're hiding.'

'Nothing! I told you already. I've told you everything I know!'

'Who's this Ben Reese? Why's he searching Carl's house and sticking his nose into everything else?'

'He knew Carl from the Symphony. They had seats next to each other. Carl never missed a concert, and when he did, this last Friday, Ben came looking for him, afraid he might be sick. He couldn't get his phone number from information, and he drove down to take a look.'

'I'm the wrong person to lie to, sweetie. You should know that by now.'

'I'm not lying!'

'You're not telling me everything.' He lit another cigarette, took a couple of drags, then French-inhaled while he watched her drawn face tense. 'Which would you prefer? Cigarette burns on both cheeks? Or getting your face sliced with a shard of glass *and* a dull knife?'

He was standing by then, holding the cigarette and the knife.

She watched him walk toward her, and said, 'Carl sent me a letter before he died with another letter inside that he'd addressed to Ben Reese. That's not exactly right. Reese's name and Hillsdale, Ohio were written on it, but not his street address. I don't know what was in it. I'd never met Reese before that. I knew who he was. I knew Carl's seat was next to his at the symphony, but that's all I knew. Carl asked me to mail the letter to Reese, to find out Reese's address and send it off right away. That he'd been rushing to leave town, and hadn't had time to get Reese's address.'

'When was that?'

'Carl mailed it the Wednesday night before he died, and then—'

'Where'd he mail it?'

'Worthington.'

'And you mailed the letter to Reese when?'

'Late Thursday afternoon. Reese got it Saturday.'

'What did the letter say?'

'I don't know, word for word. Something like he wanted to talk to Reese, and if Reese were planning to leave on vacation would he wait till Carl had gotten back and had a chance to talk to him.'

'You know more than that.' Weisberg swallowed a mouthful of Scotch, smiling at Beth, blowing smoke in her face, while he scratched the inside of his thigh.

'Only that Ben got a package from Carl on Saturday too.'

'You said he didn't have his address!'

'He didn't. He mailed it to Reese's office. From somewhere else in the state.'

'From where in the state?'

'I don't remember. Marietta, maybe. I never saw the package.'

'And what was in this package of Carl's?'

'A letter with numbers of some kind, and there were two books too.'

'Anything else?'

'No.'

'No photographs?'

'No!'

'What numbers? And what books?'

'I don't know what numbers. A string of numbers that didn't mean anything to Ben. The books were Russian. Tolstoy, I think. I don't remember which ones, but—'

'Written in Russian or English?'

'English, I think, but I don't know that for sure. Ben didn't know why he'd sent them. It didn't make any sense. That's all I know, I swear to God.'

'Is there significance in that?'

'In what?'

'The oath that rolls so trippingly off middle-American tongues.'

'I can't say in general. I mean something by it.'

'Do you.' He laughed lazily and looked at her as though he were a sophisticated older brother patronizing an idiot girl. 'What else haven't you told me?'

'Nothing. I left town right after that, when Ben Reese told me I should. I don't know anything else.'

'When do you next get in touch with Reese to tell him you're all right?'

'I don't know what you mean.'

'Don't start that crap again! He would not let you stay down here, without being reachable by phone, if there weren't a plan for making sure you're all right. Does Bobby's mom have a phone? I didn't see any phone lines.'

'No. I drive into town.'

'When?'

'No special—'

'*When!*'

'I call Ben at seven a.m., and Bobby at ten p.m.'

'Congratulations.' He leaned back in the chair, smoked the rest of the cigarette, watching the smoke curl between the two of them. He drained the flask, then put the cap on it, and dropped it into his army pack. 'I shall sleep for a couple of hours, then make your morning call.'

'I have to go to the bathroom.'

'You are *in* the bathroom.'

'You know what I mean. I have to use the toilet.'

'You're in the tub, aren't you? This is no time to be fastidious. I shall stretch out on your bed for the night.' He was smiling, lighting another cigarette, putting the pack and the matches in his pockets. 'Aren't you glad I didn't let you drink a whole glass of water?'

'Please!'

'Good night, Miss Morland. Sweet dreams.'

Seventeen

B en had been reading in bed that morning, long before the call came, going through his synopsis for references to Arthur Lennox, the FBI agent Carl had known at Arlington Hall.

The time had come to find Lennox, and tell him about Carl's death, as well as the new evidence. The pictures of Weisberg handing something to a Soviet agent and getting something different back. Climbing into a car too with another known agent. Hiding papers under a trash can, apparently using it as a dead drop.

Unless Lennox could prove what was in the envelopes, it still might not hold up in court. But that would depend on what Lennox had on Weisberg. And what that was Ben didn't know.

It was probably the photo of the list of machine ciphers they'd solved at Arlington that stood the best chance of convicting him. It was in his handwriting, and the KGB had changed all those codes shortly after he'd written it. Whether Lennox could prove Weisberg handed it on Ben didn't know. Maybe just writing that list and having it on him, outside of Arlington, would be incriminating enough.

The paper in Carl's shoe ought to help tie Weisberg to Carl's death, with Weisberg's handwriting, and Carl's dated message. And the police had the marks on Carl's wrists, finally, and bark under his nails. But that would have to be linked to Weisberg with real physical evidence.

Whether the sheriff had photographed the tree, Richard hadn't said, and Ben told himself to call and ask before he tried to get Lennox.

That was when the phone rang – at four forty-five a.m.

June Morland, Beth's mother, had taken Ben at his word and called when she'd gotten home. The widow next door had been taken ill, and she'd driven her to the hospital the previous morning, and had only just gotten home. June was extremely worried about Beth as well, especially with Beth's father away at a conference in England.

Ben told her Beth was safe, but for reasons he couldn't yet explain fully, it was important for him to know if anyone had called, or come by the house, trying to find Beth.

Then he heard about Amanda Allan's call to June Morland on Monday, and that Mrs Morland had told Amanda what Ben devoutly wished she hadn't – that Beth had said she was in Wheaton, Illinois visiting her old roommate, but that, interestingly enough, a family friend had thought she'd seen Beth at a vegetable stand in Black Mountain. June had given her that friend's name too, and directions to the cabin. And Ben started planning his drive to Black Mountain.

June Morland had been uneasy enough herself that she'd called Beth's roommate in Illinois, and she was made more uncomfortable still because she thought Ginnie was covering for Beth when she'd said Beth was out shopping. June was afraid Beth had run away with Bobby. Which Ben assured her she hadn't. He told her again that Beth was fine, that she'd left town to get away from circumstances surrounding Carl's death.

June questioned, and Ben sidestepped – till she finally said she supposed she'd have to trust him. She'd grown up with David Marshall, and he spoke very highly of Ben, but the situation frightened her. Ben told her not to tell anyone anything about Beth, for her sake, above all. And to call him, or Bobby, or Richard West, a close friend of Ben's, if anyone asked again. He made sure she'd written down the phone numbers, and then got off the phone.

Ben was ready to leave by five thirty-five – having eaten a chicken sandwich, and phoned Richard West to tell him Beth's mom might call – which was when Richard told him the sheriff had photographed the tree.

That had needed to be done, and Ben was glad they had. But what he found more useful right then was the payphone number at the Black Mountain gas station he'd gotten from Beth the day before. He could at least call her there at seven, on his way to North Carolina, when she'd be there to phone

him, and tell her to get away from the cabin and go someplace safe.

*That's if she's OK right now, and does actually phone. We
know she was fine at ten last night, and that's better than it
could've been.*

Ben had picked up his .30-06, and was reaching for his
musette bag, when the phone by the rocking chair rang again.

It was only twenty of six. Too early for Beth or Bobby. It
was probably Richard again, maybe with news from the sheriff,
so when Ben picked up the receiver he said, 'What, Richard?'
to amuse him.

It wasn't Richard.

It was William Weisberg. Calling from Black Mountain. He
started by saying, in a cold, arrogant, matter-of-fact voice,
that if Ben wished to see Beth or Bobby's mother alive anytime
in the future, he was to get himself to Beth's cabin in Black
Mountain by midnight. Eighteen hours would be sufficient,
allowing time to spare. Ben was to bring Carl Walker's papers
and photographs. Negatives, copies, and originals too – all of
them, without exception. He was to come alone. He was not
to tell anyone where he was going, or why.

'Do not attempt to tell me you don't have Walker's papers.
I have no doubt Carl got them into your hands, as evidenced
by Miss Morland's letter with an enclosure to you. If you
circumvent my instructions, two innocent women will die
extremely painful deaths. I expect you to believe that, Dr
Reese. I will *not* be incarcerated again in a US federal prison.'

'How do I know Beth's alive now?'

'Hold on.'

Ben did – planning ahead, thinking what had to get done
– till he heard Beth, telling him to do exactly what Weisberg
said.

Ben could hear the panic and the exhaustion. The fear, the
dry mouth, the disorientation. And when he hung up, he kicked
his phone book across his kitchen floor.

'I'm going *with* you, or *without* you, and I'll save you time
if we go together. I know the route. I know the mountains. I
can get us there quicker than—'

'Look, Bobby, if—'

'Save your breath, Ben. I'm going, one way or the other.

It's my momma. It's my lady friend. I've known Beth since we was children, and if you think I'm staying here, you got another think coming!'

Ben was holding the receiver with his left shoulder, staring at Alderton's only Xerox machine, his jaw shifted off to the left. '*If* you agree to one condition.'

'Yeah? What might that be?'

'I'm in charge. If you come, you do it the way I say. I'll explain some background stuff later that'll make that make more sense.'

Bobby didn't say anything for a minute. Then told Ben he agreed. 'But I got a condition too. I b'lieve we should take my car. No offense, but I've seen yours, and my Chevy's a good bit newer and faster.'

Ben laughed and said, 'Actually, I wish we could, but it doesn't make sense. The cops told you not to leave town, and you can bet they're keeping an eye on you, at least off and on. If your car disappears, they'll start looking, and you know they'll be all over us not too many hours down the road. There *is* a way you can help, though.'

'My, I surely am glad I'm not totally useless!'

'Bring something to eat and drink so we don't have to stop.'

Bobby said he'd get on to it. And Ben asked his address in Columbus, while he put the next page of Richard's long decryption into the Xerox machine. He repeated Bobby's directions, then said, 'One other thing. Wear dark clothes and shoes. I'll get to your place as soon as I can.'

Ben hung up, while stacking copies for the muniment room, extra photos included, hoping ineffectually that a second set was better than one. Even though he couldn't see a way to keep from taking the originals down to Black Mountain.

I better not call Richard now. Not till we're leaving Bobby's. If I phone him earlier, he'll kick up a horrific fuss and try to come too.

They'd been driving straight south on Route 23, and had gotten almost to Chillicothe, when the first blow landed. Bobby started to feel sick to his stomach, and Ben had to stop the car.

Bobby had a fever too, half an hour later, high and getting higher – making him doze, making him disoriented, only able to shiver, and squirm, and ask to get out of the car.

When he got back in the fifth time, Ben looked at his watch, then stepped hard on the gas, shifting as fast as the Plymouth would let him, heading south toward Portsmouth.

Bobby told him not to stop any more. To just hand him a bag from the picnic basket, the plastic bag for garbage. They couldn't afford for him to hold them back, not with Weisberg's deadline.

Ben had just said, 'I can't reach the basket without stopping,' when he saw a black patrol car coming up fast behind them.

The lights were on, but the siren wasn't. And Ben said, 'Nuts! The Highway Patrol.'

'What?' Bobby was pushing himself up in the seat, trying to see out the small oval window above the back seat.

Ben had pulled off the road, and turned off the ignition before he told Bobby not to worry, that he'd do the talking. He cranked the window down, and heard himself say, 'What seems to be the trouble, officer?' Which irritated Ben immensely – the stock phrase, repeated by everyone getting pulled over in every film ever made.

The trooper didn't react one way or the other. Tall, tailored, military-looking, polite but severe the way they're taught – he gazed at Ben appraisingly, before he asked for his driver's license, and added the usual question, 'You know how fast you were going, do ya?'

Ben said, 'Fifty-five?' Thinking, that's a relief at least. Better than an APB from the county cops tracking Bobby.

'You an optimist, are ya, by nature?'

'I wouldn't say so, no. Why?' *Just what I was hoping for, a cop who thinks he's a comic.*

'I clocked you at sixty-two.'

'I didn't think I was going that fast. My friend's sick, and I was talking to him, seeing how I could help. I'm surprised the Plymouth'll do more than sixty.'

'Sixty'd be speeding. So what's the matter with him?' The trooper was looking past Ben, bent over and staring in, trying to see Bobby's face.

'Stomach flu, I think. Either that or food poisoning. Sick as a dog, that's for sure.'

'No drinking involved with the both of you?'

'Nope. Absolutely not.'

The trooper nodded and walked away, looking at Ben's license.

Ben was watching his own watch. Tapping the wheel five minutes later, saying, 'Come on, come *on*, *come on!*'

Bobby opened his door and climbed out, slowly and deliberately, stepping away in slow motion, in time, however, to be sick again on weeds ten feet from the road.

The trooper was talking to Ben by then, saying, 'Your record's clean up till now, and I'll let you go with a warning. Do yourself a favor. Keep your eye on the speedometer. The warning'll be on your record, and next time you'll get ticketed.'

'Thank you, officer. I appreciate it.'

'Your friend need medical attention? You're gonna be a long way from a doc, or a hospital either one, once you pass Portsmouth and get down to east Kentucky.'

'I think he'll be fine. We're hoping it's twelve-hour flu.'

Bobby mumbled, 'Amen.'

And the trooper actually smiled. He said, 'You drive careful now,' and adjusted his broad-brimmed hat as he started toward his car.

Ben leaned over the bench seat, found a plastic bag in the picnic basket, and handed it to Bobby. Then he eased the Plymouth into gear, saying, 'Let's hope he doesn't follow us down to the state line.'

He didn't. The trooper pulled a U-turn, scattering gravel behind him, while Ben smiled at his rear-view mirror and shoved the car into second. 'You think you could get some sleep? When we get down toward North Carolina, I'll need directions from you.'

The next blow fell four hours later, after they'd wound down Kentucky's eastern edge, and were almost to Virginia's western tip – the narrow, jagged mountainous strip before east Tennessee. The Plymouth's left front tire blew, throwing them into the northbound lane, almost into a pick-up truck with car parts piled in the back.

Ben fought the wheel like a bit in the mouth of a bolting horse and just barely kept the Plymouth out of the northbound ditch. When the dust had settled, and the road was clear, he limped the car across it to the berm next to the southbound lane.

He didn't move for a minute, after he'd turned off the engine.
He sat with his eyes closed, and exhaled slowly, knowing how
close they'd come. He shook his head and said, 'Thank you,'
so quietly Bobby couldn't have heard. Before he got out and
looked at the tire.

When he climbed back in, he drank two cups of water.
Then he and Bobby sat for a second, scorched by the sunlight
hammering down on the metal around them, on the road ahead
where heat waves shimmered, where dust-covered weeds strag-
gled at the edges, as flies buzzed, landing on Bobby, brushed
off by an uncertain hand.

'What happened? Why we settin' off the road?'

'A tire blew and I don't have a spare. Which makes me
want to spit.'

'I can help. We'll patch it right up, you'll see. I'll be OK
in a second.' Bobby was trying to pick his head off the felt-
covered doorpost, pushing himself to sit up with a slow
floundering hand.

'There's a four-inch hole in the tire *and* the tube, and we've
got to find a new one. There's no town coming up anytime soon,
so I'll have to run back to the last one and see what I can do.'

Ben could still see it when he closed his eyes, four or five
miles back. A half-dead town dying painfully. A short string
of ramshackle houses, long unpainted, collapsing on themselves. One boarded-up Esso station. A dilapidated diner,
blistered with peeling paint, closed probably, from what he
remembered, a rusted Chevy on blocks by the door waiting
for who knew what.

Ben poured tea in a paper cup for Bobby, while he watched
Bobby's eyes try to focus on the glove compartment. 'You
OK, Bobby? You didn't hit your head?'

'Yep. Not that I know of.'

'You feel like sipping some iced tea? You don't want to get
dehydrated. Anyway, I won't be long. If you want to sit in
the shade by those trees, I can help you get there, but I can't
drive the car any closer.'

Bobby nodded, and swallowed a mouthful of iced tea, before
he said, 'You go on. I can do it myself.'

That set Ben free to start the run back.

He didn't take time to stretch the way he normally did, he
ran – looking at his watch, wiping sweat from his face, feeling

the strain in his shot-up left leg after the first mile, calculating the time they'd lost, telling himself worrying wouldn't help, to just pray he didn't make stupid mistakes and did what he could do.

He'd probably gone another three miles when he climbed around a tight right-hand curve and saw the first house, off on the left, sitting back by itself – a never-painted silver-wood cabin with a rusted-metal roof, which covered the shed-roof porch too that stretched the width of the house.

There was an old crank washer up on the porch, leaning on the uneven floor next to a tattered sofa – sunken, shredded, stuffing sticking out – covered with cats of various colors curled out of the sun.

Disintegrating cars had collapsed around the house, twenty at least, possibly more, rusted cans and corroded barrels scattered in between. Chickens pecked in the dry red dirt, and an old hound dog lay in the shade of the porch, scratching fleas and biting at a tick.

The pick-up truck in front looked like it still might run. And just beyond it was a dented maroon Dodge with a human back bent across the engine underneath a rusted hood that was propped open on a stick.

'Excuse me,' Ben said, thirty feet away, dropping to a walk, rubbing his left thigh.

The only reaction came from the dog, the black and white and rust-colored hound, who dragged himself out from under the porch to stare coolly at Ben.

'Excuse me. I wonder if you could help me. I blew a tire up the road, and need to find a spare.'

A short, thin, leathery man in grease-covered dungarees and a torn blue work shirt raised himself in front of the Dodge, wiping his hands on a rag. 'Can't hep you there none. Nothin' in town neither. Not since the Esso closed.'

'Is there anything else nearby? Close enough to run to?'

'Nope.'

'I've got somebody sick in the car, and we've got to get to North Carolina as soon as we can tonight.'

'Nothin' till Kingsport. And once you do git your car on the road, you got yourself some hard going, with the mountains and all comin' up. They can git real treacherous at night, specially if a fog sets in.'

'So we've gotta get moving fast. Right?'

'You reckon you could patch your tire? Git you down the road a ways.' He wiped sweat from his eyes with the back of a hand, then looked away from Ben. 'I might hep you with that.'

'The tire and the inner tube are both shot. It's a '47 Plymouth a lot like this. This a '48 Dodge?'

'Yep. Bought it off a fella I know just this past week. Sideswiped a telephone pole with it, and I'm fixin' it up to sell.' The man had lost his two front teeth, and seemed to be trying to keep his lip down to cover-up the gap.

'You willing to sell me the spare off the Dodge? I think it'd fit my car.'

'Reckon it would, yeah. Same chassis. Most all the rest of it too. But I ain't got no spare to sell.'

'What about a tire off the car? It really is an emergency. We've got to get to Asheville tonight. It sounds stupid to say, but it *is* a matter of life and death. I'll pay you more than the tire's worth. Extra, on top of that, if you drive me back to my car.'

'Don't know 'bout that.' He was rolling a cigarette from a tin of Buglers, looking at the beat-up Dodge, shaking his head slowly. 'Dodge don't run. Truck's got an oil leak. Not real bad, but not real slow neither. Hate to take it too far till I can git to workin' on it. And the treads on these here, you cain't rightly say how far they're gonna take ya. They ain't brand new, that's for sure.'

'Bald would be generous. But any port in a storm, right?'

'Yep. The mule you've got's gotta take you on. Though I cain't say I care a whole lot for mules.' He laughed then, and coughed, fixing his eyes on Ben.

Ben smiled back, before he said, 'I'm prob'ly a little over four miles down the road, so that shouldn't strain the truck too much, should it? And the guy who's with me is really sick. I've got to get him back on the road, especially in this kind of heat.'

'Well...' He lit his cigarette with a kitchen match and watched the smoke he exhaled stream away in the breeze. 'I reckon I could see my way for fifty bucks.' He was staring off somewhere behind Ben, pulling off his railroad cap, scratching the back of his head.

Ben knew this was highway robbery, literally *and* figuratively, since a new tire might cost him all of five bucks. He shook his head and said, 'Thirty. And that's being generous.'

'You're the one in the almighty hurry. I'm the one'll have to scrounge me another.'

'That's why I said thirty.'

'Forty-five.'

Ben looked as though he were thinking hard, as he gazed at the patches on the rusted roof, and considered the clean clothes hanging on the line – children's clothes in a whole lot of sizes – before he said, 'Forty,' as though it actually hurt. He could see the man needed it. And that he lived to dicker and trade too, and he'd lose all respect for northern males if Ben folded at $45.

'Well, mister . . .' He was squinting at Ben as he finished his cigarette, looking any age with his skin creased in every cross-hatch by a life lived in hot southern sun, his hair thin and colorless lying limp across his scalp. 'You drive you a real hard bargain, but you got yourself a deal. My name's Clinton Ray Rawlings. It's a pleasure doing bidness with ya.'

'Thanks, Mr Rawlings. I'm Ben Reese.' Ben took three bills from his wallet, and laid them into a hard-calloused hand.

'Clinton'll do, or Clinton Ray. Let's get workin' on the tire.'

He pronounced it 'tar', from what Ben could tell. Much the way he'd said 'all' for 'oil', which Ben, with all his mother's southern relatives, found generally endearing.

But the best of the tires hadn't been off in years, and the bolts fought the wrenches as though they'd been welded in place. Two got stripped, and Clinton went off to find replacements, while Ben pumped air in an inner tube in far from pristine condition.

As soon as they were ready, Clinton Rawlings called Red Bone (who'd left the shade of the sagging porch for parts unknown in the back), yelling and whistling and pounding on a fender, till the big old dog came wandering out from around the corner of the house.

'Cain't hear like he used to do, but he do appreciate a drive in the truck. Git on up here, boy, we're fixin' to go for a ride.'

The big hound hardly glanced at Clinton Rawlings before he threw himself up in the truck bed, and leaned against the cab.

Clinton tossed the tire in after him. But before he had time to climb behind the wheel, Ben asked if he had any ginger ale he could buy for the friend with the flu. '7-Up would be good too.'

'No, sir, I don't. But I got me three Cokes I'll give ya for free. They should perk him up no end. If the wife hadn't walked up yonder to see her momma, takin' every one of the children with her, she'd a fixed up somethin' right quick that woulda cured his ills.'

Clinton talked the whole time he drove, mostly about cars – about tire treads he'd thought well of over the years. About oil pans, and oil leaks, and reboring an engine.

Ben nodded and said, 'Really?' from time to time the way he did when he talked to his brother, who rebuilt used cars too, for extra money, and had sold Ben his Plymouth.

'You take you a Chevy, one of them new models they got today, automatic drive, and all that, it spoils acceleration. It ain't gonna last. Give me a stick shift any ol' day. What she'll do in the quarter mile, that's what folks care for.'

'*I'd* just like a defroster that works.'

'They are a good bit better in the new cars than they was in yours and mine, but they still got a ways to go.'

They were there then, finally, pulling behind Ben's Plymouth, fending flies off, as they droned around their heads, while they changed the blown tire.

When Clinton Rawlings was gone, taking the old tire with him, Ben washed off with wet paper napkins, then changed into a clean black shirt, and climbed behind the wheel.

He stopped in Kingsport and bought a spare, but didn't take time to put it on then. It was there for the next emergency – the one he hoped didn't come.

It started drizzling an hour and a half later, somewhere in Virginia, in the Jefferson National Forest, in some part of the Appalachians, as they headed toward Tennessee.

It was getting dark by then, in the shadow of the hills, in the rain and the woods, with clouds hanging low, while Bobby slept without being sick, a traveling breeze blowing in the windows across his parched-looking skin.

Ben drove around a quick climbing curve and downshifted

into second, and when he looked at Bobby, who'd just shifted on the seat, he saw his eyes open.

'How long I been out?' Bobby shoved his hair out of his face and held it there with both hands.

'Couple hours. Feel any better?'

'Yeah. Some. Give me five minutes and I can take over. You must be real tired.'

Ben had been yawning when Bobby spoke, but he said, 'I'll need you more later. I don't get a lot of sleep anyway. Haven't since the war.'

'Yeah, me neither. I work a lotta hours, but I know what you mean about the war. It's been getting some better lately. Least that's what I tell myself.' He smiled, but didn't say anything else. Not for three or four minutes, till he asked Ben if he'd mind if he smoked.

'Won't bother me. If you think you're up to it.'

'One, anyway.' He was pulling a pack of Camels from his shirt pocket, feeling for his lighter in the pocket of his brown chinos. 'So where was you in the war?

'Europe.'

'D'you go over in '45?'

'Summer of '44.'

'D-Day?'

'Night before.'

'How was that? I thought—'

'It's kind of a long story.' Ben didn't say anything else.

And Bobby left it alone. 'February of '45 for me. Green replacement, that's what I was. Didn't have time to train us like they did you guys. Real glad I went, though. 'Specially right about now.'

'Why now in particular?'

'Getting combat under your belt can be real useful. This jackass who's got Beth and my momma? He's beggin' to get his clock cleaned.'

'He is that. Yeah.' Ben's smile was cold and quick, and he watched Bobby out the edges of his eyes.

Bobby sat up straighter, and ran a hand back through his thick black hair, before he pulled out the ashtray. 'So what was you doing last night and this morning? You said you was working till real late, and early today too.'

'Carl got me some information that explained who this guy

Weisberg is, but my friend Richard had to take that and put
it in a form I could read, and then—'

'Was it in some foreign language? Or some kinda code?'

'Right, and I wanted to type it up so it made better sense.'

'So this guy was a Nazi, was he? A sympathizer or
something?'

'Not exactly. I can't really say.'

'Sorry, I shouldn't've asked.'

'Not too long before he died, Carl discovered some evidence
which might make it possible to prosecute Weisberg. That's
what Weisberg wants from me. That's why he's got Beth and
your mom. Carl moved to Worthington because he knew
Weisberg was looking for Sylvia, and that eventually Weisberg
would find her. Carl was making sure he'd be there when
Weisberg did.'

'Quiet ol' Carl. Who woulda thought?' Bobby shook his
head, and laid his elbow on the car door across the open
window. 'So what's this guy want with Sylvia?'

'You'll have to ask her that. But there *is* a lot you can help
with.' Ben pushed a pad and pencil across the seat toward
Bobby. 'Draw me a picture of Beth's cabin, inside and out,
and the lay of the land around it. Draw your mom's place too.
From what you said before it must be close by. Then talk to
me about both houses. We'll be seeing them in the dark, and
I need to get a good feel for them, as well as the land they're
on.'

Bobby described the spit of land he'd grown up on. How
his house was built on a fairly flat piece that dropped off in
the back down the side of the mountain. That the front porch
on the east end was three steps above ground level, and it
went on to wrap around the south side too, running that whole
length.

He then drew a floor plan of the downstairs room and the
two upstairs bedrooms, and how the only stairs to the second
floor were on the outside. He showed how Beth's house sat
in front of his, up closer to the road, separated by a wedge
of woods eighty or a hundred yards deep. He told Ben that a
toilet and tub had been added on to his momma's house that
winter. That he and his brothers and sisters had gone together
to pay for it, but he hadn't seen just where they'd put it, though
he knew it was on the north wall. He thought out at the west

end, the farthest away from Beth's. 'There's a sink too, and they fixed up some other stuff. I was coming to see it this fall. You can laugh, if you want, us never havin' a bathroom, or electricity either. She's got it now, though. A real refrigerator setting right there in her kitchen.'

'I'm in no position to laugh. I was raised on a dirt-poor farm in northwestern Michigan. My dad was gassed in World War I, and if I hadn't shot squirrel and rabbit, starting when I turned six, we would've been hungrier than we were.'

Bobby glanced across at Ben, and crushed his Camel in the ashtray. 'That's where Beth and me met, you know. Beth's cabin belonged to her aunt at that time, and Beth used to spend the summer there. My daddy was a caretaker for them when they wasn't there. He'd drain the pipes in the fall, then open the shutters up, and turn on the bottled gas and the water come spring. Funny . . .' Bobby stopped and smiled to himself, looking out his side window well away from Ben. 'I never said Beth was my girlfriend till I talked to you this mornin'. Lady friend, I guess I called her. Kinda surprised myself.'

'I thought you'd been dating for a long time. I guess from the way she talked.'

'Nope. No, she was real different than me, growin' up. Her daddy's a surgeon. Mine never got to school. On the one hand, I was kinda embarrassed about Papa, and the way we lived. Real poor compared to her. Made me madder 'n heck when I saw myself acting that way, but I s'ppose I took it to heart some, even if I knew better.'

'On the other hand?'

'What? Oh. Well, it's kinda hard to explain. We never did see cash money as much of a measure of what kinda folks we was. You can be fractious, and mean, and have plenty of money. You can be a coward who'd curl up his toes in a thunderstorm, and drive a big car. Courage, and loyalty, and being real hospitable, that's more what we held up at home. So I guess it was knowing how they'd look on us, that was some of it, her folks, and their friends. If I was to get real involved with Beth, it'd be kinda like I'd joined 'em. Turned against mine, almost. Folks who'd be looking down their noses at southern folk like me.'

'Because you're southern? Because you—?'

'You know what I mean, the ones who run the government,

and the colleges, and the banks today. The folks who write
the newspapers, and shoot their mouths off on TV, most all
of 'em are northern. You know how it is. They ridicule us
every chance they get. We come over here from hard times
in Scotland, two hundred years ago a lot of us, Ireland too,
as you know. And we been fighting for America ever since,
starting with the Revolution. Sergeant York. Audie Murphy.
Look sometime at the records. See how many Scotch-Irish
mountain folk been real important in the military, and all
through the government.'

'I know that's true, from experience, and from reading too.'

'Folks like that, they're tough. They made the wilderness
a place fit to live. They never did own slaves, they was money-
poor as much as them. And northerners, then and now, they
look down their noses like we're stupid. Like we're all moon-
shiners, or senseless like the Hatfields and McCoys. And I
can tell you, havin' been lots of places since, we ain't so easy
to pigeonhole, and we ain't so easy to fool.'

'My mom was a farm woman from Georgia. That's not
exactly the same, but it's close. A lot of the same prejudices
apply.'

'That's one fine thing the war did. World War II, I'm
speaking of now. Give a lotta folks an education we wouldn't
a got without it.'

'I'm one of those too. I'd started before the war, on a scholarship, working all the time too. But the GI Bill got me as
far as I went.'

'But ya know,' Bobby was picking at a shred of tobacco
sticking to his bottom lip, 'seems like the thought of Beth
getting scared by some yardbird, getting hurt too, maybe even
getting killed, God forbid, it's *real* painful just to think about.
More than I'd expect. Personal. To me. I don't reckon you
can imagine that, but it's been a big shock to me today, to
see how it makes me feel.'

'Oh, I think I can imagine it.'

'Yeah?' Bobby Chambers started to ask, then looked at Ben,
and didn't.

'My wife died in March. Delivering a baby who died too.'

'Mercy!' Bobby stared across at Ben with sad, shocked
eyes. 'Beth never told me.'

'I don't suppose she knows.'

Neither of them said anything after that, till Ben asked Bobby, two minutes later, to tell him about Beth's place.

'Sorry. I forgot to draw it out.' He did then. And described it, inside and out, and talked about the woods there, and the clearing in front. 'Don't your defroster work any better?'

'Nope. But there's a rag inside the glove compartment.'

Ben turned for a second and looked at Bobby, then back out at the road. 'There's one other thing we gotta talk about before we get down there. How we'll deal with Weisberg.'

'I was thinking that—'

'I was a Ranger. I helped train British Commandos in Wales before the invasion. I went into Omaha Beach in a sub with a Canadian strike force the night before D-Day. I was a behind-the-lines scout for army intelligence across a lot of Europe. I'm not as emotionally involved in this situation as you. It's not my girlfriend, *or* my mother. And I meant what I said when I told you that I'd be in charge. If Weisberg sees there're two of us, he may start killing people. I've got to be able to trust you to do exactly what I say, and with you not feeling well, it makes it even more critical.'

Bobby said, 'I see that. I'm not up to par. Better than I was, thank God, that's something.'

'But—'

'You got the experience too, I recognize that. I wasn't in combat all of nine weeks, and it makes the most sense. Like I told ya already, I agreed to let you lead, and I'll stick by my word.'

'I'll go in and assess. You hold up where I put you, and back me up when I ask. You don't do *anything* without asking me first. You agree to that?'

'Yessir. Anything you say, sir.' Bobby saluted and smiled. 'What rank did you end up?'

Ben laughed and said, 'Master Sergeant.'

'Hunh. I woulda figured higher.'

'Don't you know sergeants run the army?'

'I hear what you're saying, but I—'

'I did turn down a promotion or two.'

'Why?'

'I didn't want to tell other guys to do things that could kill them when we were following other men's orders and

I couldn't control the situation. If I got hurt, that was my problem, but other people, no.'

'I can understand that. Knowin' what we saw.'

'I got busted down to private three times too.'

'Drunk and disorderly?'

'Nope. Telling officers what I thought when they were doing something stupid that could get a lot of men killed.'

'We surely had both kinds, didn't we? Officers who were real stupid, real arrogant. Others that were so good, that could read every combat situation just right, and see exactly what it took. Men that pulled stuff off you couldn't believe, and led from the front the whole time.'

'I never stayed with any one outfit. I got shipped wherever they needed me, so I didn't have a platoon, or a bunch of guys I got to know well.'

'I had buddies I went all through with. They're closer to me than most of my kin. Too many got left over there, that's for certain sure. So. You got hit, did ya? That's what's wrong with your hand there?'

'Yep.'

'All I got was shrapnel in the shoulder when we was taking Barby, Germany . . . Neck too. Right here.' Bobby touched the scar below his ear and lit another Camel. 'Couple more inches, and I'd be over there too.'

Ben nodded, but neither of them spoke. Till half a mile further on when Ben asked if he remembered right that they'd be going through Asheville.

'Yeah.'

'I left a message this morning for a fellow Carl knew named Lennox at his office in Washington, and I want to call him from Asheville and see he's left one for me. What's your sister's number? Carlie. The one we talked about earlier. Write that on the paper too. Does that look like a truck stop to you, up ahead on the left?'

'Yep.'

'I'd like you to call Carlie from there and make sure she's home. She's got to stay home tonight too. Say you've absolutely got to talk to her when we get to Asheville. If she's not home now, or she can't be tonight, at least that'll give me time to figure something else out.'

'Got a lotta mountains to get through before we get to Asheville. Let's just hope the fog ain't too bad.'

It was. And it held them back. It made driving ten feet an act of faith, when they couldn't see that far. They crawled south on nerve and knee-jerk notions of what the other drivers would do. They swallowed a lot, and squinted at the fog, straining to see what they couldn't.

Bobby drove through part of it, pale and pasty, wiping his forehead with a clammy hand, temperature back nearly to normal, strength lagging behind – but with three bottles of lukewarm Coke staying where he'd put them.

He knew the roads, which helped considerably, with the hairpin turns, and the tailgaters, and the nutcases driving too fast.

It was after they'd actually made it around a very treacherous right-hand turn (in spite of a semi coming straight at them, driving right in their lane, with another idiot two feet off their tail) that Bobby said, 'Look at that sign.'

'Ah. "Repent, the End is at hand!"'

'They paint 'em where it's scariest. Momma's uncle Web used to write stuff like that on the Knoxville road west of Asheville. I used to figure he meant real well, but it's nothin' I'd take up myself.'

Ben had slept for almost an hour, but was sitting up by then, pouring coffee from a thermos into the metal cap. 'I don't know that it does what they intend. It makes a lot of people cringe.'

'Yep. Though it does do good with some folks.' Bobby concentrated for the next few minutes, bucking the roads and the fog, before he said, 'There was one old fella my granddaddy knew who was driving drunk one night years ago, and he lost control and ran into the cliff right under one of them signs. He swore it made him stop drinking. That reading that warning got him to think when he was scared enough to pay attention. Prob'ly depends on your background. It didn't put him off the way it would with some folks. Does your car always handle this bad? Seems like the rear end's kinda squirrelly. Could be the front tugging on me too.'

'Pull over when you can, and I'll check the tires.'

'Can't for a while. No berm on our side.'

They were quiet after that.

Feeling the car.

Listening to every noise.

Till Bobby pulled off in the first place he could. And Ben jumped out of the car.

Clinton's tire was flat.

Ben opened the trunk fast, and grabbed the jack and the spare.

Eighteen

By quarter of eight that night, Weisberg had finished a fried-egg sandwich at Beth's kitchen table.

Beth was still in the bathtub, but sitting by then on a kitchen chair since he'd loosened the chains enough that she could. She'd drunk three glasses of water, and swallowed a piece of wholewheat bread held by William Weisberg.

While he'd eaten, he'd asked more about Mary Chambers and her family ('Who lives nearby? Who's likely to visit?') – even after he'd spent the day listening and watching every movement on the mountain.

'So Mary doesn't have a phone?'

'No. I told you that before.'

'The daughter, Carlie, you're sure she's the only one who's likely to drop by?' Weisberg was finishing a piece of wild blackberry pie Beth had made the day before.

Beth nodded limply, slumped against the back of the chair, arms chained behind it, feet up on the side of the tub to keep them as clean as she could.

Weisberg could see her through the door, but he said, 'Don't nod. Answer me verbally.'

'She's the only one still in town. There's another daughter who lives here, but she's out of town on a visit. I told you that before. I don't think Carlie'll stop by. She came yesterday morning and drove Mary to town to do her marketing. She won't come back for two or three days, if she sticks to her normal routine.'

'She knows you're here?'

'She and Mary both know, and know not to tell anyone. Let me get a shower and clean up the tub.'

'Later. Perhaps. *If* you acquit yourself precisely as I ask. We could take a shower together after this is over. That's something to look forward to, wouldn't you say? Coffee, now, however. Concentration's required.' He drained his cup, then stood up abruptly and picked up the Colt .45 he'd kept in plain view on the table.

He reloaded and replaced the magazine and laid the gun down. Then he tore a linen dish towel into strips and tied the butcher knife he'd sharpened that morning above his right ankle on the outside of his leg.

He pulled on his leather gloves and checked the contents of his army pack. He took out a spool of fishing line and dropped it in a grocery bag, adding several discarded tin cans he'd punched holes in earlier. He put lids from Beth's pots and pans into another paper bag. Then he slung the pack across one shoulder, slid the .45 in his pocket, and grabbed both paper bags.

'I'll be back soon. Nobody's near enough to hear you, so don't waste your breath screaming.'

It was nearly dark when he stepped on to Mary Chambers' front porch, and knocked softly on the home-made screen door with screen sagging on the top two-thirds and solid wood at the bottom.

He could see a low-burning kerosene lamp at the back of the downstairs room, and he heard a radio playing too – 'Just As I Am', being sung by a choir, while a male voice talked over it. 'Mrs Chambers? Can you hear me? I don't want to startle you. I apologize for arriving so late.'

The radio clicked off at the far end of the room, and slippers padded closer. A tall sinewy weathered-looking woman stepped up just inside the screen. She said, 'Yes sir?' in a quiet voice. 'Is there something I can do for you?'

'Mrs Chambers? I'm Bill Randolph. I've got a message for you from Bobby. I've just arrived from Columbus. I'm on my way to Florida, but I told him I'd stop by. He's all right. He doesn't want you to worry. He won't be in the hospital long, but—' Weisberg smashed the door into Mary Chambers, taking her by surprise as she started pulling it toward her.

She stumbled and fell back, her face hit hard by the wooden frame, as Weisberg charged in and spun her around, pulling her arms behind her, tying her wrists with rope.

*   *   *

It was nerve-wracking for Ben and Bobby, with the dark, and the fog, and the slick roads and the rain, fighting too with the images in their minds of what was happening to Beth and Bobby's momma.

They watched them in silence. Neither of them wanting to make it worse by naming probabilities or painting pictures in front of each other that gave shape to their own worst fears.

They'd lost more time than they could afford – they both knew that, but didn't mention it. For it was almost ten thirty when they pulled into a gas station on the eastern edge of Asheville.

Ben phoned the FBI night number in Asheville he'd gotten from Lennox's office that morning, and was greatly relieved to hear that the night-duty officer had a message for him from Agent Lennox.

Lennox had just gotten into Washington that afternoon from California. He'd get to Black Mountain and consult the local police as soon as he could – with luck sometime before dawn. Ben should leave messages at the FBI number in Asheville, and/or the police in Black Mountain. Lennox also wanted a phone number where he could reach Ben.

Ben got the FBI man to agree to call the police in Black Mountain, tell them Lennox would be arriving, probably sometime during the night, and that if he, Ben Reese, hadn't arrived at the Black Mountain police station by one thirty in the morning, they should phone Carlie Roberts in Black Mountain for further information that he knew Lennox would want. Ben gave them Carlie's number, as well as the gas-station payphone number as the one where they could reach him. Then he dropped a dime in for Bobby and handed him the receiver.

'So you want me to tell Carlie that if the police call after one thirty she can tell 'em we're at Beth's, but she can't tell 'em before that. Nobody at all. And she can't come herself. Not under any circumstances. We'll take care of the situation, one that's got some danger to it, and explain as fast as we can.'

'Exactly.'

'Carlie won't give in to them. She's the stubbornest woman I ever met. But we both better pray I can put it to her right, so she don't get her dander up, like I'm not trusting her the way I should. Or like she needs to get involved herself to protect Momma and Beth.'

The call went as well as Bobby thought it could've.

And they climbed back in the car.

Bobby parked it in a patch of woods down the mountain from his mother's cabin. He pulled in where underbrush would hide it, then crawled out slowly, as though every muscle in his body ached.

Ben took two boxes of ammunition and four loaded magazines out of the glove compartment and laid them on the front seat, then pulled a sheaf of papers from his briefcase and put them in his musette bag.

He tied a length of rope around his waist, over his belt and his long-sleeved shirt, having checked the wires in his belt that morning before he'd put it on. He pulled a black watch cap down over his ears, poured a cup of water in a patch of dirt and smeared mud on his face, and his neck, and the back of his hands, then slung his binoculars around his neck on a strap he'd shortened that morning.

It was hot on Black Mountain. Muggy. Still. And he listened to the sounds in the woods, floating, some of them, up from the valley, as he checked the contents of the musette bag – lock-picks, wire-cutters, fountain-pen-sized flashlight, Swiss Army knife with attachments – wishing he had the two-sided hatchet that had helped him live through Europe.

But he did have the Springfield .30-06 he'd bought for himself in high school, the Olympic competition sight as accurate as ever. He'd carried one just like it all through the war, and he could've assembled it in his sleep, even though he hadn't shot it in the twelve years since.

He dropped three six-slug magazines into the leather ammo pouch attached to the side of his belt. Then pulled the Springfield out of the trunk and slipped the last magazine in place, emptying six sealed military slugs, casings nearly three inches long, into the spring-based chamber. He slung the rifle on his left shoulder, with his mind fixed on Weisberg.

Bobby said, 'Man, that's an unforgivin' gun.'

'Sounds like a cannon going off too. Movies never get it

right. Tell me again about the inside of your house. The stairs on the outside coming off the porch go upstairs to the bedrooms. All there is on the ground floor is one big room. Kitchen in the front toward Beth's. Eating area in the middle. Sofa at the back, right?'

'Right. If your back's to Beth's, the long wall going back on the left's got a whole lotta windows. The far wall too, so there're views across the mountains. The window in the front above the kitchen sink, on the short wall closest to Beth's, that's kinda small, with the door set off to the left. The screen door's on in the summer. The bottom part's solid wood, the top two-thirds is screen.'

'So whoever's standing in that room can see out the west, the south, and the east?'

'Yeah, but there's no glass on the north wall, where the stairs go up on the outside. The bathroom's at the far end there, coming off with a shed roof. The cook stove's on the north wall too, kind of in the middle, and there's a big work table there, right in front of the stove.'

'And the porch goes across the east and south walls?'

'Yep. Eight feet deep, the floor built up on short stone pillars. There's fieldstone pillars supporting the whole house. Different heights depending on how the ground drops off.'

'So there's open space under the house?'

'Sure, but there's a lotta pillars.'

'But no screens on the porches?'

'No, open all the way 'round. Got a fuel-oil space heater right square in the middle of the downstairs, close to the table where we eat. Don't reckon I said that before.'

Ben nodded, as he handed Bobby his handgun, a loaded Webley Mark IV .455 revolver, with a full box of shells. 'Ready?'

'Yep.'

'Glad to see you're feeling better.'

'Oh, man, me too.'

'So take us up to Beth's.'

Once they stepped out on to the edge of the road, they didn't speak again. They climbed along in the shadows, where the verge met dusty underbrush, stepping off into the woods as soon as they heard a car crawling slowly down Black Mountain.

Fifteen minutes later, Bobby led Ben toward the back of Beth's house, taking him through the woods – thick woods, dense with heavy old trees – where her house sat hidden away from the road.

Bobby stopped, and pointed toward it, fifty yards away. And Ben nodded, signaling him to stay where he was, while he watched it silently for several seconds, before he started toward it, sliding from tree to tree.

The windows on that side were open, but screened, and every room was dark. Ben had seen that where he'd started, before he'd crouched and crept toward it, the wooden grip of the .30-06 balanced in his right hand.

He studied the ground in front of him – weaving his way across ferns and mountain plants, smelling the spice scent of unknown shrubs, stepping on moss and well-rotted leaves toward the north-east window of the house.

He laid his back quietly against the trunk of a big maple, and listened while he watched the woods, hearing the sounds he expected – leaves rustling erratically, insects droning and buzzing, small animals scuttling unpredictably, one solitary great horned owl somewhere off in the distance – nothing that gave him pause, inside the house, or out.

Part of the reason they'd made Ben a scout was his night vision was better than most, and he used it every way he could (the way he had looking for signs of tracks, and mines, for booby traps and trip wires) – so that when he lay down on his gut in the dirt, and crawled closer to the corner of Beth's house, he saw a nylon fishing line a foot above the ground.

It was strung between that north-east corner and a tree twenty feet east of where Ben lay, and when he followed it across to the tree trunk, he found two metal pan lids strung close together camouflaged by leaves.

Ben cut the line, and laid it down silently, then stepped up to the house.

There were others, just as he'd expected – the first on the far side of three darkened windows at the north-west corner of the cabin (windows screening empty rooms, from what Ben could see from outside).

He found Shep dead, inside a small shed not far from that corner – dead for probably a day at least. And he pulled a gunnysack across the floor and laid it over the body, fighting a quick hot flood of anger that clenched his jaws tighter and got him moving even faster.

Shutters were locked across the windows on the front – where there were more fishing lines strung between trees and the house, hung with cans and pot lids, meant to give Weisberg warning that someone was on the way in.

Ben cut the ones he found, then moved around to the north side again, and waved Bobby in.

When they'd circled back and were standing by the front steps, Ben used hand signals to tell Bobby that he, Ben, would go straight in, while Bobby covered his back.

Ben climbed the stairs and opened the screen, carefully, silently, holding it with his foot, while he tried the handle on the wooden door, keeping himself well to the left, off to the side of the frame.

He had it unlocked in a matter of seconds, and then he was turning the handle, his Springfield in his right hand, his back against the wall.

He pushed the door wide with the rifle barrel and stared east into the living room, nerves stripped as he listened, adrenaline firing his senses, making him harder to stop.

Bobby was up on the other side of the porch, his back against the wall by then, straining to see the west side of the room before Ben went in.

Ben moved fast, in, and then on, from room to room, making no sounds, searching behind doors, under the beds and the sofa.

There was no one there, in the sticky heat, in the still stale air. And after he'd closed the curtains on the windows where there were open shutters, he clicked on his pen-size flashlight and scanned every room.

There were no signs of a struggle in the bedrooms, though the double bed had been slept in. The living room looked more or less normal. And Ben stepped up to the front door and motioned Bobby in, whispering, 'Weisberg smoked a whole lot of cigarettes, so he was here awhile.' Ben dropped Beth's flashlight into his musette bag, keeping his small one in his hand as he headed back to the kitchen.

There was broken glass on the far side, on the floor in the doorway to the bath. He'd stepped on it, on his first trip in. And he stood shining his light on it.

Bobby came in behind him – right after Ben had seen the blood in the tub. The blood, the urine, the feces. The raw places too, in the two exposed studs from newly drilled holes.

Bobby said, 'I'll kill him!' quietly. A second before Ben grabbed his arm.

'Knock it off, Bobby. Study what's here. We need to know who we're up against.'

He pointed the flashlight at the broken drinking glass sitting on the edge of the sink, at the cigarette stubs dropped on the floor, at the others burned out in the bottom of the tub, at the paring knife on the edge.

Ben studied the stain on the knifepoint, then laid it down on the sink. He started to say, 'I'll scout the woods between here and your mom's' – but his voice died in his throat as soon as he saw the words written in blood on the mirror:

BETH'S NOT A
BAD SCREW

Bobby made it out the door, through the kitchen and the living room, and was hurtling down the wooden steps when Ben threw him to the ground.

He crouched on top of him, straddling him sideways, pinning Bobby's face in the dirt with one knee, while twisting his arms behind him. 'Listen to me! NOW!'

It wasn't a shout, but a hiss – a quiet, threatening, sharp-edged assault an inch above Bob's ear. 'I will tie you up and leave you here! You got that? I'm not gonna let you screw this up!'

Ben didn't say anything else for a minute. He watched, and let it sink in. 'He's taunting us. He's egging us on. He wants us to make mistakes. You want to rescue Beth? Get yourself under control! You can *help* them. You know things about the place I don't. But you're a liability now. You're a danger to them and us!'

Bobby was panting, but he'd stopped fighting Ben. And when he finally said, 'OK. You're right. I'll do whatever you say.'

Ben countered with, 'Yeah? You mean it?' But didn't let him go. He leaned down closer again, and whispered, 'Weisberg shot Shep. He's in a tool shed on the west end. There're trip wires all over the place. To slow us down and warn Weisberg. There'll be plenty on the path to your mom's. He told us he's got them both, and he knows we'll go there after Beth's, so we can't use the path. The woods on the south of the path, the left side as we're looking toward your mom's house, they come up closer to her house, right?'

'Yeah.'

'You'll go in on that side. I'll go in on the north. The north's closest to the vegetable garden and the outhouse, correct?'

'Yeah. If the outhouse is still there. There's a real small garden shed too. I forgot to mention before.'

'I'll check out the south side, and then scout the rest, then come back here and get you.' Ben stood up and watched Bobby.

Who rolled over and got up, then picked up the Webley he'd dropped. 'How much time is scoutin' gonna take?'

'If you want to get it done and stay alive, you scout and you plan. I've got what Weisberg wants, Bobby. He knows he won't get it if they're dead. He's gotta wait on us. Right?'

'Yeah. OK. I reckon you're right.'

'I *hope* I'm right. That's for sure. How's the flu?'

'I'm doin' better. Well enough to help.'

Ben cut seven more trip wires on his sweep of the woods, three on the path, two on either side.

He'd seen signs of struggle on the path, a woman being dragged and pushed, leaving a lot of unpleasant information scratched into the dirt.

Shep wasn't the only dog who'd been shot and killed. Another lay dead in hard-packed clay between the vegetable garden and the east-end porch. A big dog, long-haired and yellow, old and scrawny and ill-looking. Who'd died on the chain he'd lived on. Presumably. Based on the bare dirt circle.

It made Ben ask himself what else Bobby hadn't thought to tell him, as he watched the house from the south-side woods, lying in weeds, on moss and dirt, his eyes riveted on the cabin.

The house was dark inside. But he stared hard anyway at the long wall of double hung windows lining that long side porch, watching the screen door and the window on the east – considering all those open windows helping Weisberg hear.

Ben's binoculars were better than nothing, but what he could see was limited. Till one quick glimpse of movement told him what he'd expected – someone was inside waiting, watching for him.

Ben faded back into the woods, and worked his way around, till he was hidden on the north side, behind the wooden garden shed, on the east end of the house.

He crouched and ran to the north side of the house where the outside stairway climbed to the bedrooms. He stayed still and listened, staring at the length of that wall without windows or doors.

The bathroom had been added on the far end, where the ground fell away and the stone piers supporting the floor were tallest. But several feet before the bathroom was what looked to be a dumb waiter positioned under the first floor.

Ben slipped closer, and studied it. It was all new wood and untarnished pulleys. The dumb waiter shelf sat at ground level, kindling stacked on top of it, under ropes and pulleys and a trap door overhead that opened to the downstairs room.

Ben moved the kindling silently, taking his time, setting it far enough away from the dumb waiter that he'd have room to maneuver. Then he stepped inside, bending his neck, not able to stand straight, reaching up to the trap door, pushing slowly and carefully, just enough to be sure it would move.

He stepped out and listened for a minute. Then worked his way east to the woods.

Ben signaled Bobby from ten feet away, toward the east edge of Beth's clearing, where he told him what he'd seen – the dog, the path, the movement inside – speaking so quietly Bobby had to strain to hear.

Bobby said, 'Momma don't have a dog. Hers died last March. That might be Sarah's. She prob'ly left her dog with Momma so she could go outta town.'

'There's something on the north side that looks like it's got possibilities. It's new construction, this side of the bathroom. It's a dumb waiter that had kindling on it, with a trap door overhead that looks like it opens into the downstairs room.'

'Must be for the cook stove. Momma didn't want to give up the old wood-burner, and I bet they put that in so she don't have to carry wood so far.'

'If I stand in it, I can shove the trap door open and get my head up above the floor. So if we both go up through the north woods, and then curve around west on that side, you can crawl up toward the east-end porch. You'd crawl along the length of that, heading south, staying low below the porch, then sight in on him at floor level, at the steps in front of the door. He won't be able to see you till you stick your head above the porch, with the wood on the bottom of the door, and the window above the sink.'

'Yeah, I can see that. But—'

'You take the rifle, I'll take the Webley. You aim through the screen door, keeping yourself out of sight, while I get his attention from the dumb waiter on the north. I'll point Beth's flashlight at him, so we can see to aim.'

'So gettin' from the woods on the north, that's prob'ly the hardest part.'

Ben smiled, and said, 'One of them. Timing's as important. I'll cover you till you're in place, then we'll pick a time to go in. You've gotta get the barrel up on the porch the same time I jump out the trap door. You oughta say something too at the same time I throw up the trap door. "Get away from the women. Throw down your weapon!" Something like that.'

'We risking too much here? Beth and my momma? What if he shoots 'em before we can stop him?'

'It's a risk, but if we don't screw up he won't know we're near him, and there won't be time for him to do anything before we've got him giving up his arms, or getting himself shot. We can't just give him the papers he wants. He'd shoot us all to protect his own skin.'

'That's the way it looks, don't it? But it's still a risk for the women.'

'I'm open to other suggestions.'

They were both silent.

Ben choosing not to look at Bobby.

Bobby staring at the woods. Till he said, 'Should we synchronize our watches?'

'Yep.' They did that in less than a second. Then Ben started into the woods with Bobby right behind him.

Nineteen

They were lying on the edge of the north woods watching Bobby's house. They'd already settled on eleven forty-eight for the two-pronged assault, and Ben was ready to cover Bobby when he headed for the east-end porch.

But then – just as Bobby started to get up – something moved behind the screen door. Ben touched Bobby's arm, keeping the binoculars trained on the door, shaking his head at Bobby, who'd stopped the second Ben touched him.

Something tall and broad, on the other side of the screen, had stopped, in the dark, back a ways from the door, the upper outline lighter than the room behind it, and only just visible with Ben's binoculars.

They could hear each other breathe, lying there in dirt and dry leaves, with the breeze picking up and beginning to roll toward them, carrying a trace of cigarette smoke, while their lips got dryer and their eyes strained harder to see beyond the screen.

Then the shape was gone. And all they could hear were soft summer leaves rustling over their heads.

They still waited, thirty yards away from the house, watching and listening for whatever more might happen. Till Ben motioned to Bobby, to the dial on his own watch, then signed eleven, and fifty-six, and waved Bobby off, pointing toward the right, signaling him to get further north before he came out of the woods.

Bobby was running then, carrying Ben's Springfield, crouching, hustling, hiding behind the shed – while Ben kept his handgun trained on the house, binoculars searching the windows and door.

Bobby sprinted fast toward the porch – safe finally on the north side, his back against the old wooden wall under the outside stairs.

He dropped to the ground a few seconds later, crawled east along the porch's north end, then turned the corner, crawling south toward the porch steps.

He lay there, where he couldn't be seen from the house, three feet down from the floor of the porch – when Ben moved out, covering ground fast, Webley gripped in his right hand, eyes sweeping the land and the night between the woods and the house.

He was past the shed, heading for the north wall, making himself hold back the adrenaline – slowing his heartbeat, controlling his breathing – even when he was standing still, listening under the stairs.

He edged his way to the dumb waiter, and stepped in silently, crouching under the overhead door, watching the phosphorescent hands on his watch hit eleven fifty-four.

Ben slid his left hand along the trap door, feeling for the hinges, checking that he'd gotten it right, that they were there on his left, testing the door to make sure it still moved – carefully, slowly, getting himself ready to shove the trap door when it was time and launch himself into the room.

He stayed bent over, staring at his watch, Beth's flashlight clamped in his left hand, listening for Weisberg, for the women, for Bobby – gnashing his teeth at having to wait the way he always had.

Then it was time – and he shoved the trap door, letting it fall with a crash – the same second Bobby shouted, 'Get away from the women!'

Ben stood, head and shoulders in the room, ten feet away from Weisberg, catching him in the flashlight beam – at almost the same second Weisberg fired a semi-automatic through the screen door.

Ben shot Weisberg in the arm closest to him, the left arm holding the gun – so that the handgun clattered across the floor and slid toward the porch door, away from the women who were slumped together, on the other side of Weisberg, but off on Ben's right.

Weisberg spun away from Ben, grabbing his injured arm, as Ben vaulted out of the dumb waiter yelling, 'Stay right where you are!'

Weisberg didn't.

He crouched and jumped toward the women.

Ben lunged into him, knocking him off balance, smashing his weight down with the edge of his shoe on to the arch of Weisberg's foot – just as a butcher knife sliced through his own shirt, grating against his ribs.

Ben dropped the flashlight to free his left hand, telling himself not to kill him, as he chopped the edge of it next to the vertebrae at the base of Weisberg's neck. He knocked the knife out of Weisberg's grip, then dragged him away from Beth and Bobby's momma to the back corner by the bathroom.

'You OK, Bobby?' Ben's eyes were pinned on Weisberg's, watching agony wash across his face, the Webley pointed at Weisberg's chest, as Ben's left hand examined his own ribs a hand's breadth above his waist.

The screen door slapped shut behind Bobby, just as he said, 'I'm OK. He nicked my shoulder when I was crawling up the steps, but it's no big deal, I promise. Beth? Momma?' He was hurrying toward the two crumpled figures on the far side of the space heater, though he stopped first at the kitchen table and took the chimney off a kerosene lamp as though he hadn't had to ask himself, 'If there were a lamp in this room, where would it be now?'

A globe-shaped glow of pale light exposed the damage Weisberg had done to Beth, and Mary Chambers – both of them, bruised and sweating, chained together in two chairs, backs almost touching, mouths stuffed with wadded rags tied with strips of cloth.

Bobby Chambers ran across the room and smashed Weisberg in the face, knocking him back against the bathroom door, before Ben grabbed his arm.

'It's not gonna help, Bobby!'

'Then how come it made me feel better?'

Ben didn't say anything.

But they both smiled, as Bobby ran back to Beth, and began untying the gag. He got the other off his mom, who made him show her his shoulder before he looked at their chains.

Beth started crying quietly, gulping in air past bleeding lips, torn and cracked at the corners. Mary Chambers coughed before she said, 'It'll be all right, honey. Bobby's here now. We're gonna be just fine.' Her voice broke and her throat sounded dry, but she looked better than Beth.

Bobby talked to both of them, stroking their hair and patting their backs, while he started working on their chains.

Ben watched Weisberg, keeping him pinned in the corner, as he told Bobby he had wire-cutters, if there wasn't a turn-buckle, or a link he could bend.

'It's a combination lock. Cutters would work, but—'

'So, we need the numbers from him.' Ben cocked the Webley, raising his eyebrows at Weisberg, the bones of Ben's face looking sharp-edged and hostile, his eyes like slivered ice.

Weisberg smiled, a slow insolent one-sided grin, before he said, 'You're bluffing. You won't shoot me, not in front of witnesses.'

'Not to kill. Without provocation. I'll start blowing out body parts. Knees, probably, first.'

'And yet your secretary says you're such a kind man!'

'Maybe she doesn't know me nearly as well as she thinks.' Ben aimed his .455 at Weisberg's right knee. 'I don't *remember* that it pulls up and to the right, but I can't guarantee it. I haven't shot the Webley in years, and then I could use my left hand.'

Weisberg studied Ben's face. And half-nodded his head. 'Even if you win this hand, you won't win the last. You need to remember that, Reese. I meant what I said. Eleven left. Forty-two right. Seventeen left.'

'You got that, Bobby?'

'Yeah.'

Ben carefully released the Webley's hammer, the muzzle still pointed at Weisberg's chest. 'So, you ready to go back to prison?'

'I'm *not* going back. I told you that on the phone.'

'You murdered Carl and Miriam. Why would you think you'd get off? Bobby, take the rope around my waist and tie his hands behind him.'

'Just a sec.' Bobby finished unfastening the chains, then walked over to Ben. 'His arm's bleeding kinda bad.'

Ben pulled a handkerchief out of a back pocket.

And Bobby tied it around the wound on Weisberg's left forearm. 'Should we use the rope to cut the blood flow? It's thin enough, and pliable. I can make a tourniquet above the gunshot, and tie his hands to that. It'd be easier to do in front, because of where the wound is. Course, we could let the sucker bleed. Whatever you want to do.'

'Do the tourniquet and tie it to his hands, in back if you can. Take care of your shoulder too. Your mom must have something you can use.'

'It ain't nothin', Ben, but a real small graze of a flesh wound.'

'So tell me,' Ben said, staring at Weisberg, breathing slowly, holding himself back, watching every look that started on Weisberg's face. 'When did you decide to kill Carl?'

'I'm not dignifying that with a reply.' He gazed at Ben with casual interest, smiling into his eyes, his hands tied in front of him now, on top of his blood-smeared pants.

'Bobby, I think we should get Beth and your mom up to Beth's house. Take 'em away from Weisberg, and find them some food and water. Beth's not looking too good.'

'Momma, can you walk up yonder and fix the two of you something to eat? I don't trust this jackass as far as I can throw him.'

'Nothin' happened here that we can't care for. You can walk, can't you, girl?'

Beth was standing already, leaning against the kitchen table, a blouse buttoned on top of her gown, ballet flats on her feet, her hair tangled and wet with sweat, her eyes fixed on Bobby.

'Hey.' He went over to her and wrapped his arms around her, then whispered something in her ear.

Her arms went around his waist, and she nodded her head against his chest. Ben heard her say, 'Me too. I'm OK. I want to go get cleaned up.'

Mary Chambers looked surprised, as she stared at Bobby's face – then she turned away, smiling to herself, before she gazed across at Ben. 'Beth and me, we'll go make us some sandwiches, and get a pot of coffee on the fire. We'll have it ready for y'all right quick.'

Ben's back was still to the rest of them when he said, 'Don't make anything for us. We're taking Weisberg into town, and I don't know how long we'll be gone. You two make yourselves comfortable, and we'll get back when we can.'

'Whatever y'all think best.' Mary was looking at Ben again, smoothing her gray hair back toward the bun at the nape of her long thin neck. 'Proud to make your acquaintance.'

Ben laughed, and said, 'Me too. Can either of you handle a gun?'

Mary said, 'I been shootin' squirrels since before you was born.'

'Bobby, why don't you give Weisberg's gun to your mom? Pick the knife up too, and put it someplace safe.' Ben was using his left hand to test the rope tying Weisberg's arms. 'So my bet is that you tied Carl—'

'Yes?' Weisberg eyes were locked on Ben's, his wide thick lips set in a smile that looked like it came from pride and conceit, and something else as well.

'What are you looking so smug about?' Ben could feel it. A resilience somewhere in Weisberg. Some fact keeping him going. Making Ben uneasy.

'Why would I tell you?'

'You tied Carl to a tree, then shot him and faked the suicide.'

'You're talking through your hat. You've got no proof of any kind.'

'I've got the proof Miriam had, which makes suicide highly unlikely and points directly at you. I've got everything Carl put together as well, plus definite proof now that Carl was tied to that tree. If we go through your things, we'll find evidence that you were there. Dirt on your shoes. Bark fragments on something you own. The belt of your raincoat, if you used that to tie him? The gloves you were wearing? A piece of rope you haven't thrown out? There'll be something to tie you to Carl. The paper they found in his shoe? Yes, I somehow suspect that's important.'

'What paper? I know nothing of any paper.' There was wariness in Weisberg's eye that hadn't been there before.

'REMEMBER KRIVITSKY. REMEMBER REISS. R-e-i-s-s. Mean anything to you?'

'No. Certainly not. Why should it?'

'Written in block letters? The warning you sent Carl?'

'I had nothing to do—'

'I don't know when you gave it to him, but sometime before you murdered him. Maybe you tried to use threats to shut him up, so you wouldn't have to kill him. I'm giving you the benefit of the doubt there, even making the suggestion.'

'And yet I'm unimpressed. Yes?'

'That would only have been a ploy to try to throw him off

guard, saying you would've left him alive when he knew as much as he did. I've done some research since I got my brain back after we collided in the barn. Krivitsky was a Soviet agent working in the US in the thirties. A GRU agent who defected to us, back before the GRU was renamed the KGB. He was found dead in 1940 in suspicious circumstances meant to look like suicide. Many believed then, and more believe today, that Walter Krivitsky was murdered by his Soviet runners. Ignatz Reiss was killed by the Soviets in Switzerland after he defected. He was shot in the country and left to die.'

'I know nothing of any Krivitsky *or* Reiss. You're grasping at straws.'

'Handwriting experts won't think so. The note was written by you. Carl wrote the date on it, plus, "Weisberg. Tell Lennox", making sure we'd find it no matter what happened to him. There's also the issue—'

'You don't grasp the true significance of this situation. Unlike you, *I* have succeeded in high-level critical operations, at great personal risk, that have benefited all mankind in the twentieth century and beyond! I, personally, have been instrumental in keeping the United States from perpetrating on the rest of the world the destruction it rained on Japan. Without my efforts—'

'No one might've died in Korea. Is the coast clear, Bobby?'

Bobby had been watching the two women walk across the clearing, into the path through the woods, and he said, 'Give 'em another minute maybe. What're you two talkin' about?'

Weisberg laughed.

And Ben ignored the question, asking Bobby if he wanted to get the car, or make the creep walk. Ben was feeling his ribs again, when Bobby wasn't looking, trying to measure the size of the gash and how much blood he was losing.

'I figure it'll do him good to walk. Give him a chance to enjoy the outdoors before he's locked up for good.'

'Frisk him first, OK?'

'Sure.' Bobby did, without finding anything that could've been used as a weapon. 'Let me just light me a cigarette before we head out. He's had his last smoke for a while, if I have anything to do with it.' Bobby lit the Camel four feet from Weisberg, his eyes laughing at Weisberg's face when Weisberg looked away.

Ben asked Bobby to take the handgun and give him the Springfield. 'The Webley'll be easier for you to use with a wound in your right shoulder.'

Ben took the rifle from Bobby in his right hand, then grabbed Weisberg's shoulder with his left, and shoved him toward the screen door.

Bobby opened it for Weisberg, then went back and blew out the lamp before he stepped on to the porch behind Weisberg and Ben.

'You get a big thrill out of killing dogs?' Ben had glanced at the old yellow dog sprawled where he'd died in the dirt, before he followed Weisberg down the stairs, rifle barrel in his back. 'Not as much as torturing Beth, but then you see yourself as a ladies' man.'

'Don't presume to lecture me—'

'Making women hurt, that's the appeal, right? Make them care about you. Make them think you love them. Then mock them one way or another, and torture them when you can.'

'You're confining yourself to the plight of individuals who have no bearing on the larger issues confounding nations today.'

'Nations won't last for ever. Human beings will.'

'*That* is unworthy of even the—'

'Wonder why Susannah can't stand you? Was that your one failure? No. And there'll be more the older you get. Jail will actually save you from that. From seeing revulsion in their eyes.'

They were halfway across the clearing, Ben behind Weisberg, Bobby behind Ben, walking beside the vegetable garden, when Mary Chambers came hurrying out of the woods, still carrying Weisberg's Colt, calling out to Bobby. 'I was just walkin' into Beth's when your sister drove up, and she says—'

Weisberg ran straight at her, his hands still tied in front of him, knocking her down, grabbing at the Colt – when Ben shot him in the right thigh with the .30-06.

The roar was deafening, but Ben didn't notice. Weisberg had fallen on Mary, and Ben was jerking him up, dragging him away through the garden, dropping him forty feet off, seeing him smile as he raised his hands to point at one of his shirt pockets, his eyes smug and taunting.

Weisberg motioned Ben closer with the fingers of one hand till his face clenched, suddenly, from what looked like overwhelming pain.

Ben leaned toward him, in time to hear him whisper, in an accent he hadn't had before, 'I win the last hand . . . as I . . . foretold.'

Then his body contorted, the whole long length of him, clenched into a spasm, his head lolling off to one side once the rest went limp, leaving the eyes fixed and empty, a trickle of blood between his lips.

Ben stared at him for half a second, then knelt and searched his shirt pocket.

He pulled out a single ampoule, a large thin-sided glass capsule meant to be bitten and broken, filled with a milky liquid.

A spare, apparently, from the evidence in front of him. Maybe cyanide. Maybe something else. Something that killed as fast.

Twenty

Ben was sitting on Bobby's momma's side porch when the sun came up. He was facing south, and he couldn't see it hit the horizon on the east side of Black Mountain, but he saw what it did to the gray around him – the folds in the mountains like pleats in a tapestry, the wandering waves of blue shadowed hills, the pale mist carpeting the low places – as purple, and pink, and salmon-colored fingers stretched across the sky.

He watched the lights in the valley below him, flickering on as another day dawned, while he rubbed his hands across his scalp over a tired brain. He turned too, when a quiet voice said, 'Hey,' twenty feet away – in time to see Arthur Lennox walk around the corner of the house.

Lennox sat on the porch on Ben's left, his feet on the same stone step, and lit a Lucky with a dented lighter, then pushed the pack toward Ben.

'So now you're reading my mind?' Ben stared at the half-empty package, before he looked over at Lennox.

'Sure, it's part of the job. See you got the mud washed off your face.'

Ben smiled but didn't reach for the Luckys.

'Well?'

'Well, what?' Ben had to work to keep his head up. His feet weighed a thousand pounds. His hands hung between his shins, his elbows planted on his thighs.

Lennox's large, square, big-boned face was cocked toward Ben, his thick brown eyebrows raised above his glasses, his dark eyes watching intently, his chapped-looking lips pressed in a tight thin line. 'I made a phone call on your behalf.'

'Yeah?'

'Carter Clarke. The brains behind Arlington Hall. Miriam

Gold's boss. Former Director Army Security Agency, retired 1954.'

'And?'

'We composed a document for you to sign. Carter Clarke is a happy man.' Lennox opened his briefcase and pulled out a sheet of paper, FBI insignia embossed on the top, three paragraphs in single-spaced type.

Ben read it, nodded as he turned toward Lennox, and asked if he had a pen.

Lennox was staring across the valley below, pushing his tortoiseshell glasses up his nose, as he pulled a ballpoint from an inside pocket of a tired tan linen suit.

Ben signed the paper and handed it back along with the Bic pen.

'I've got another copy for you to take to your friend. What was his name? West? The one who helped you decrypt Walker's messages? Give it to him when you get home and have him mail it to me in this envelope.' Lennox handed Ben the envelope with the letter enclosed, then snapped his briefcase shut. 'I'll be along to interview him early next week, when I meet with you to retrieve the materials from the muniment room.'

'Fine.'

'What else we gotta talk about now? We've covered Venona and what Weisberg did, passing it on to the Soviets.'

'So was Carl right that Philby confirmed that we'd broken the codes from '43?'

'Yeah, but they started writing changes to the codes on Weisberg's word alone. It took 'em a while. There were different versions of Venona, plus a number of unrelated codes. Military, diplomatic, trade traffic too, that they used with embassies and trade delegations, that they changed because of him.'

'Is it true that if they hadn't the Korean War might've been avoided?'

'Avoided, or prepared for. One or the other.'

'What's Weisberg been up to since then?'

'Don't know. He served that year in federal prison. All we could do was charge him with contempt of court without revealing what we knew about him from Venona. At least we got him stopped, him and that agent he was running who was selling high-level aeronautical secrets. An agreement was made not to use Venona to prosecute anyone, as I think you know, and they've stuck to that to this day.'

'Isn't that frustrating? Knowing who's guilty of what, and not telling the rest of the country?'

'Yeah, it is. But that's between you and me.' Lennox inhaled his Lucky, and rubbed his eyes behind his glasses.

'So after Weisberg got out of jail?'

'He disappeared, we think through Canada. You know about the report that he was seen in Moscow, and a year later in Alexandria?'

'Yes.'

'There was nothing after that till Carl Walker called me and left a message the end of May asking me to call when I could, that he had a new lead. He didn't say it was an emergency, and I was out of the country, vacation, and then business, and once I got back and called him he never answered his phone. I figure he must've called when he found the photographs and note from Miriam Gold.'

'You'd think he would've called after he'd seen Weisberg. Unless he wanted to take care of him himself.'

'I'd bet that's what it was. I didn't get another message. Course it could've gotten lost in the shuffle, with me gone as long as I was. So this Susannah Adams woman, she says Weisberg was working for Armand Hammer?'

'Yep.'

'You know about Hammer?'

'Some.'

'He took daddy's money from pharmaceuticals, moved to Russia, drummed up trade for Stalin, made money in pencils, if you can believe it, and came back with half the Romanovs' treasures. He owns Occidental Petroleum.'

'Was Weisberg still an agent? Now? Since he's come back?'

'Don't know. We don't have any evidence that he was. They gave him a code name in '48 that he'd be able to use for life, along with a method for getting in touch directly with the KGB. That's not a common occurrence. Weisberg was very much valued, and a fairly high-level operative.'

'Carl Walker wrote me that Weisberg had gone through basic in the US Army, but that he was just a linguist during the war with no combat experience. Did he have any other training? Moscow-based espionage stuff?'

'*I* think it's likely. There're three years we can't account for when he was in his twenties. *I* think he was getting trained in the Soviet Union as a GRU agent. I have information to that effect, but nothing that's conclusive. Let's just say it's an educated guess.'

'I see.' Ben watched Lennox take a last drag on his Lucky, and crush it under his shoe. 'Carl said the FBI who tried to work with the Army Signal Corps people during the war, the ones working on Venona—'

'What later became the National Security Agency.'

'Right, he said that the FBI were often arrogant and sometimes slipshod, jumping to conclusions and throwing their weight around, but that you were easy to work with, and fair and honest in the work.'

Art Lennox laughed and said, '*Carl* was easy to work with. Meredith Gardner too. Venona's major book-breaker. The way Carl dedicated himself to watching over Susannah, and looking out for Weisberg, that was a huge help. I couldn't've done that. Too much other work.'

'Why did Weisberg do it? What was the appeal of the Soviet Union?'

'That's a question I've asked for years and still can't answer. Miriam Gold, now, she *really* understood the climate of the times. How it affected immigrants from Russia. Jews in particular, which she was, of course. New York especially was a hotbed of communism. City College of New York in the thirties? You wouldn't believe what it was like. When they held student elections, seeing how the students there would vote, you know the way they do in a lot of colleges, comparing how the students vote to the actual national election? The two parties at CCNY weren't Democrats and Republicans, but Bolsheviks and Trotskyites.'

'Are you kidding?'

'No, that's absolutely true. The immigrants in New York then, many had come from Russia. They'd been persecuted by the Czar. Some were Bolsheviks, some were Trotskyites, some were Zionists. They'd get here without the language, like plenty of immigrants before them, sure, but they're Jews too. There's anti-Semitic hostility. Then the Depression hits, and they think capitalism's dead. They believed the Soviet system was the final answer. That there was real freedom and equality there, plus complete and equitable employment. Lots of them swallowed it hook, line, and sinker.'

Ben was shaking his head when he said, 'But the evidence was trickling out early in the thirties. The massive exterminations. The famine and starvation. The genocide of Jews, especially the intelligentsia, which got even worse later, but—'

'You shoulda seen what the KGB runners, handling the Jewish agents here, called them behind their backs in the actual Venona messages. "Rats", that was the Zionists. "Polecats", that was the Jewish Trotskyites. And this was while they were making use of them here in very substantial numbers, turning them into agents who pumped scientific and political information into the USSR, before, during, and after the Second World War. They got Jewish groups here to send money to Russia too.'

'Sad.'

'Yeah. But there was more with Weisberg. What he believed I can't tell you. His parents were Bolsheviks, so he was probably raised a believer. They were non-practicing Jews, and he hated religion, we know that. All religions, across the board. That was a huge issue for him. What he experienced as a kid in Egypt, I don't know in detail. When he got here his dad became a jeweler and his younger brother went into the business.' Art Lennox shrugged, and lit another Lucky. 'His dad died young, his younger brother too, and when Weisberg was at Arlington Hall, he flashed a lot of jewelry around he'd inherited from the business. He was more than happy to impress the ladies, and he'd let his girlfriends wear some expensive piece when they went out in the evenings. But the other deal with him, *I* think, was he wanted the excitement of being an agent, of "being in the business".'

'The appeal of being a part of the elite?'

'That, but the intelligence business per se. Imagine what it's like. Your life makes a mockery of everyone around you. Everything you say is a lie, and the stupid suckers believe you. It makes you feel smarter than everybody else, and you live your life laughing at their gullibility. Weisberg enjoyed that tremendously, I'd say. And he also got to tell himself that what he was doing was noble. Danger and risk overcome for a greater purpose. It made him a larger than life hero. At least in his own mind.'

'I've known people who'd like that fine.'

'You bet. And on top of that, he knew secrets. He could tell himself he knew how the world *really* turns, because *he* was on the inside and brought about change himself. Unlike the rest of us schmucks who're stupid enough to believe what we read.'

'And we've all seen the appeal of that. C. S. Lewis wrote an essay about the desire to be part of the "inner ring", to be "in" with the ones who are really in control. I think that's something we all face. Probably time after time. The temptation to choose our career, for example, for power and prestige, not for love of the work itself. So on top of that elitist appeal, Weisberg could add the intelligence issues.'

'Yeah.' Lennox lit himself another Lucky, then looked over at Ben. 'I didn't see the altruism that motivates some KGB agents. Most of the Soviet agents here gave away secrets for free. And let me tell you they did us real harm. Microwave radar, the atomic bomb, the work that's led to these room-size computers, the slaughter that came from the Yalta Agreement. Rosenberg, Hiss, Curry, Duggan, they all did it for free. Weisberg, no. Weisberg got paid. Weisberg was a gambler. He inherited plenty from his dad, and gambled it all away. Horses. Cards. The high life. Weisberg wanted it both ways. Money first, and maybe foremost, while calling himself a moral hero.'

'Where does sadism come in?'

'Fairly close to the surface, I'd say. All you gotta do is look at Beth.'

'What happened between him and Carl I can't prove today, but I think he shot him and faked the suicide. I have to give old Carl credit, he didn't give Weisberg what he wanted, and that couldn't have been easy for Carl, who'd never been in combat, or anything much like it.'

'Don't forget Miriam Gold either. She had guts. Her death was a big motivation for Carl. I really admired Miriam. She would've been good for him.'

'*He* certainly thought so. I don't think he ever got over her. What about the Krivitsky note they found in Carl's shoe?'

'I figure Weisberg was baiting him, threatening him and demanding a meeting, and Carl put it there in his shoe to incriminate Weisberg in case he didn't live to tell us, pretty much as you suspected. What about Beth? He didn't rape her, did he?'

'No, thank God, he didn't.'

'You figure she'll be OK?'

'I hope so. I think the threats of what he *would* do to her, cutting her face and that kind of thing, which in the end he didn't actually do, traumatized her as much as what he did. He cut and burned her back, and one leg, and both arms, and she's not going to get over that overnight. But she will, I'd say. And now she's got Bobby paying attention, and I think they'll be fine.'

Art Lennox laughed and crushed his half-smoked cigarette on a fieldstone step.

'Not that I *know*, of course. I'm no expert on any of it.' Ben yawned, and leaned back, his elbows on the porch floor, his legs stretched straight down the steps.

Lennox was staring at the mountains rolling away from that spit of land, at the mist swirling and dissolving in front of them, at the thick blue-green forests lit by streaming sun. 'Wouldn't be a bad place to live and raise your kids.'

'No, it certainly wouldn't.'

Neither of them said anything else for a minute. They listened to the woods wake up while they sipped the hot black coffee Lennox had brought from town.

Ben asked when Weisberg had shot the dog.

And Lennox told him Mary had said that Tug had been born deaf. 'He was sleeping under the house when Weisberg got here. When Weisberg left to go get Beth, Tug was standing by the porch, and Weisberg shot him. Wanted him out of the way.'

'You think he used cyanide?'

'Potassium cyanide, something like that. Definitely an intelligence-type suicide pill. Composition varies.'

'Weisberg's easy way out. No humiliation. No lousy prison food. No hard mattresses in cold concrete cells.'

'One other thing. When I come up to see you next week? And I'm giving you some leeway here, 'cause I'm going with my gut in this. You need to have *every single scrap* of paper, and *every strip of celluloid* ready for me to take away that has *any* bearing of *any* kind on Walker and Weisberg and the code-related matters. You and your friend, this Richard West.

You both got fairly high clearance from the war, and that makes it less complicated. But the Venona information is going to get buttoned up, believe you me.'

'I understand. But they will reveal it some day, won't they? I mean the real scoop on the spies? The world's as dangerous as it is today partly because of them.'

'I'll say! They helped hand Eastern Europe over to the Soviets, and made life worse for all of us in ways the public can't comprehend. I *hope* they'll reveal it. I *think* the time will come, though when that'll be I don't know. And what our news folks'll do with it, I wouldn't want to guess. Truth doesn't always get told. And this is truth I know firsthand. Anyway, thanks for all the help, Ben. I understand why you did it yourself, and didn't get the police in.'

'Thanks for your help with *them*. That could've gotten nasty, here, *and* back home.'

'If it's any consolation, I think we would've put him away. The machine ciphers are in his hand. I think he would've gotten time for that. And with the paper in Carl's shoe, and what the labs could've come up with, searching Weisberg's stuff for physical evidence, I think we could've come pretty close to getting him for Carl's murder.'

'I'd like to think so. That some kind of justice would've been done.'

'You get your side stitched up?'

'Yeah, it was no big deal. Seven or eight stitches, maybe. Looked worse than it was.'

'Good. I hear Bobby Chambers was a lucky guy too, luckier than you. I'll call you in a couple of days, and set it up for the first of the week.' Arthur Lennox was standing by then, pushing his Luckys in his shirt pocket. He leaned over and shook Ben's hand, then turned and walked toward the path that led through the woods to Beth's.

Twenty-One

Ben had lifted weights in the basement, weeded his strawberries, staked his tomatoes, and run three miles. He'd seen two does, four fawns, one bald eagle, and a woodchuck waddling away from the barn before he'd made scrambled eggs.

He'd eaten on his front porch, balancing his plate on his knees, while he'd reread Jessie's last letter, even though half of him saw it as a weakness. The rest just said, 'Life is too short, do what you want to do.'

It was Bobby who'd made him think about it when he'd called at seven that morning to tell Ben that he and Beth were getting married in September.

Ben had been really glad for them. And he thought they'd do well together. But there'd also been a second or two of self-centered envy that'd left a disgusted storm in his stomach that still hadn't blown over.

What he needed was work, to keep his mind off himself.

He ought to transcribe the Ordway. Or investigate the bull-with-big-horns watermark on the paper in Alderton's 1400 Bible. Or help somebody with something else that was worth doing too.

He should also ask himself why he felt guilty, for the times he was busy with Carl's death and didn't think about Jessie. As though every minute that was halfway normal was something to be ashamed of.

What did he think it should be like? That he'd miss her the rest of his life the way he did the day she died? Jessie wouldn't have wanted that for him. And he wouldn't want it for her.

They weren't in a class by themselves either. All marriages ended this way, unless you were killed together, with shutting your mouth, and shuffling along, the same way everybody else does.

Stop sniveling, and call the vet, and start looking for a dog.

The phone rang in the kitchen – the first of two phone calls, cutting into his morning, that changed a lot about his life.

Vernon phoned to say his oldest son was coming home from the army and would need Ben's house starting in October. Vernon felt terrible, making Ben move. But Ben told him not to worry, to just ask around for another farmhouse – one that wasn't crumbling, on ten acres or less.

He was standing on his front porch again, drinking a glass of water, watching the sheep scatter and bleat, as a car rumbled up the drive.

It stopped in a cloud of dust in front of the old barn – seconds before the door flew open and Richard West climbed out. He started toward Ben, clutching a paper bag, shouting, 'I've made a double batch of chicken curry, and I've put half in small containers for you to freeze and reheat.'

'Thanks, Richard, I appreciate it. What would I eat if it weren't for you?'

'Nothing very appetizing, though—' Richard stopped on a flagstone in front of the porch and stared fixedly at Ben. 'You all right? You're head isn't hurting again?'

'No, I'm fine. But I've got to find a new place to live.'

'What?'

Ben told him.

And Richard nodded. Before he said, 'This is clearly more than fortuitous! What you need is a project. A compelling, disrupting, uprooting, that will challenge you as much as Walker's death.'

'Wait a minute. Why would—'

'You now have a reason to drag yourself away from this isolated bucolic life that offers so little intellectual stimulation!'

Ben closed his eyes, before he shook his head, then looked up at a great blue heron flying toward Vernon's pond. 'I don't get enough stimulation with the work I do every day?'

'Well—'

'And how 'bout peace, and open space? How 'bout woods, and wild animals, and fields blowing in the wind, and the quiet to hear them talk to you when they do. How 'bout a chance to read what's worth reading too, without mindless noise and constant interruption from nearby neighbors, and loud TVs, and car radios in the road!'

'Well. I can see I've hit a nerve.' Richard was smiling cryptically, holding his curry and squinting at Ben.

Ben laughed and said, 'Yeah, I think you have.'

'One can read anywhere. What you need is a challenge.'

'Easy for you to say. You, who haven't asked a woman to dinner since 1946 in case she might interfere with you doing your daily crosswords!'

'That's not entirely true. And besides, my personal life is not your concern.'

'Mine is yours?' Ben laughed and punched Richard amicably on the shoulder, before he opened the door for him.

Richard had recognized Jessie's handwriting on the letter lying on the table, and Ben had seen him do it. He still looked Richard in the eye, though, while he held the door open.

Richard smiled shyly, and lowered his voice. 'Don't mind me, Ben. You know what a busybody I am. I shall leave you your curry, and beat a hasty retreat. I'll see you with Lennox next week.'

The second call was from Walter Buchannon, a farmer friend of Ben's, who didn't explain what kind, or why, but asked Ben to drive over and give him some help right then.

When Ben drove into his driveway, Walter (looking taller and tougher and maybe even broader than Ben remembered) was standing by his pick-up, rolling up a shirt sleeve and looking at his watch.

Ben had climbed into Walter's truck before he asked him what the call was about and why he was acting mysterious.

'Well, I've got this friend . . .' Walter cleared his throat, as he turned out of the driveway – then he smiled fast, and started over, after glancing once at Ben. 'He's more of an acquaintance, I guess. He's an odd bird, but an OK guy, and he's crazy about horses, and he called me all hot and bothered 'cause he bought him a buncha horses in a group sale at an auction. That's where they sell a bunch real cheap, and you have to take 'em all to get the one you want.'

'And?' Ben was watching Walter over his own dark glasses,

thinking he knew where this was headed, and how it ought to end.

'Well, he likes sulky racin', and he don't have a whole lot a money, or land either one, and he can't afford to keep 'em all, and there's one, this thoroughbred, and this guy's gonna have to send him to a rendering plant tomorrow with the others that're lame and broke down, and yet he figures this one's . . . I don't know, he kinda figures this one shouldn't get put down, but he don't know what to do with him.'

'Walter—'

'We don't need another horse. June don't ride, and Buster's got one, and I got Oliver, the big guy I drive, and I thought about you. I mean I know you rode on the farm and all that, and I thought you might want to take a look. I could keep him at my place, if you wanted me to.' Walter glanced at Ben then, sheepishly, as though he weren't sure what kind of reception this was going to get, or what kind of reception it *ought* to get from someone he didn't know any better than he knew Ben.

'I'm not planning to get a horse, Walter. I mean, I like horses, you know that, and I'd like to have one sometime, but this doesn't seem like the time to me.'

'I figured that'd be the case, but we've only got till tomorrow, and I didn't know who else to ask. I thought maybe, if you didn't want him, you might know somebody who would that I don't know to ask.'

'Nobody comes to mind. But I'll give it some thought.'

They were quiet then, watching the land slip by – the woods, the cornfields, the winter wheat, the just-cut timothy ready to be baled, the streams winding through low places, the one herd of black-and-white cows grazing on smooth green hills.

'How've you been?' Walter asked, with his eyes on the road.

'Oh, pretty good. You know.'

'Yeah. Here we are. His name's Henry Rivers. He's got a big heart, but he's real impractical. Bites off more than he can chew. Can't take care of what he's got. I don't mean to be hard on him, but I don't like to see it.'

Walter pulled into a rutted mud track, then drove past the side of a small dilapidated house into a mud-and-gravel parking area between the house and a shed-like barn with holes in the roof and walls.

It was surrounded by postage-stamp-sized paddocks packed with milling horses. There was mud and manure halfway to their knees, and they looked beaten and listless, when they weren't pinning their ears. Some had wounds and bald spots on their hides. Most were skin and bone.

'Walt! How you doin? Good to see ya.' He was small and thin, with a bandy rooster sort of set to his chin, wearing ripped jeans and beat-up boots, hurrying over to Walt and Ben from hitching a rusted six-horse trailer to an older rustier pick-up. 'Glad you could come so quick. Sad bunch, huh? Ones in the front here are from the group sale.'

Walt introduced Ben, and the three of them shook hands.

Henry said, 'He's a real good-looking horse,' while he wiped his forehead with a handkerchief that he'd been using for a while. 'I got him in a stall in back. Got a real sad story behind him. Hurt his leg on the track. Run pretty good till he done that. You can look at his papers and see what he won. Small tracks, though, nothin' fancy. Looks like he cut the leg on wire, or a startin' gate or something, and the folks that owned him give him away to some fella from up in Michigan. Story goes that he put him in a field and didn't feed him for three years, let him scrounge what he could off the land.'

Walter shoved his hands in his pockets, his big tanned face turning bright red, his eyes looking hotter still. 'That guy oughta be horsewhipped!'

'Yep. Think what that horse went through in the winter. It's a wonder he's alive. Musta been a stream there, where he'd kick the ice in and get himself water, you know how they do. But he went right down to bone. Weighed eight hunnerd pounds when some guy bought him in a big sale up near Detroit.

'I got him in this group here, last week like I said, and I been fattenin' him up on corn for the killers, 'cause they pay by the pound as you know. But there's something about him. I don't know. You can see the leg wouldn't a held up for racin', but he could be a saddle horse, I figure, for somebody. But if you folks want him, you gotta decide today. I'm taking him to the killers tomorrah mornin', him and twelve others I can't pay to keep.'

Walter said, 'Can we take a look at him?'

'Sure. Sure, I'll get him right out.' Henry ambled around to the back of the barn, where he moved two geldings from a tiny fenced-in space into the one next to it, starting a dust-up that didn't last long with the two mares already there.

There were two stalls in front, and two stalls in back, that backed up against each other with no aisle-way between. All four stalls had top-to-bottom doors to the outside, with no windows, and no other light. And the stalls were so small a normal-size horse could barely turn around. When Henry opened the stall door, Ben saw exactly what he'd feared – the floor was more than a foot and a half deep in filthy mud and muck, and the heat and flies were horrible.

The mud-encrusted hindquarters of a medium-sized chestnut horse were right up against the door too, and as soon as it opened, he backed out a foot, and turned his head toward the outside, blinking his eyes time after time, trying to adjust to light. He was wearing a rag of a halter that was too small for his head, so the webbing pressed into his hide, and had for quite a while.

He started to try to turn around, but Henry squeezed in, wading through the filth, carrying a threadbare lead rope, and backed the horse straight out, holding him there in the fenced-in space in foot-deep mud and manure.

The gelding had no muscles anywhere, and there were bones sticking out where they shouldn't be, and a stomach too, hanging underneath him, from no exercise and too much corn, to fatten him fast for the killers.

'His name's All Sun. He got bred down in Arkansas. The left fore got cut on the track. See how thick the leg is? Fetlock up to the knee?'

Ben was staring at All Sun's face, the broad-browed copper-colored head with a long white blaze that was turned toward his. He was filthy and sweating and matted with unbrushed winter hair, but the eyes didn't look mean or crazy, and he let Ben stroke his neck. He didn't try to bite or kick. And with everything All Sun had had to put up with, plenty of horses might have.

He looked resigned, to Ben. Stoical. Self-contained. Without illusions, or expectations, or respect for the likes of men. Ben knew he was anthropomorphizing, as he took the lead rope from Henry. But he'd lived with horses growing up, and he saw what he saw from experience, and the kind of instinct for animals that roots when you're a kid.

He led All Sun through the mud and the muck into the drive by the trucks. He patted his neck, and felt his injured leg – the scarred tendon, the thickened splint bone – before he walked him around in a circle watching the way he moved.

All Sun watched him back, and did what he was told. 'Ho . . . Walk . . . Ho.' He let Ben pick his feet up, which stank with thrush, from standing in crap for weeks. And he held his head reasonably still and let Ben examine his teeth.

'Henry, do you have a lunge rope I could use for a minute? And a place big enough to lunge him?'

'Sure. You can take him behind the barn. My neighbor don't mind if we use his land. I'll go grab you a rope. Did I tell ya he's twelve years old?'

Ben talked to All Sun while he waited. Then snapped the twenty-foot lunge line on his halter, and led him back to the patch of muddy grass where there was space to get him trotting in a circle and see more about how he moved.

All Sun was so out of shape, and so nervous, he was breathing hard as he trotted around Ben. And yet Ben still cantered him a few minutes later, not quite half a circle, careful not to ask too much, but wanting some kind of an idea how he'd move at the canter.

His gaits weren't nearly as regular as they would be if he were fit, but Ben could see enough to know All Sun wasn't lame, and he might move reasonably well, once he got in shape.

He was quivering when Ben stopped him, and Ben patted his neck, and told him to settle down, that he'd be OK, that he'd been a good boy, that he was done for the day.

As they walked toward the parking area, another truck drove in, and All Sun shied sideways. It was hard to tell if he was spooky by nature, with him cooped up and eating corn, with sugar making him hyper.

But he'd jumped away, instead of into Ben, and Ben was glad to see that. If a horse is going to act silly, you want him to choose to do it in a direction other than yours.

When the truck door opened and the man got out, All Sun stood and studied him – and then began to calm down.

Henry said, 'Hey, Doc. I didn't expect you this morning.'

'I was in your neck of the woods, and thought I might as well stop. You still want the Coggins test done on the Morgan you want to race?'

'I do. Sure. You wait there and I'll go get him. Can I leave All Sun with you folks a minute?'

Ben said, 'Sure,' and then nodded, as Walter introduced him to Dr Jack Martin. Ben listened when he talked to Walter, describing a colic he'd just treated. And then Ben, who'd been watching All Sun, turned to Dr Martin. 'Have you got time to check this guy out? The leg that got hurt on the track especially. The usual stuff too. Heart, lungs, teeth, gut. Henry wants to sell him. He bought him last week in a group sale.'

'Hold on just a minute.' The vet got his bag and stethoscope from the truck seat, and walked back to Ben.

He started with the old injury, and said it probably wouldn't be much of a problem. 'The big scarred tendon's been healed a long time. The splint bone's healed OK too. It's nothing you'd want him to stress on the track, but he'd be OK to ride as a pleasure horse for quite a few years to come. Probably. Meaning, I can't guarantee that. I might not buy him for a kid who'd be crushed if things turned out differently. But the cannon bone, that's critical, that was never injured. His eyes are fine. His heart and lungs and his gut-sounds are normal. He's anything but fit, as you know, but he could be again, with the right food and exercise, once his feet get attention.'

Henry arrived leading a small bay Morgan, and Martin stepped across to him, taking a syringe from his pocket.

Ben asked Henry how much he wanted for All Sun.

'I gotta get me fifty bucks, to pay for what I got in him. I'm not looking to make nothin'. I'd like to find him a home.'

'I'll take him. If Walter's still willing to keep him at his place.' Ben looked at Walter.

He smiled and said, 'Sure. We can go home and get the trailer now, and be back in close to an hour.'

'Dr Martin, could you give him whatever immunizations he needs while you're here? Look at the papers Henry's got and fill in whatever's missing? Check the thoroughbred number tattooed inside his lip with Henry's papers too, to make sure we've got the same horse. Leave medication for his feet too, if you've got it with you.'

'Sure. No problem at all.' He gave Ben his business card, and Ben wrote his address on the back so Martin could send him the bill.

Walter and Ben were back an hour and a half later, having gotten a stall ready, and brought Buster's horse in so All Sun would have company when he arrived and know he wasn't alone. Ben had also borrowed two carrots from June Buchannon and stuck them in his back pockets.

He didn't need them at Henry's. All Sun loaded into the trailer exactly like what he was – a pro who's been loaded a hundred times going to and from trainers and tracks.

He was dripping with sweat though when he got out. And he was very nervous in Walter's barn. He circled constantly in the big clean stall, pawing at the sawdust, not touching his hay at all, while Ben and Walter watched.

Ben told Walter he'd stay with him for a while, then stop by the house before he left to pay his board for the month. 'I'm changing his name to Journey, by the way. All Sun doesn't do much for me.'

Walter stood in his kitchen where he could watch both barn doors, and dialed a number he had to look up. He waited for someone to answer, and then said, 'This is Walt Buchannon, Dr West. I figured I oughta tell you Ben bought the horse. It's lucky you gave me a call last week, 'cause this one come up just at the right time, and I wouldn't't've gotten in touch with Ben if you hadn't gotten me looking for one . . .

'No, that's what I'm tellin' you, he bought it right then . . . Nope, once he saw that horse, and how he was livin', and heard what he'd been through, Ben bought him right then. The vet showed up like I asked him to, and he give the horse the once over, and that kinda clinched the deal . . . Ben'll have to spend a good bit of time working with him, but I figure that could be a good thing . . . No, don't thank me, I'm real glad you thought of it. I wouldn't have on my own.'

Ben stood by the stall door and watched the mud-caked chestnut stare anxiously out the open window at the back of his stall. It was covered with stiff metal fencing so he couldn't break the glass, and he felt the wire with his nose from one side to the other.

He stretched his head up to the top of the stall and stuck his muzzle over the heavy horizontal boards that separated him from the old bay gelding in the stall next to his. The bay raised his nose and snorffeled at Journey – an interested, easy-going, goodwill kind of greeting – before he walked to his own half-door and hung his head over the top to watch Ben in the aisle-way.

Journey twirled around twice, then peed in a back corner, before he looked out the window again, trumpeting nervously four or five times, calling to every other living horse who might be anywhere near him.

He sniffed the feed box, and the floor of the stall. Then, finally, he turned his head toward Ben, who was still standing, silent and still, by the closed half-door.

Ben looked away from Journey, as soon as their eyes met. He turned his back to the door. And waited for Journey to come to him.

He did. After a few minutes. And Ben paid no attention, except that he talked in a low quiet voice. Speaking slowly and soothingly, keeping his voice deep and rumbling, talking on about nothing whatever, without looking at Journey.

After another four or five minutes, Ben finally turned slowly and opened the half-door. He stepped in and closed it again, turning to face the aisle-way, till Journey stopped circling and stood still behind him.

Ben said, 'Come here, kiddo. You want a carrot? Come on. I won't hurt you. You're not going to have to worry about that ever again.'

Journey was absolutely drenched with sweat, and Ben told himself to bring towels when he came back, and to give him a really good iodine bath once he'd begun to calm down.

'You're a good boy, aren't you, Journey? All you need is a home. You need to get fed, and turned out so you can run around, and get brought in when it's cold, or hot, to live in a big clean stall.' Ben stopped, still staring at the aisle-way, while Journey paced behind him.

'We'll get you fit, and we'll have fun together, and you won't have to worry again. Not as long as you live.' It wasn't that Ben thought Journey understood any of that. He was talking so Journey could hear his voice and get used to the care and the calmness.

He was talking to himself too.

Committing himself to the future. To everything Journey would need.

'You want another carrot?' Ben held the carrot up, and Journey stopped pacing long enough to eat it. Ben reached over and stroked the side of Journey's nose, then blew softly into Journey's right nostril, which Journey moved even closer, so he could smell Ben better.

Journey stood there, as long as Ben breathed on him. Then he rushed over to the window and stared out at the yard.

'I'll be back later. You be good. Don't give Walter a hard time.'

Journey didn't look at him when he left.

Journey didn't trust anyone. Journey would have to have reason to, and that was going to take time.

Ben wrote Walter a check, and got the phone number of the cavalry colonel Walter knew too, who trained horses and taught dressage, now that he'd retired. Ben started out the kitchen door, then turned and looked back. 'Thanks for all the help, Walter.' He stood there for a second or two.

Till Walter said, 'It's nothing. You two are gonna get along real well.'

'Yeah. Maybe. Yeah, I think we are. I'll be back this afternoon.'

Ben started his car, and put it in reverse. Then sat and stared at the hands stuck tight to the wheel. He said, 'What've I done?' out loud out the window, with the clutch pinned to the floor.

I don't make snap decisions like that. Not with this much commitment attached. What if I can't afford him?

He had no idea what a saddle cost, even a beat-up used one. He didn't have a clue where he was moving, or how much a house would cost, or what kind of work would be involved in fixing up another place.

I've saddled myself with a broken-down horse who's so unfit there's no way to know what he'll be like when he's strong.

Geeze. Only Richard would know if there's a term for that. Saddled myself with a horse.

Ben smiled, shook his head, and finally stepped on the gas. 'Yeah, well, why not?'

He'd always been a sucker for a challenge, and life with Journey wouldn't be dull. Which was probably a good thing. First of all, he could use the help. And that would get Ben up, and get him out the door.

Journey couldn't talk, either. That was something in his favor. He'd be much easier to be around than Richard West on a good day.

And now that Ben stopped to think about it, he'd bet Richard had something to do with this. Why would Walter phone him out of the blue, when he didn't know Ben any better than he did?

Richard called him, that's why! And I should've thought of it sooner. I'll get the truth out of Walter and tell Richard to back off.

Yeah?

Why? Let him have the pleasure of thinking he pulled it off. It's not like he doesn't deserve it. With everything he's been doing for you ever since Jessie died. If he gets really uppity, you can spring it on him later when he thinks he's gotten away with it.

Ben grinned briefly at the end of Walter's drive, then turned left toward Hillsdale.

He wished Jessie had had a chance to know Journey, whether she rode or not. That she'd learned about Carl and the Venona code too, because she would've grasped the significance. Especially with the refugees she'd helped, and the uncle who'd died under Tito.

OK, so I've got to buy a saddle, and the rest of the tack. Then find a house I can live with, and do the fixing up it'll take to get myself moved before school starts.

Even if I can't by then, it won't be a slow summer. And I'll do better with that than I ever would with boredom.

I better not get a dog yet, though. I don't know now if I'll have enough land for one to really run around on.

Historical Notes

Although Carter Clarke, as chief of the US Army's Special Branch (part of the War Department's Military Intelligence Division), essentially ran Arlington Hall's code breaking and decryption program from its inception in 1942, he didn't work exclusively at Arlington Hall until 1949.

The fictional character William Weisberg is based loosely on William Weisband, a linguist at Arlington Hall – *and* a Soviet agent – who did spend time in Federal Prison for refusing to appear before a grand jury after having been identified by Jones York as his Soviet 'handler'. Jones, a jet aircraft scientist who was apprehended for stealing top-secret information, handed the information to Weisband to pass on to the Soviets. Both Weisband and Jones York were paid for the work they did for the Soviets, unlike the vast majority of agents here and in Britain.

Weisband worked in the Russian Program at Arlington, initially as an army officer, starting in late 1944, when the Venona traffic was only one part of a larger mix that included diplomatic, military, civilian trade and lend-lease messages. After the war, Venona was separated from the rest of the Russian Program. Weisband *was indeed* standing behind Meredith Gardner when Gardner decrypted the first important Venona message, which revealed the Soviet intelligence infiltration at Los Alamos. Weisband did tell the Soviets Gardner had read that message (and subsequently a great deal more), which Kim Philby corroborated later.

Weisband also did tremendous damage to the US and Britain by telling the Soviets, probably in 1947, that we were having significant success in decrypting all high-level codes (military, diplomatic and civilian trade). As a result in 1948 the Soviets changed *all* their codes, thereby keeping us from learning of the planned attack on South Korea, and much more besides.

Weisband was known as a gambler and a womanizer, and did loan his inherited jewels to girlfriends at Arlington Hall. He did not leave the US after his release from prison, however. He became an insurance salesman who married and raised a family in Washington DC. He died there of natural causes in 1967, much loved by his family. There's no evidence that he continued to spy for the Soviets after he was released from prison, though he *was* given a password he could use for life to communicate with the KGB, which was *not* a common occurrence.

The fictional Weisberg's murderous behavior is entirely imaginary, and not related in any way to the real William Weisband.

Neither was Weisband known to be in contact with Arman Hammer, though Hammer's activities in relation to the Soviet State as described in the novel are very well documented.

Arthur Lennox, the fictional FBI agent, is based on a real FBI agent named Robert Lamphere, who did work extensively with the book breakers and the Venona material, and was much respected at Arlington Hall for his fairness and accuracy.

Both the Russian and American recently released Venona decryptions did reveal what *Code of Silence* claims they revealed. There *were* over 300 agents working here for the Soviets. And every real-life person identified by name in *Code of Silence* as a Soviet agent – Harry Dexter White et al – was, in fact, exactly that.

For information on the Venona Code and its decryptions I would highly recommend: *Venona: Decoding Soviet Espionage In America* by Dr John Earl Haynes (20th Century Political Historian, Library of Congress) and Dr Harvey Klehr (Andrew W. Mellon Professor of Politics and History at Emory University). They uncovered the Soviet side of the Venona telegrams in the KGB archives in Russia when those archives were first opened to outside researchers after the Soviet State collapsed. Senator Daniel Patrick Moynihan, after reading Haynes and Klehr's early writings, did much to persuade the American intelligence community to release our Venona materials, which have since been published in three separate batches. Up until that time, only the President of the United States and the very highest level of our intelligence people knew of our Venona work and its revelations.

The Venona Secrets: Exposing Soviet Espionage and American's Traitors by Herbert Romerstein and Eric Breindel is also well worth reading.

In Denial: Historians, Communism & Espionage by John Earl Haynes and Harvey Klehr offers a very interesting and careful analysis of twentieth-century American attitudes to the issues involved in Soviet espionage. *The Haunted Wood* by Allen Weinstein and Alexander Vassiliev is an excellent source of information on Soviet espionage in the US, as are the works of David Kahn and Nigel West.

Acknowledgments

First of all, I want to thank Robert Louis Benson, who, unlike his fictional *Code Of Silence* namesake, is much too young to have worked at Arlington Hall in the 1940s. Lou oversaw the release of the US Venona decryptions and wrote the official history of the Venona Project. He patiently submitted to my extensive questioning, read a very rough draft of *Code Of Silence*, met again to identify and clarify mistakes, yet encouraged me throughout. Any inaccuracies in the finished novel are very much mine alone.

John Earl Haynes helped me immeasurably as well. He let me question him relentlessly – and also put me in touch with Lou Benson. John wisely suggested I visit the National Cryptologic Museum and attend both the 2005 National Cryptologic Museum Foundation Meeting *and* The National Security Agency Center for Cryptologic History 2005 Symposium – then helped make my attendance possible.

John recommended me to Rowena Clough, who was at that time the archivist/librarian at the National Cryptologic Museum. She spent an entire day pointing me to, and hauling out, the documents I needed to get an accurate picture of Arlington Hall, and its Venona book-breakers in the 1940s. She introduced me to Bill Haines and Norbert 'Ski' Simozymanowski (volunteers at the museum) who had worked at Arlington Hall in the 1950s. They gave me many everyday details that helped me a lot. Rowena introduced me to Dr David Hamer too, an authority on code and book breaking with a long-time interest in Enigma. David gave me very useful information, and he and his wife graciously drove me to and from the symposium.

David Kahn, internationally known author and authority on espionage and code breaking in America, very kindly answered my questions at the symposium, as did Nigel West, a well respected British author who's written extensively on British intelligence and related fields.

The North Carolina part of the plot comes from three summer visits I made as a child to a cabin like Beth's on Black Mountain. Bobby's father is based on the caretaker, who did live on a spit of land behind it in a cabin like the Chambers'. He did wake me and take me to see 'bees dancin''. I did make a suggestion about the shed's roof and the oldest son was upset by that in ways I contemplated for years.

I didn't get back to Black Mountain for half a lifetime but found the cabins – against all odds – and got a chance to tell the caretaker's widow how important knowing him *and* them had been when I was a kid.

The Cabins at Cedar Falls are based on the very pleasant Inn at Cedar Falls, which is right where I describe it.

As always, of course, this novel couldn't have been written without John Reed, who gave me the character of Ben Reese, and still helps tremendously.